She found the spot, A23, and approached, only to find a man sitting in the car. What the...?

She banged on the car window, then stepped back as Hot Guy—Kavan—turned to look at her. He broke out into a smile as she looked at her phone, quickly scanning the confirmation email from the rental company.

Yep, this was definitely the right spot.

"Um...what are you doing here? This is my car!" she demanded, stepping aside so he could open the door.

He unfolded himself from the vehicle, but not without bumping his head a bit—side effect of being so tall in a small car. Despite the incident, he had a slight grin on his face.

"Actually, this is my car." He was calm and undisturbed by her demand, much the way he had been undisturbed by her need for the outlet.

She waved her paperwork at him and pointed to the number painted behind the parking spot. "I have A23."

He oh so calmly reached into the car and pulled out his paperwork, which indicated he indeed had A23. And he was already in the car.

He looked at her with those eyes and she started to sweat inside her winter coat. "We can share. We're all going to Dublin."

She paused and narrowed her eyes at him. "What's the catch?"

He pursed his lips and did no "You have to drive."

Dear Reader,

I am always thrilled when someone opens the pages of one of my books, so thank you for choosing *Road Trip Rivalry*! Poorvi and Kavan's story is rivals to lovers, on a road trip and let's throw in a fake relationship on top! It's the first of my books that takes place overseas, so I hope you enjoy the scenery.

Like all my books, this one can stand alone, but unlike the others, it is not part of a series. You are meeting all-new characters in a new setting.

Poorvi Gupta and Kavan Shashane find themselves stuck together on a road trip across Ireland to get an older woman traveling alone home to her daughter before the start of their respective conferences.

Together, Poorvi and Kavan navigate the roads, the sites, an opinionated grandmother and whiskey as they make their way across Ireland.

As a bonus, my first-ever novella, *Detour to the Gingerbread Inn*, is right in the back! It's Christmastime, and Naina and Jais are snowed in at a dilapidated inn on their way to a wedding. Their own marriage has been rocky for a while, but a little holiday magic and Indian sweets can help even the grumpiest bah-humbugs.

I hope you enjoy reading *Road Trip Rivalry* and *Detour to the Gingerbread Inn* as much as I enjoyed writing them.

Please connect with me on social media: Instagram @monashroffauthor; Facebook, Mona Shroff, Author; and TikTok @monaseesandwrites.

Happy reading!

Mona Shroff

ROAD TRIP RIVALRY

MONA SHROFF

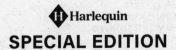

SPECIAL EDITION

Harlequin®
SPECIAL EDITION™

ISBN-13: 978-1-335-40197-7

Road Trip Rivalry
Copyright © 2024 by Mona Shroff

Detour to the Gingerbread Inn
Copyright © 2024 by Mona Shroff

Harlequin Enterprises ULC
22 Adelaide St. West, 41st Floor
Toronto, Ontario M5H 4E3, Canada
www.Harlequin.com

Printed in Lithuania

MIX
Paper | Supporting responsible forestry
FSC® C021394

Mona Shroff has always been obsessed with everything romantic, so it's fitting that she writes romantic stories by night, even though she's an optometrist by day. If she's not writing, she's likely to be making melt-in-your-mouth chocolate truffles, reading, or raising a glass of her favorite gin and tonic with friends and family. She's blessed with an amazing daughter and a loving son, who have both left the nest! Mona lives in Maryland with her romance-loving husband and their rescue dog, Nala.

Visit the Author Profile page
at Harlequin.com for more titles.

To Jyothi and Kosha for making me laugh
at my own drama. No, no one is sick
and I am not having an affair.

CONTENTS

ROAD TRIP RIVALRY

Chapter One

Poorvi Gupta pushed her glasses up her nose as she ran her gaze over the crowded gate area, looking for a place to charge her laptop. Her flight to Dublin was running about an hour behind, and patience was wearing thin around her.

Toddlers were fussing. A mother with a small baby was wearing a hole in the carpet as she paced back and forth trying to keep her baby asleep. Teens sat on the floor hogging the outlets to scroll social media, their legs outstretched. A middle-aged, brown-skinned man was informing an airline representative that his elderly mother would be on the flight alone.

Poorvi's stomach was in knots, but mostly about presenting her paper at the Irish College of Ophthalmologists conference in Dublin. It wasn't her first presentation abroad, but the International Conferences were always a bit more complex than a presentation locally at university like Hopkins.

She still needed to make some adjustments to her presentation, but doing so required an outlet to keep her fading laptop charged long enough to run the slideshow. As she searched, she noticed a man looking her way. She continued to look for an outlet, but her glance at him revealed a tall figure with medium-dark skin, a perfect nose and a chiseled jaw sporting a balanced amount of scruff—not so much that it was a beard, not so little that it appeared as though he had neglected to shave. He was dressed in nice-fitting jeans, a long-sleeved

T-shirt and a ball cap. The way her heart pounded in her chest, as well as the fact that she broke out in a sweat, confirmed it.

He was hot, hot, hot.

Which meant she needed to steer clear of him. It wasn't that she was awkward around handsome men, it was that she was *ridiculously* awkward around handsome men and had no desire to sweat profusely and trip over her words in what would certainly be an embarrassing attempt at conversation with a guy who she'd probably end up sitting next to for the duration of the six-hour flight to Dublin.

Never mind all that, she needed to be convincing in her presentation of the possible detrimental side effects of the latest refractive surgical procedure, C-MORE. As it was right now, C-MORE should be discontinued until the side effects were addressed.

At least in her professional opinion.

Her new boss, Dr. Bobby Wright, had made it abundantly clear that he had wanted to see the presentation prior to the conference. He wanted to make sure she struck the proper balance between recommending further study, while not pushing too hard for the temporary discontinuation of the procedure. He was afraid that all the clinicians would come down on him for taking away their paycheck.

Whatever. Bobby's priority was the lab. Her priority was the patients. And as the lead investigator, her recommendation carried the most weight.

Success had been drilled into her since she was a child. The reality was that she really loved ophthalmology and doing research gave her great satisfaction. Not to mention the added bonus of not having to talk to anyone for long periods of time.

Someone across the aisle stood up and unplugged their phone. Finally! Poorvi made a beeline for the outlet, while reaching into her bag for her charger. She passed the middle-aged man who had been talking to the airline representative and did a double take as she heard him speaking to an old woman in Gujarati. Her parents had made sure that she was fluent in the language. But she didn't hear it all the time. The old woman was wearing a sari, much like her grandmother had up until her recent passing. No matter how hard she had tried to convince her to wear pants, or maybe even a salwar, her grandmother remained true to her sari.

That second of hesitation cost her. She failed to navigate the maze of extended teenage legs and children's paraphernalia, and tripped over a tossed sneaker, nearly falling headfirst onto the ground. She didn't fall, though the flailing of arms and legs was considerably less than graceful. She managed, however ungracefully, to reach the outlet just as another charger was plugged into the open socket.

"I need that outlet," she blurted out. Laptop charger in hand, Poorvi brushed flyway strands of hair from her face. She looked up to see Hot Guy standing there. Great. She immediately flushed, sweat breaking out all over her. "You took my outlet."

"The outlet was open, wasn't it now?" His voice was butter smooth and tinged with that Irish accent. He drew his gaze over her. In a different situation, Poorvi would have melted into ghee. But she *needed* that outlet.

"I was running for it," she declared, pushing her glasses up her nose again as she tilted her neck back to really see him. Damn. He was taller up close.

"You weren't quite there," he explained.

"You saw me running for it," she spat at him. Handsome or not, this man had no manners. "And I nearly fell."

"I saw no such thing," he insisted.

"You just said I wasn't there yet, so you clearly saw me running for it and you took it anyway," she fired up. She really needed to charge her computer before they boarded so she could work on that presentation.

Hot Guy sighed and leaned toward her. He even smelled amazing. Like soap and leather. "Listen, my phone is dead and my brother is fixing to call any minute—"

"Well, I have to work on a presentation. Catch up with your brother on your own time," she snapped, inhaling deeply. Damn but he smelled great.

He furrowed his brow over beautiful dark brown eyes. The irises were so dark, they blended with the pupils. It only made him more handsome. "I'll not be giving up this outlet until my call is through." He spoke kindly, but there was no doubt that he was not budging.

She opened her mouth to protest, but his phone rang, and he answered it, turning away from her.

She glared at the back of his head for a second, his audacity infuriating. She decided he really wasn't all that handsome after all. Not only did she not get her outlet, she was sweating.

"I'm fixing to get on the plane, Bhai, I—" Kavan Shashane never should have answered the phone. But if he didn't, Naveen would just keep calling and texting. He spotted the beautiful, but irritating, woman stalking off in his peripheral vision, presumably to continue her search for an open outlet in the crowded gate area. If she'd hung about, he'd have been happy to let her have the outlet after his phone call.

He watched her push her blue-framed glasses up the bridge of her nose as she continued her search. Her dark hair was tied into a thick side braid, though some pieces had come free when she'd tripped. Clearly, she hadn't even seen him reach for her in case she had fallen over that sneaker. But there you had it— he tried to be kind, and no one noticed. Story of his life now, wasn't it? She was comfortably dressed in dark jeans with just the tiniest of intentional cuts and a white button-down, tucked in just so. He was distracted enough by her that he missed the beginning of what his brother was telling him.

"Say it again, Bhai. I'm not hearin' you," Kavan said, still looking at the woman.

"Just listen. You're on your way back from the States, anyway. I got you registered at the ICO conference in Dublin later this week. I need you to go on to the meeting, find this P. K. Gupta and be sure to convince him not to present that paper." He paused. "And I scheduled a photo shoot for you. We are needing to update."

"Bhai, this is ridiculous. If there are issues with that procedure, we should investigate it, there are other procedures—" Kavan paced back and forth while drinking his cooling coffee. Forgetting that he was attached to a cord, he took an extra step and was yanked backward, spilling his coffee.

"Crap."

"What did you do now? Spill coffee?" Naveen sighed into the phone. "Seriously, Kavan."

"It's fine, Bhai." Kavan said. The coffee had only spilled a few drops on his sneakers, and a few more on his T-shirt, so no harm done.

"Fine. Then, stop thinking, you'll strain something. This procedure is becoming our highest earner. We need it, yeah? That paper will lead to research, and research takes time. And during that time, patients will be hesitating to try the procedure. They'll want to wait for the research. And the reality is that all current studies support the use of the procedure."

"Bhai. Have you even looked at the newest research? It really does suggest that—"

"Honestly, Kavan. I've been taking care of things in the clinic for years. Trust me. You should be doing this procedure as well. You're literally the only one in the clinic who isn't doing it, because you're waiting for more studies. And you know as well as I do, that there are *always* new studies coming out. They aren't always relevant. That's what I need you to convince this P.K. Gutpa of. That the relevant studies of our

time contradict his research, so there's no need to present it."
He paused. "I don't have to look at the research when I have a
nerdy brother to do that for me."

"Exactly." Kavan let the dig slide. He'd been called worse
than nerdy. Besides, that was hardly an insult these days, was
it? "There's a reason I don't do C-MORE," Kavan said.

"It's the same reason you still live with Mom. You have
no guts. Honestly, little bhai, if it wasn't for me, you wouldn't
even have finished high school, let alone university and medical college."

Kavan inhaled. Naveen wasn't wrong.

"If we—I—stop doing C-MORE, what do you think happens to our bottom line, Kavan?"

Kavan stayed silent. He didn't have to speak. Naveen would
do all the talking.

"It goes away," Naveen said. "We lose money—not a good
thing. Just go and do what I ask, like a good lad, eh?"

Kavan closed his eyes and inhaled. Naveen had run everything since their father died. He'd learned long ago that it was
easier to give in.

At least to some degree in this case. P. K. Gupta's data
looked interesting. It certainly implied that a temporary hold
was to be considered. What he needed to do was actually talk
to this P. K. Gupta, see their results and discuss the best options
for the patients. This was what conferences were for, weren't
they? "I can talk to them." Kavan agreed. He'd never win the
argument with Naveen if he didn't have proper facts.

"That's a good lad, then." Naveen assumed Kavan would do
as he was told, like he always did. Fine. He'd deal with Naveen
later, if need be.

"Yeah. Bhai, sure." Still aggravated with his brother, he
ended the call and grabbed his charger, all thoughts of the
beautiful woman gone.

Chapter Two

Poorvi found an open outlet at the adjacent gate. She opened her computer and pushed up her glasses again. She didn't actually need them; she'd had refractive surgery (the older, more studied procedure—a perk of being in the business), but she liked the feeling that there was something between her and the world, so she had multiple pairs of glasses. It was her one nod to fashion, making sure her eyeglass frames matched her clothes. So blue for blue jeans today. She'd even bought a few new pairs to go with her outfits for this conference. That wasn't for a few more days, but her little sister, Niki, had wanted her to go early and maybe do a bit of sightseeing. Poorvi had no interest in seeing anything while this presentation hung over her head. So while she had agreed to come early, she was going to use the time to fully prepare for her presentation at the ICO Conference.

She worked until she heard the announcement for boarding. She got on the plane and noted that Hot Guy was seated across the aisle from her. And that he must have spilled coffee on himself. Whatever. He was inconsiderate and she had little time for another self-centered man. Her boss, Dr. Bobby Wright, fell into that category, and she had no choice but to deal with him. Her ex, Brooks Handel, was another. But she no longer had to deal with him, as he had ghosted her months ago.

She had just opened her laptop again when a small commotion broke out in the aisle just behind her. A passenger and the flight attendant were having trouble communicating. Mostly because the passenger was speaking Gujarati, which the flight attendant did not understand.

Taking a closer look, she realized it was the older woman she had seen at the gate. She was dressed in a light-colored sari, was neither thin nor heavy. Her gray bun was pulled tight at the nape of her neck, much the same style Poorvi's grandmother had worn. Her arms were free of bangles, and her forehead had no chandlo.

Poorvi grinned as she noticed what could only have been a slight eyeroll on the part of the older woman, as she tried—yet again—to communicate in Gujarati to the flight attendant. Her own grandmother had shared similar frustrations from time to time.

People were still filtering onto the flight. Poorvi stood, and turned back to the older woman. "Ba," Poorvi immediately refered to the woman as grandmother as opposed to auntie. She missed her own grandmother enough that seeing a woman who seemed close to her grandmother's age, the endearment just tumbled from her mouth. "Tell me what the problem is," Poorvi asked in Gujarati, just as another, much deeper, smoother voice did the same. She glanced behind her and sure enough, Superhot Guy was talking to the older woman in Gujarati.

Huh.

He rasied an eyebrow when she spoke. Poorvi rolled her eyes. "I got this," she told him.

"You sure?"

"Yes." She was the fixer in every area of her life. Of course she was going to help. She turned back to the older woman and again asked her in Gujarati how she could help.

The passenger explained that she was afraid to sit in the middle seat and preferred the aisle.

"She can have my seat." Hot Guy addressed the flight attendant. He pointed to somewhere behind Ba. "The aisle seat back there." He dropped his phone as he gestured, his computer slipped and a few papers fell from his bag.

Poorvi stared for a moment. Was this guy for real? "Not necessary, she can have mine. It's right here." Poorvi was unclear as to why she was fighting him, especially when he was doing something so selfless, but she was. She started gathering her things when the older woman spoke again.

"I want to sit near both of them," she said, looking at the flight attendant and pointing at them. "They both speak Gujarati."

Poorvi translated. The flight attendant pressed his lips together, but Poorvi stared him down. *Let the woman sit where she's comfortable.*

The flight attendant nodded and started the chess game that was involved in moving seats around to accommodate Ba. Some people were willing, others not so much.

"I really don't see why I have to move to accommodate anyone." One particularly stubborn man set his jaw.

Hot Guy glanced at Poorvi before addressing the man. "You don't have to, now do you? Completely understandable."

What was he doing? They needed that man to move. Poorvi was about to step in, but Hot Guy continued.

"You don't have to, but you could anyway, yeah? And then you'd be the hero here, because then that woman would be able to fly to our great city of Dublin and boast about the kindness of the Irish bloke on the plane." Hot Guy smiled softly and gave a shrug as he glanced at Poorvi.

His eyes told her this was a shot in the dark and he had no way of knowing if the young man would be convinced.

She couldn't help her small smile back at him, but she should have hidden it, because as soon as she smiled, Hot Guy smiled back as if they now shared a bond.

The man glared at Hot Guy. "Nice, so if I don't move now,

I look like the arsehole." He grumbled, irritated. He huffed as he gathered his things and made to move.

"Thank you," Poorvi said.

"Whatever." The man harrumphed as the flight attendant ushered him to his new seat and offered him a complimentary drink.

However it happened, Poorvi was now in a window seat, Ba was next to her in the aisle, and Hot Guy was just across the aisle from her.

"Do you know each other?" Ba asked. Poorvi had automatically started thinking of her as a grandmother.

They shook their heads.

Ba eyed Poorvi, her eyes narrowed. "You are married?"

Poorvi smirked and shook her head. "No."

A small crooked smile appeared on Ba's face, and she turned to her other side.

Oh no... Poorvi knew where this was going.

"And you." Ba pierced Hot Guy with her grandmother powered eyes. "You are married?"

Hot Guy chuckled and shook his head. "No, Ba. I am not married."

Ba's grin widened as she turned back to Poorvi. "You are a doctor?"

Poorvi sighed. "Yes, but—"

"But nothing." Ba held up a hand to Poorvi as she turned to Hot Guy. She opened her mouth, presumably to ask the same question, but Hot Guy's attention was on the flight attendant who was giving instructions.

"So," the flight attendant was saying, "Mrs. Patel's daughter, Devi, will meet her at the airport in Dublin, but if you all could help her through baggage claim and all that, it would be lovely."

Poorvi nodded and Hot Guy said, "Of course." He needed to stop using his velvety deep voice and fabulous Irish accent. Or was it British? It seemed to change. Why did she care?

The flight attendant flushed and did a double take at him. "Don't I know you?" she asked.

"Um…I'm thinking not," Hot Guy said quickly, pulling the cap down further on his head. "Thanks. We'll be sure she gets to her daughter."

We? Poorvi nodded. "Ba? I will take you to your daughter after we land, okay? Do you need anything?" Even though her parents spoke Gujarati with her and her sister, Poorvi likely had an accent. "I'm happy to make sure she gets to her daughter." Poorvi made eye contact with Hot Guy.

"Very good." Ba bobbed her head at Poorvi. "What is your name, beti?"

"Poorvi." She gave her name with a smile and returned to her laptop. She heard Ba ask Hot Guy his name.

"I'm Kavan." She heard him say, then his hand was hanging in her peripheral vision.

She looked up to see him offering his hand in introduction. He was Irish. And Indian. Oh Lord help her. She sighed and shook his hand. "Poorvi."

Ba grinned openly turning her head from one to the other. "You would make a beautiful couple." She bobbed her head. "Atcha. Okay."

Poorvi flushed, but she rolled her eyes and returned her attention to her computer. A glance at Hot Guy showed him still looking at her.

"Sorry about the outlet. My brother and I are in business together, and we have a big meeting coming up—"

His excuses hardly made up for his rudeness earlier. She shrugged. "Whatever."

"I'm trying to apologize here," Kavan said.

"That's rich, considering you got what you wanted," Poorvi retorted. "And I got stuck standing in a corner, balancing a computer on my knee."

He furrowed his brow obviously irritated with her. "Never mind." He sat back and returned to his phone.

"He's very handsome, no?" Ba whispered loudly to her in Gujarati.

Poorvi flushed. Kavan, of course, could hear—and understand every word. "Hmph," she said, shrugging.

Ba's eye widened. "Open your eyes, beti," she continued. "And he wears expensive T-shirt and jeans. Too bad about those dirty sneakers." She rubbed her forefinger and thumb together, then gave Poorvi a hard look. "And you don't seem to be getting younger."

"Ba!" Poorvi glared at the older woman as if she really were her grandmother. She certainly acted like her real grandmothers. "I'm not interested in getting married. I have my work."

Ba harumphed. "Work is not going to give you love." But she seemed to give up on Poorvi, instead turning her attention to Kavan. "She's beautiful, isn't she?"

Poorvi groaned internally. She did a side-eye glance at Kavan. He was flushed.

"Quite. But she's also rude, isn't she?" he answered.

"Excuse me?" Poorvi fired up, and turned her attention to him.

"You heard it. I tried to apologize, and you blew it off." His gorgeous dark eyes flashed at her from across Ba.

Ba turned her head to each of them as they argued. Like she was watching tennis.

"I'm not rude because I didn't accept your apology. That's my choice," she hissed at him.

"A choice to be rude." He went back to his phone.

"It was rude to take that outlet," she shot back. Seriously? Who was this guy?

"I was there first." He glanced up at her from his phone,

and she genuinely expected him to stick his tongue out at her. "Wasn't I?"

She opened her mouth to continue her retaliation. And then she shut it. Who cared what this stranger thought of her? Though she noted that her irritation had overcome her tendency to fluster around attractive men. At least that was something, she wasn't sweating. Anymore.

"What are you both saying?" Ba shook her head, speaking in Gujarati, and then sized up Kavan as well. "You are not getting younger. Give your mother some peace. Get married." She turned to Poorvi and nodded at her to include her in her chiding. "My daughter was like you both. Then she got married and had children, and now she is very happy. Also my son." She gave them both the side-eye and then waved a dismissive hand. "It's your life," she said and put her head back and closed her eyes with the superiority of someone who knows she is right but is surrounded by idiots.

They both stared at her, stunned, then looked at each other. Poorvi was beginning to wonder what she'd gotten herself into, agreeing to look after Mrs. Patel—and she wondered, just slightly, if Kavan was thinking the same thing.

Well, it didn't matter. Helping Ba was the right thing to do. It was how she'd been raised, and clearly Kavan had *some* manners if he'd been brought up to help an elderly woman on a long flight.

Still, Poorvi was not about to let some random grandmother mess with her head. She had stood up to both of her real grandmothers and her mother and was still happily single. Well, single.

Chapter Three

Kavan had work to do. It wasn't easy to concentrate with gorgeous yet irritating Poorvi just two seats over. She had given no indication that she was interested in him, or that she even found him attractive. Which was…odd. Not that he was full of himself, but growing up, he'd always been known as the "good-looking brother." To the point that Naveen exploited his looks by having him do ads for their office.

He wasn't conceited about it; it was a fact, and had been since he was a child. Everyone had fawned over him, how cute he was, and then as he got older, how handsome he was. Quite frankly, he found it off-putting at times. Particularly the way his brother tried to pull him off as being not much more than a "pretty boy" and downplaying his academic strengths, by referring to him as nerdy and awkward.

The fact was that Kavan had done better than his brother at every level of schooling. He had faltered only after their father died, when he was fifteen and Naveen was eighteen. It was true, Naveen had been the one to kick him in the pants to get him back on track, but Kavan had done the work. Something Naveen never seemed to remember and basically ignored.

Even the few girlfriends he'd had seemed to care less about him than how he looked. As a result, he hadn't really ever had a long-term relationship. They'd always been more than happy to have him escort them to a party, their arms draped possessively in his. They had no trouble sharing his bed either. But when it came to any kind of real connection, those women simply hadn't seemed interested, so the "relationships" such that they were, always ended.

He wanted more than a beautiful woman on his arm. And he wanted to be more than that handsome guy on hers. He was looking for true connection, someone he could be himself with, someone who was his *person*.

Kavan was working on a paper. Or rather data for a paper. His brother and two other surgeons in the office had been doing the C-MORE refractive procedure for a few years. In fact, they did more of that procedure than any other practice in the country. Kavan was compiling the data of side effects over time. He had included everything from age and gender to refractive error to tissue health. He had started because patients were coming back with side effects that were not necessarily going away with time, as they did with other refractive procedures.

Naveen had given him an impossible task. If Dr. Gupta was coming all the way to Dublin to present this paper, he must at least have compelling enough data to warrant further study. He did need to meet with this P. K. Gupta, but maybe not for the reasons that Naveen wanted him to.

He refocused his attention on his data. The distraction here—he glanced over at Poorvi, who had pushed the glasses on top of her head—was not simply how attractive he found her. It was more about the fact that he was almost instantly attracted *to* her, despite the fact that she seemed to instantly loathe him. She appeared engrossed in her work, so he did not try to engage her. Besides, Ba was asleep next to her.

The fact that he had to do a photo shoot wasn't helping, either. Naveen had realized long ago that Kavan's looks somehow made people trust him, so Kavan became the literal face of their little practice, which was fast becoming a large clinic. Kavan's face was everywhere in Dublin and in the surrounding area. Hence the ball cap. It was irritating and embarrassing, but Kavan did whatever Naveen asked him to. After all, he owed Naveen everything.

Naveen had taken over the family after their father passed. Their mother was grieving, and she was a tough lady, but the first year was hard on her. It had been during that first year, relatively unsupervised and grieving, that Kavan had gotten into the wrong crowd of people. The boys he hung out with ditched school, smoked everything and by the time Naveen caught on, Kavan had started experimenting with drugs. Naveen then had made sure that Kavan found better mates, had no access to drugs, got to school, did his homework and ate.

And he never let Kavan forget it.

He glanced up. The bathrooms were free. Normally he avoided the airplane loo because it was a small and cramped space, but he'd been chugging coffee for hours before boarding. And—he glanced at his phone—there were still three hours left before landing.

He inhaled and stood. Small, confined places just were not his thing. He wasn't Batman; he did not have a childhood trauma to blame this on. But his heart raced and his palms started sweating any time he had to go into a small space. Like now.

He entered the small vestibule, controlled his breathing as he had been taught and did his business, all the while telling himself he was fine. He went to unlock the door and pull it open it to the wider space of the plane, and the door wouldn't open. No!

He tried again. His heart thudded in his ears. He locked and unlocked the door, but still the door wouldn't open. He broke out in a sweat, it was getting hard to breathe. He was starting to feel lightheaded. No! No! No! He jiggled the handle to no avail.

He knocked on the door. "Some help, please. I seem to be stuck." He could feel the panic entering his voice. Someone pulled the door open. He had been trying to open it the wrong direction. Of course he had. His heart rate calmed and he looked up to see who his savior was.

Poorvi was standing there with eyebrows raised at him. "You okay?" she asked, her voice gentle for the first time since he had laid eyes in her.

"Fine," he mumbled, mortified that of all the people on the plane, the beautiful Poorvi had caught him stuck in the bathroom having a panic attack. Her kindness only made him more embarrassed. He brushed past her without another word.

"You're welcome," she muttered under her breath.

Still embarrassed, he headed for his seat, planning to hide in his computer for the remainder of the journey.

Chapter Four

Poorvi just made it back to her seat when the jostling started. She glanced at Kavan as he stood to let her back to her seat, a slight flush still in his cheeks. She wasn't sure why he appeared to be so flustered, a lot of people have trouble with those doors. He avoided her gaze, which was not consistent with his behaviour so far, either. But what did she know? She'd exchanged a handful of words with him, most of them were unpleasant. At least they had been on her part.

Whatever. She needed to go over her slides and make sure her numbers were up to date for her presentation.

Again.

A lot was riding on this event.

And Ba kept on chatting. She had slept the first half, but now she was going on about her daughter and how they will celebrate Holi with a huge feast and a huge variety of powdered colors to play with.

At first, Poorvi fought it, but finally, she gave in. She and her parents had never really celebrated Holi.

"Oh. You must celebrate," Ba said, her eyes lighting up. "Everyone knows it is the festival of spring and color. But it is also the festival of love. Holi celebrates divine love, but—" she raised her eyebrows and bobbed her head toward Kavan "—anything can happen, eh?"

Poorvi pressed her mouth shut and shook her head. "Nope. Ba. Not in a million years."

Ba grinned at her and gave her an exaggerated frown and shrugged. "Okay. What do I know?"

"I have other priorities," Poorvi insisted.

"Okay." Ba nodded. Ba closed her eyes and rested her head back against the seat.

Poorvi reached for the last dregs of her cooled coffee just as the plane jerked, spilling the last sip on her white blouse. That was going to stain. A collective gasp from the other passengers, followed by concerned murmuring. What the— The plane jerked again and continued to bump and rumble.

Poorvi gasped as her heart rate accelerated. Ba took her hand. "Beti. All is fine," she said. "This happens."

Poorvi knew about turbulence. She just did not like it. Nausea started to set in. *Please don't throw up. Please don't throw up.*

"This is your captain speaking. We have hit some severe storms and will have to make an alternative landing. Dublin is not an option at this point, so we will be making an emergency landing in Cork." Her voice was calm and competent.

Poorvi relaxed for a moment, until the captain's words registered with her. Cork? "Where the hell is Cork?" She turned to Ba, but it was Kavan who answered.

"Cork is south and west. About a two- to three-hour drive to Dublin," he said. He leaned over. "Are you okay?"

She nodded, forced a smile. "Of course." But she held Ba's hand as if she were her child while Ba chanted her prayers softly. It was soothing.

Kavan glanced at her, pointing at the stain on her blouse. "Is that coffee? I know how to get that stain out."

Poorvi stared at him. The plane was rocking around and he was talking about coffee stains? She turned away from him.

The flight attendants made one last pass of the cabin and then seated themselves. The oxygen masks popped down in the roll of turbulence, and they were instructed to use them.

Ba was chanting her prayers, still calm. Poorvi was feeling much better, and she reached over to help Ba with her mask and bumped hands with Kavan doing the same thing. He had actually stood up and was fixing Ba's mask now. A ping of electricity should not flow through her just because she touched a handsome stranger's hand, but it did all the same. Kavan caught her eye as if he'd felt the same thing. Not likely.

She had no idea what her face revealed, but Kavan's next words were soft and kind. "I'm okay getting Ba settled. You go on and tend to yourself."

She nodded and managed to get her own mask on, just as the flight attendant approached Kavan, his lips pressed together in reprimand. "Sir. Please sit down."

Kavan met her gaze and raised his eyebrows as he sat down, mocking the reprimand he'd just gotten. Like they were friends.

He was mistaken.

They were thrown around in their seats as the plane tilted and bumped in the heavy storm. Every so often, a baby would cry, but other than that, the plane was silent. Poorvi was jostled when the landing gear hit the runway. She was then yanked by what felt and sounded like a screeching stop. The plane finally came to a halt and there was a second of silence as everyone realized they had landed safely.

Poorvi joined the other passengers as they broke into relieved applause. She caught Kavan looking over at them and flushed, before they both looked away. She and Ba got to work gathering their things.

Poorvi and Ba made a stop at the restroom before heading to baggage claim.

"Hey. Pretty scary flight, yeah?" Kavan drew up next to them.

"Um, yeah." She looked at him. "You okay?"

"Me? Yeah—especially now that we're on the ground. How about you?"

"I'm fine," she said, clipped. "Just not a fan of turbulence." She flushed and turned away.

"Are you okay?" he asked.

"Yes. Why wouldn't I be okay?" She stared at him.

"Well it just seemed… I mean you looked a bit…pale…"

"I'm fine." She stared at him. "Anything else?"

"Um well, yeah. See, I grew up in Ireland." He raised his eyebrows in what could only be pride. "So I'd be happy to help…with Ba, yeah?"

The last thing she needed was to be on a road trip with this man. No good could come of it, really. "Oh, that's okay. I was heading to Dublin for a conference anyway," said Poorvi. "So I'm happy to take Ba along with me, if she chooses to come."

"You call her Ba, too?" He grinned at her.

"Not really a long shot. She's certainly acting like my grand-mother," Poorvi quipped, pressing her lips together. "Trying to get us married." She rolled her eyes.

Damn. Why'd she have to go and mention the woman's matchmaking?

"You sure you don't want the company?"

"Absolutely positive," she answered, pushing up her glasses.

Kavan sighed, disappointment on his face—or at least what she could see under his ball cap.

"Very well then." He reached into his backpack and handed her a bleach stick. He pointed to the coffee stain on her white blouse. "Just soak that in cool water, apply this and wash. Should be good as new. Good luck. Have a nice stay in Ire-land, yeah?" He waved, walking backward and bumping into a woman. The woman's face turned angry, but as soon as he turned to face her to apologize, she broke out into a huge smile and waved off his clumsiness.

Who was this man who gave out bleach sticks at the air-port? Poorvi did an internal eye roll. "Have a nice life," she said as he left.

Chapter Five

Poorvi splashed water on her face in the bathroom. She was still shaking from the plane ride. The turbulence was terrifying. Poorvi inhaled to calm her nerves. It hadn't helped to have Kavan breathing down her neck. Though it did seem as though he was genuinely concerned. But she could never admit to him that she had been afraid. If she'd learned anything in the last year, it was how to not show weakness.

She shook her head as if to clear the nice thoughts of him. The last thing she needed was a distraction in the form of an outrageously handsome and sweet Indian-Irish man.

People were everywhere. It seemed theirs was not the only flight that had been detoured to Cork due to bad weather. She needed to be at that conference in Dublin by Friday. According to Google, Dublin was just a few hours' drive from Cork. Today was only Wednesday, so no problem.

They made their way to baggage claim, which at first glance reminded her of any one of the apocalyptic movies she had seen. Further investigation revealed it was simply organized chaos, which was only mildly better. Announcements about flight delays, where to find baggage and other things crackled and popped from speakers in various places. Airport representatives had taken to the floor to guide people. Their voices mingled with the announcements, assuring that nothing could be heard. Machines whirred and clanked loudly as the baggage belts started and stopped. People milled about in all directions, looking for bags, family members or the car rental desk. Various languages mingled in the air.

The belt number for their luggage was changed twice, forcing them to run from one end of the baggage claim area to the other. Ba kept close to her in the chaos. People crowded around, nearly ten deep, in the area where the bags were spit out. She never understood that. The bag was going to come around anyway. She went to where the crowd was thin and grabbed her bag from there. A large red hard-shell bag with duct tape on the corner came around and Ba made a break for it. Poorvi followed and got Ba's bag off the belt, but not without a small struggle. Lucky both their bags had wheels, as there weren't any carts available.

"If you had let him, Kavan would have helped with the luggage," Ba said. Was there some kind of grandmother class they all went to? Why did they all say the exact same things?

"We're fine, Ba," she said. "Let's call your daughter. Can she come get you?"

Ba called as they made their way to car rental. She stood apart from Poorvi and had a conversation that Poorvi could not hear. "No, she cannot come," Ba reported as she joined Poorvi in the never-ending car rental line. "Her husband is out of town until Holi and her children are too small to leave alone."

Poorvi sighed and groaned internally. Of course she would help this woman, but it would be easier if she could just be on her way. "I'll drive you." There was no way she was going to leave an old woman who didn't speak the language alone at an airport with no way to get to her family.

The rental lines were worse than the bag claim lines, if that was even possible. This day was trying her patience.

"What do your parents do?" Ba asked as they waited in the infinite line.

"They are both cardiologists," Poorvi replied.

Ba smiled and bobbed her head. "Both parents are doctors. How lovely."

Poorvi shook her head. Both parents being doctors had really left no other options for her. Luckily, she hadn't really wanted any other option. She had always been fascinated by the eye, so it was a natural choice to go into ophthalmology. They weren't sure what to make of her decision to do an MD-PhD as opposed to patient care, but research had always been her passion. Her favorite classes were always those that had a lab. She'd even played "lab" as a child. The other children thought playing lab was no fun, so she used her stuffed animals as the "staff" and examined everything from grass to lint.

There were times when she missed those days. At least her teddy bear and stuffed elephant didn't accuse her of having slept with the boss. No, correction, the boss's boss.

"How about siblings?" Ba asked.

"I have a sister, Niki." Poorvi smiled. "She is not a doctor. She's an event planner." Niki was a year younger than her, and they had an apartment together in Baltimore. "She's like my best friend." Poorvi gushed a little over Niki. "Also, she can cook. Which helps because we live together and I do not cook."

"Henh?" Ba was impressed.

A free spirit and always the life of the party, Niki was currently working as an event planner for nonprofit organizations. She also had the biggest heart of anybody Poorvi knew.

"How about you? What kind of doctor are you?" Ba asked.

"Oh I'm an—"

"Next!" the agent at the car rental called them.

"Oh. It's our turn." Poorvi went to the desk. "Hello," Poorvi said to the attendant in her most patient voice.

"All I have left is manual," the agent said by way of greeting. Her hair was frazzled, her name tag—Shannon—was skewed. Shannon had not counted on turbulence either. "It's a small SUV."

"No problem. I'll take it." Poorvi had learned to drive a stick shift from her masi. Her mother hadn't really seen the need to learn the skill, but her mother's sister had insisted, saying it was a life skill.

Thank you, Kosha Masi.

"Really?" Shannon was surprised and seemed to relax. She had been ready to argue with Poorvi.

"Yes." They just needed a car. And a look at these lines indicated that getting a car—any car—might be harder than it should be.

"Perfect." The agent typed away, and in a few moments, Poorvi had the location of the car. She, Ba and their luggage slogged their way to the garage to locate the car. The garage was cold and damp; she was grateful for her winter coat.

She found the spot, A23, and approached, only to find a man sitting in the car. What the…?

She picked up her pace and went to the car window. She banged on it, and then stepped back as Hot Guy—Kavan— turned to look at her. He caught her in that gaze of his and broke out into a smile as she looked at her phone, quickly scanning the confirmation email from the rental company.

Yep, this was definitely the right spot.

"Um…what are you doing here? This is my car!" she demanded, stepping aside so he could open the door.

He opened the door and unfolded himself from the vehicle, but not without bumping his head a bit—side effect of being so tall in a small car. Despite the incident, he had a slight grin on his face. She stepped back out of his space. He was really tall.

"Actually, this would be *my* car." He was calm and undisturbed by her demand, much the way he had been undisturbed by her need for the outlet.

She waved her phone in front of him and pointed to the number painted behind the parking spot. "I have A23."

He oh-so-calmly reached into the car and pulled out his phone, wincing as he bumped his elbow. "A23. My spot."

He turned his phone toward her. Sure enough, he indeed

had been assigned A23. And he was already in the car. "Well, I suppose that according to your elementary school rules, you were here *first*, so…whatever." She shook her head and shivered. Ba waited patiently. She looked around in case the company had a kiosk in the garage to see what else they might have.

"A car is not the same as an outlet." He looked at her with those eyes and a small smile and she started to sweat inside her winter coat. "We can share. We're all going to Dublin."

She paused and narrowed her eyes at him. "What's the catch?"

He pursed his lips and did not quite meet her eyes. "You have to drive the whole time."

She looked at the car and then at Kavan, then back into the car. She saw the gearshift. "Oh, I get it. You don't know how to drive stick."

He said nothing, just stared at her.

"What were you going to do?" she asked, amused.

"I was going to figure it out." Irritation laced his words and Poorvi took some satisfaction in making him admit something he did not want to. "I need to get to Dublin, don't I?"

Poorvi chuckled.

"But now you're here. It's mutually beneficial. I have a car that I can't drive, yeah? You can drive it, but don't have a car. And we're going to the same city."

She really did not have a choice. This was her best chance to get to Dublin as soon as possible. She sighed. "Okay."

He came over and grabbed Ba's bag. "I'll handle this. You both get in, yeah?" He quickly reached for their bags. She really tried not to notice his muscles as he lifted the bags, but come on, how was she *not* supposed to notice beautiful brown-skinned muscles flexing like that? "I know these roads fairly well, so I'll be navigating."

Poorvi took off her winter coat and tossed it in the back seat. She sat down in the driver's seat. Whoa. This was weird. Shifter in her left hand. She pressed the pedals. They were the same.

"You'll be driving on the left," Kavan said as he clicked his seat belt and turned to the back. "All buckled up, Ba?"

Poorvi caught Ba's expression in the rearview. The older woman was positively beaming. She bobbed her head side-to-side, a large grin on her face. She seemed very excited.

"We need your daughter Devi's address," Poorvi said into the rearview.

"We go first to Blarney Castle," she stated in Gujarati.

Poorvi turned to find Kavan staring at her. "This is the first I've heard of this." She held up her hands in surrender. Kavan narrowed his eyes at her. "I'm not lying. I need to get to Dublin as soon as possible. I am not here to travel." And she didn't want to be stuck with this man any longer than she had to be. A small—very tiny—but signifcant part of her was starting to *like* him. And she just couldn't have that.

"Ba. We need to get to Dublin. We both have to work," Kavan explained, a hint of desperation in his voice.

He didn't want to dawdle anymore than she did. Which was perfect, but made her a bit sad. She did not want to investigate the reasons for that.

"Ba," Poorvi added. "Devi is waiting for you."

"No. She isn't." Ba pressed her lips together and avoided Poorvi's eyes.

"Of course she is. Your son said—"

At the mention of her son, Ba tsked and waved a dismissive hand. "I told my daughter I will be there on Friday." She grinned, proud of herself.

"Ba—" Kavan started, the desperation in his voice obvious now.

"We really need to just get to Devi—" Poorvi said.

"I will see Ireland." She nearly smirked at them. She had the power and she knew it. "You both will show me. Blarney Castle is only twenty minutes away."

Chapter Six

Kavan just stared at the older woman. What was happening? As lovely as it may be touring his country with this beautiful and pleasantly irksome woman, he didn't have time to show Ba or anyone all of Ireland.

Once he found P. K. Gupta, he needed time to go over the data.

He glanced at Poorvi. The expression on her face made it clear that she hadn't had any idea that this was Ba's plan.

"I have never kissed the Blarney Stone. It won't take long." Ba said to them.

"Give me your daughter's number, please." Poorvi had her phone ready. She sounded clinical and authoritative. He certainly might have handed over whatever she had asked for.

"No." Ba clamped her mouth shut.

"Ba. She's probably going out of her mind," Kavan added.

Ba narrowed her eyes at them. "No, she isn't. I called her."

"What did you tell her?" Poorvi asked.

"I told her that I was with a tour group seeing Ireland. I would see her Friday," Ba said.

"You did what?" Poorvi spun around in her seat.

"I want to see Ireland," Ba repeated.

Poorvi stared at Kavan in disbelief. And, he realized, maybe a bit of panic, too. "But *we* need to be in Dublin in two days."

"Then we will see what we can in two days," Ba said triumphantly.

Kavan looked at Poorvi. She made eye contact with him and his heart rate increased. "Let's just drive to Dublin." Maybe after he settled this issue with P. K. Gupta he coud figure out what he was feeling about Poorvi.

"And do what?" Poorvi's already large eyes bugged out. "Drive around and see who claims her? She hasn't given us the address."

"Ba," Kavan started in his most charming voice. He had been known to charm an auntie or grandmother in his day to get permission to stay out late or ride a motorcycle. "I'm sure Devi is missing you very much, and your grandchildren must be excited to see you. Both of your children would want you to be safe, don't you think?"

Ba narrowed her eyes at him. "I may be old, but I am not stupid enough to fall for your act." She set her jaw. "I am seeing Ireland." She mumbled something to herself that Kavan did not quite catch, but she was clearly agitated.

"Nicely done." Poorvi rolled her eyes. "Now she's angry."

"When is your conference?" Ba asked.

"Friday," Poorvi answered at the same time as him. They made eye contact again. He gave a side smile. He could get used to this.

Ba grinned. "Perfect. We will all arrive on Friday. You drop me at my daughter's and then go to your conferences."

Naveen was going to kill him if he didn't get to P. K. Gupta before he presented his paper. "Thursday," he spat out quickly. "I meant I have to be there on Thursday."

Ba shook her head at him. "Friday. It's an auspicious day anyway."

"Is it?" Poorvi asked.

Ba's face lit up. "It's Holi! My daughter always has the most amazing Holi party. That's why I came."

"So you should get there early and enjoy the preparations," Kavan tried again.

Ba waved a hand. "They can manage until I get there. And you can both come to the party." She clapped her hands together and her face lit up. "It will be fabulous. It's the festival of color and spring, but it also celebrates love." She looked meaningfully at Kavan. "The moon will be full that night. Anything can happen."

Kavan flushed and avoided looking at Poorvi. Ba pulled out a well-worn travel guidebook with a few dog-eared pages in it and handed it to Kavan. He opened it to find that Ba had made a checklist. Blarney Stone. Cliffs of Moher. Aran Islands (all three). Dublin. He showed it to Poorvi.

She widened her eyes and glanced at him. Her look said it all. She needed to get to Dublin, but she didn't want to hurt Ba. This itinerary was not part of her plan. She had other priorities. His thoughts exactly.

She opened her hands to him in a silent gesture of surrender, whispering to him, "What are we going to do? We have no choice."

He pressed his lips together and caught her eye yet again. She was right. In that moment they were on the same side. They had made a connection. Unwanted tour of Ireland and Naveen's assignment notwithstanding, that connection felt like a beacon of light.

Chapter Seven

Taking a road trip with a spunky grandmother and a highly irritating, though admittedly attractive, man was not how Poorvi had imagined seeing Ireland. She'd had a plan and she very much liked sticking to her plans. But she wasn't about to abandon an old woman. Something about Ba and her insistence on playing tourist was deeper than it seemed, though Poorvi could not place why. Kavan's desperation to reach Dublin mimicked hers, but she had the feeling he was going for more than just a conference.

Not that it was any of her business. Or that she cared.

Poorvi had her own conference that started on Friday, which put knots in her stomach just thinking about it. She wasn't presenting until Saturday, but Bobby wanted her there by Friday to go over exactly what she was going to say. Honestly, she had half a mind to blow him off and just get there on Saturday.

She pushed aside the feeling that this connected her to Kavan in any way. They were two separate people with separate lives who happened to be sharing a car. Trying to get an old woman home. While taking in the sites in Ireland.

"Do you know where we're going?" she asked.

"That, I do," he said without looking up from his phone. "The question is, can you put up your part of the deal?" He cocked a smile at her.

Irritating man.

She narrowed her eyes at him. "Of course," she stated with much more confidence than she felt.

Poorvi spent an extra moment familiarizing herself with the car. Once she figured out where everything was, there was nothing left but to drive. She put the car in gear and gave it some gas. They eased out of the spot and into the lane. There. That wasn't so bad.

Hot Annoyance was still tapping away on his phone. Whatever. How hard could it be to drive on the—

"AHHH!" Her passengers screamed and she slammed the brakes just inches in front of a set of headlights. Her heart hammered in her chest. She had narrowly avoided a head-on collision.

"What part of drive on the left do you not understand?" Kavan barked at her.

"You're supposed to be navigating, not pretending to be a teenager with their phone!" she barked right back at him, her eyes wide and jaw set. So to drive on the left, one had to actually drive on the left.

He narrowed his eyes at her. "The left lane…is. On. The. Left."

She turned her gaze forward. The other car had gone. She moved the vehicle into the left lane.

"Now turn left here," Kavan said in a quiet rumble, his phone still in his hand. Notification dings were coming through rapidly. Then his phone rang. "We're leaving the garage, and it drops right into the highway, yeah?"

She was too occupied by driving to care who was calling him, but clearly someone was trying to reach him. He ignored his phone and continued to direct her. She nodded that she understood.

Her instinct was to shut him up. But there was none of the expected superiority and cockiness in his voice. She turned left. *Shift, check the lane, hit the gas.*

"Turn right here," he mumbled. She checked traffic both ways before making the turn and driving slowly out of the airport. It was dark, despite the morning hour, and rain was coming down in buckets.

"Now. You're going to merge, but everything here is opposite of the States, yeah?" Kavan's phone was still dinging, but he seemed unconcerned by it.

Probably because she currently held all their lives in her hands as she attempted to drive in what could only be described as an upside-down way.

"So the far left is the exit or slow lane, while the right lane is the 'fast' lane," Kavan explained.

Again, she bit back her glib response; her instinct had been to go to the other side of the road. She nodded without glancing at him, intent on the quickly approaching highway. She turned the wipers faster, gave her signal, checked her mirrors and the side of the road she was on, shifted and accelerated.

The car stalled.

What the? She could drive a stick with her eyes closed. She glanced at the shifter. She had moved it in the wrong direction.

She waited for Kavan's bark. But instead, he spoke gently. "You're still getting used to the gearshift." Kavan was checking traffic around them. "You're clear. Go ahead."

Poorvi started again and this time made it to the highway. It was difficult to see, but she decided they could just take their time. No rush. She could do this. She shifted and sped up, staying to the left.

Kavan continued to give soft direction, which helped Poorvi keep her mind on shifting and staying left.

Every time she switched lanes or took an exit successfully, Ba let out a call to thank God. "Hai Ram!"

She glanced at Kavan and caught a small smile on his face as Ba praised God for the umpteenth time. "Ba," he said. "She's fine. You go on and take a nap."

Ba was not having it. She shook her head and held her prayer beads in her hands with white knuckles. Poorvi rolled her eyes but couldn't help the smile that fell across her face.

They drove in relative silence for a small stretch; the only sound was Ba's soft praying and Kavan's "stay left" chant. Which, while annoying, was helping her remember to stay left.

"Relax. You got it now." He sounded excited for her.

"I'm relaxed," she retorted.

"Uh-huh." Kavan raised an eyebrow as his gaze shifted to her white knuckles clutching the wheel. She loosened her grip a bit.

"You'll go straight for a few kilometers, then take the exit for Blarney Castle." He put his head back and closed his eyes.

"What?" Poorvi panicked. "You can't sleep! You have to navigate!"

"Ha." Kavan put his head up. "So you do need me."

She glanced at him. "The same as you need me, Mr. I-can't-drive-a-manual."

"Ahh! Look at the road!" Ba screamed from the back seat.

Poorvi turned back in time to see that she was just fine. "Ba! I'm fine."

"Hmph. Just checking."

Poorvi shook her head as she tried to calm her heart rate. Although, between Ba screaming in the back and Kavan speaking softly in that amazing voice of his, that was hardly likely to happen.

Chapter Eight

"She's something, eh?" Kavan said softly while Ba continued chanting her prayers.

"She got us to take her to the Blarney Stone," Poorvi answered. It took her a minute, but she realized that she wasn't snapping at him anymore. Huh. "She reminds me a bit of my grandmother." She couldn't keep her voice from cracking, so she inhaled and paused. "We, uh...lost her last year."

"I'm sorry."

Poorvi shrugged as if it were okay. "She had a long life. She died peacefully in her sleep. *My* Ba lived on the same block as us, and we went there every day after school while our parents were at work." Her grandmother was tough and sassy.

"You're smiling at something." Kavan said.

"Am I?" Probably. Thinking of her grandmother always made her smile. "She was kind of sassy." She tilted her head toward Ba. "Like Ba here."

"Ah. So that's where you got it from." Kavan let out a warm chuckle.

"Well, yes." She continued looking at the road. "My mom always says I am most like her mother, which was why I drove her crazy."

"What about your siblings?"

"A sister. Niki belongs to my mom." She spared the gearshift her tight grip for a second to cross her fingers. "They're like that."

"Do you get along with your sister?"

"What's with all the questions?" She frowned at him. He had gotten her to talk about her family. To what end? This was too close for her own comfort.

"Just making conversation."

"Well, we don't have to do that." She changed the tone of her voice so there would not be any doubt as to the sincerety of her words. "We're just two people who are stuck taking an older woman on a tour of Ireland. We don't have to get to know each other. We can just coexist," she said. She didn't have the time or space to get friendly—on any level—with anyone right now. She side-eyed him. "We're not going to 'bond.'"

He stared at her a moment, something akin to confusion on his face. Without a word, he abruptly turned in his seat and started chatting with Ba. "Tell me about your daughter and her family."

Poorvi should have been relieved that he acquiesced so quickly to her request, but she could not shake the feeling that she had somehow hurt him. Maybe if she explained why she didn't want to share that might make it better. But she wasn't ready to share all that.

Ba, however, was more than happy to talk about her family. "My daughter is my eldest, Devi. She married Yash, a wonderful man. And they have my grandchildren. Dharm is eight, and his sister, Mira, is five." Her son in the States was married but no children.

"So why Blarney Castle, Ba?" Kavan asked, seemingly entranced with what Ba's answer might be. But instead, Ba looked out the window, refusing to answer. She must have her reasons.

Wow. Not a good day for Kavan. Poorvi glanced at him quickly.

"Well, I'm excited. I've never been here either." Kavan filled the silence. "The castle was built over six hundred years ago. The famous stone has many stories on how it came to be in the castle, but however it got there, its powers are undeniable." Kavan smiled at them. He continued to talk, basically about the castle and the stone.

"Your exit is in one kilometer," Kavan pointed out gently. "On the left."

Poorvi followed his directions and turned up the winding road. "Oh! We're here. Blarney Stone!" Considering she'd had no desire to come to the castle, her excitement surprised her. The castle sat among green grass, with trees on the periphery.

"It's about twenty-seven meters—uh, ninety feet high." Kavan told her as they all exited the car.

Poorvi simply stood there for a moment and took in the majesty of this castle.

"And technically this is Blarney Castle, but yes, the stone is up there." He pointed toward the top of the castle. The rain had stopped and the sky was still gray, but the sun must have risen because it was definitely lighter out.

The air held some moisture and a chill, a typical March day in Ireland, according to Kavan, their unofficial tour guide.

"It is gorgeous, yeah? I've never seen anything so beautiful." Kavan had paused to look up at the castle.

It was beautiful. Even in the gray of the day, the green was brilliant. The rectangular stone structure stood high and strong among the greenery.

Ba walked past them, her considerable purse on her elbow. With respectable speed, no less. The woman who had needed to sit next to them was no longer here. In her place was a spry lady with an agenda to see the castle.

"Wait up, Ba," Kavan called. "There are lots of stairs."

She waved him off. He and Poorvi finally caught up with Ba when she paused to take in the beauty.

"How do you know there are lots of stairs if you haven't been here before?" Poorvi asked.

"Well, I could tell you." He smirked at her. "But then we might actually 'bond,' and I know how you feel about that." He fell into step with Ba as they approached the narrow stone stairs. Poorvi was behind them. The stairs (125 of them, according to Kavan), located at what seemed to be a side entrance, twisted up in a spiral to the top of the castle.

If the view from below was majestic, the view from up here was simply breathtaking. Poorvi tore her gaze from the endless greenery and followed Kavan and Ba to the line of people waiting to kiss the Blarney Stone.

"Ba. They say if you kiss the stone, you become more…" Kavan paused and turned to her as the Gujarati word for eloquent eluded him. "What's Gujarati for eloquent?"

"Vathordyu," Poorvi said.

"That means talkative." He corrected her.

"True, but the straight translation of 'eloquent' is chatadara. Which really means more like 'declamatory.'" She shrugged. "Talkative is more like 'gift of gab,' which you clearly have."

"And which you do not." His bluntness seemed out of character, but what did she know, she just met him a few hours ago.

She side-eyed him. "As long as we understand each other." She shrugged. "Though your Gujarati is pretty good."

"My dad used to make us speak Gujarati at home all the time."

"Used to?"

"Well, he had to stop when he died, didn't he?"

"Oh." She snapped her head to him, shocked he'd been so flippant about that. But the look on his face defied his words and his tone. He still hurt from that loss. It was obvious. "I'm… I'm really sorry."

He shrugged. "I was a teenager. And after he died, we just sort of deferred to English."

"Gujarati reminded you of him." She sighed.

"Yes. Exactly." He furrowed his brow, surprised. "I tried to practice Gujarati, since it reminded me of him. But my brother and my mom…" He shook his head.

She nodded, understanding. "Too hard."

He stared at her as if that had not occurred to him. "Or it was Naveen not wanting to do anything he wasn't the best at, and Mom going along with him, as usual." There was more than a hint of bitterness in his voice, and Poorvi found she was curious to know why. She opened her mouth then closed it. No. She didn't have time for all that in her life.

"Well Kavan does not need to kiss the stone, then," Ba said with a smirk.

Poorvi burst into laughter.

"But you do," Ba told her.

"I communicate just fine, Ba," Poorvi countered.

Ba raised her eyebrows and widened her eyes. "No, beti, you don't."

Kavan laughed out loud while Poorvi shook her head at both of them. Ba joyfully took her turn when it came.

Two volunteers stood by what appeared to be a large whole between the floor and the wall. There were iron rails to grip on either side.

Ba lay down on her back as instructed and gripped the iron bars. The two volunteers held onto her as they gently lowered her head to where the stone was embedded in the castle wall, so she could kiss it. They then gently pulled her up and she stood. The whole process took maybe sixty seconds.

Poorvi took her turn (they'd come all this way) lying down on her back, allowing the two volunteers to lower her down into the small opening that led to the stone. She kissed it and they pulled her up.

Kavan's heart pounded in his chest and he broke out in a sweat just watching Poorvi and Ba being lowered into the gap between the wall and the floor. Sure, there were iron railings to hang on to, but that was really all. For once in the past few hours, his physical response had nothing to do with Poorvi. He started to walk past.

"Uh, you're going to miss your turn." Poorvi pointed at the stone.

"I'm good. Ba said I didn't have to."

"But you've never been here before," she insisted. So she was listening to him.

"Well, yeah. But—" he glanced warily at the hole that led to the Blarney Stone "—I'm good."

"You're kidding, right?" Poorvi smirked at him, but stepped closer to him, studying him. Her smirk disappeared and was replaced with concern. "It's a really…small space." Her mouth gaped open as she put it all together.

He stared at her. She must think he was weak. That's what Naveen had thought of Kavan's fear of small spaces in any case. Naveen was forever trying to get Kavan into small spaces, convinced that if he faced his fears, he would overcome them. All it did was make Kavan trust his brother less and less.

Poorvi turned back and he followed her gaze. Ba was waiting for them, but had seemingly engrossed herself in the scenery. She turned back to him and watched him a minute before she moved closer to him and spoke softly. She smelled of floral shampoo, which was incredible considering they'd been on a plane overnight, and truth be told, he enjoyed her proximity. "It is a small place, and it is high, but it's only for a second. However, I think you already have a pretty good gift of gab, so no harm skipping it." She gave him a one-armed shrug and a small smile. Poorvi took a few steps away from the opening, so they coud allow others to have their turn.

Kavan followed her as if he'd always followed her, before glancing over again, clearly apprehensive. "I lied… I was here once before. With my whole family." Rather when his family was whole. "I couldn't do it. Naveen, my older brother, teased me the rest of the trip. Made me feel…"

"Weak," she said. Something in her eyes related. Anger flashed through them, and then she focused on him again. "No offense, but your brother sounds like an asshole."

He chuckled, relief flooding over him. Yes. Naveen was an ass at times. He inhaled. "Maybe. But that asshole raised me."

She quirked a smile, unapologetic that she had insulted the person who raised him. "Hard to believe." She squeezed his arm through his coat. He wished he wasn't wearing the coat so he could feel her hand. "In any case, it's up to you. No judgment."

"Really? Because you can be pretty judgy." He grinned at her.

"True." She chuckled. "But not for this. You saw how I was with the turbulence," she said quietly, her eyes huge as she let him in just a little. It felt like a door opening, and he found himself leaning into that feeling.

Ba approached him, motioning for him to bend down so she could reach him. "You never know when a chance will come again," she whispered, looking him in the eye. Apparently she had been listening. He had the distinct feeling she was not just talking about kissing the Blarney Stone.

He looked at Poorvi over Ba's shoulder and she nodded and smiled.

He walked back over to the staff and sat down, his back to the gaping hole in the floor that he would be lowered into. His heart raced and he broke out in a sweat. Ba stood by him and nodded encouragement. Poorvi stood on his other side. He had assumed she would mock him, but the only thing coming from her was encouragement.

Fear of small spaces be damned, he was doing this. He grabbed the railings, closed his eyes, and allowed the staff to lower him the few inches. He kissed the stone and they pulled him up. He stood, feeling a bit lightheaded and nauseous. Ba squeezed his shoulder and whispered to him, "If you can do that, you can do anything." She winked and glanced at Poorvi before moving on.

Poorvi approached him, her brow furrowed. "You okay? You look like you might vomit."

He looked up at her. "I might." But God, please don't let him vomit in front of her. "Ba is very convincing."

She grinned. It nearly stopped his heart. "Which is why we are here to begin with." Poorvi rolled her eyes.

"I guess we're both just big softies at heart," he said.

"Speak for yourself," she said with a half smile, turning away from him. "Let's go if you're done. The sooner we finish her tour, the sooner we move on with our lives."

"Yes, ma'am," he said under his breath. She had let down her wall for a split second and let him see her fear, just so he would know that he wasn't alone. She wasted no time putting the wall back up, but that moment was more intriguing than he had imagined.

Chapter Nine

"Chalo. Cliffs of Moher is next." Ba plowed ahead to the car, leaving Poorvi behind with Kavan. When she looked at him, he seemed completely fine, lighter even, after his experience kissing the Blarney Stone. Maybe the stone's magic was more than simply doling out the gift of gab.

They'd bonded. Against everything she'd intended, yet they'd bonded over their fears. It was only a tiny moment, but still…

It wasn't as horrible as she might have thought it would be, showing vulnerability like that. Surprisingly she wasn't the least bit mortified at having revealed her fears. And it had seemed to help him.

The sky was still gray, and the chill was hanging around. Poorvi pulled her winter coat tighter, as did Ba, and they all seemed prepared.

"Really?" Kavan asked Ba. "Because it's cold there this time of year. And no guarantee on visibility."

"How cold?" Poorvi asked. Not that it mattered, Ba seemed determined.

"Cold. But more than that, the fog can be thick." Kavan said. "The Cliffs of Moher is where the Atlantic meets Europe. The Cliffs are millions of years old, and the views of the water and the land are like nothing you've ever seen, trust me." He grinned. "It's an incredible experience, walking over them, the water just directly below you, yeah?" He grinned and his face lit up, all irritation from two minutes ago replaced by his boyish grin and accompanying enthusiasm. "You'll not want fog, because you want to see the ocean come right up on those cliffs. There's nothing like it." He rested his gaze on her for a second longer than was necessary, but it was long enough to stir something in her.

Ba nodded as if giving her approval. "Can't miss it."

"How far is it?" Poorvi asked.

"About three to four hours to the cliffs, give or take." He glanced up. "Though it looks like rain." He checked the weather app on his phone. "But not for a bit."

"We need to eat," Ba said as she opened her large purse, pulling out a ziplock bag that held something wrapped in foil.

Poorvi met his glance and shot him a quick smile. The spicy flatbread was a staple to travel with in case one needed a snack. "Perfect," she said. "We'll just have tepla while I drive." The sooner they finished this tour the better. She might have liked seeing the castle and the stone, but she was here for a reason. And it wasn't sightseeing.

Kavan raised his eyebrows at them. "Tepla? We can have that any time. We're only twenty minutes from Cork downtown and the English Market. Let's get something there. The food is amazing."

"It's an extra stop that we do not need to make." She motioned to the tepla. "Besides, Ba didn't say anything about the English Market."

"We're like twenty minutes away from this amazing meal—"

"Which we do not need," Poorvi insisted. "It's not on the itinerary."

"None of this is planned, is it?" Kavan retorted, maybe a bit more insistent than was necessary for a trip he was being forced into.

Ba eyed him a minute and her expression was unreadable. She sat down in the car. "Chalo. Kavan baraber kayche."

Poorvi sighed and shook her head at Ba's instruction to do what Kavan wanted. "Nicely done. We'll never get to Dublin at this rate."

Poorvi tried to hide it, but she was sure her anxiety was clear in the sweat on her brow and the way she clutched both the gearshift and the steering wheel. He couldn't blame her. He hadn't even bothered to learn how to drive a manual car.

Poorvi put the car in gear and pulled out. City driving was different than highway driving. She was not thrilled with having to drive into the downtown area, especially when she still wasn't familiar with driving on the opposite side of the road.

At home she was fine. But here… "Watch that pedestrian!" Kavan warned, somehow without raising his voice. Poorvi slammed the brake and the car stalled.

"All good," he said. "Just start her up."

Poorvi did that and they proceeded, with only a rude hand gesture from the pedestrian.

"The English Market is just a block away." Kavan looked at Ba as Poorvi parked. "You good with walking, Ba?"

"I may be old, but I am not feeble," Ba retorted as she bounded from the car and started walking to the market.

The English Market was a large market filled with various stalls ranging from savory food to sweets to paintings to pubs and everything in between. Sights, sounds and aromas of varying intensity surrounded them.

Poorvi inhaled deeply and, despite all her many reservations, her stomach rumbled.

"Coffee and a sandwich," Kavan stated to the group. "The meats here are amazing, as are our Irish cheeses. And the bread." He made the chef's kiss.

"Yeah, well, let's get the food quickly and get moving." Poorvi said. She shivered slightly, but it wasn't particularly cold. Maybe in the fifties. She glanced at the overcast sky. Sun would be nice.

Ba shook her head, a smile coming across her face. "You're missing out on the experience. Look around. Forget Dublin for a few minutes."

Poorvi stood and watched her. She was exhausted from the flight and the driving, but apparently Ba was not going to give in until she experienced the market. Poorvi had no choice.

Poorvi inhaled and looked around. Stall after stall of food, crafts, sweet treats, coffee, tourist knickknacks went on and on. They walked a bit and all the different aromas hit her. People were having coffee, buying trinkets or simply doing their daily food shopping. Movement and sound were constant. An obvious tourist destination, various languages from around the world hit her ears, a few familiar words here and there. The excitement in the air was palpable.

Kavan led the way to a large sandwich stall with a long line. "Worth the wait," he said as he got in line.

Poorvi rolled her eyes.

The line moved quickly and soon enough they each had a sandwich and a drink. Poorvi grabbed her sandwich and water and began walking back to the car. She got a few steps before Kavan called out to her.

"Poorvi!"

A spark shot down her spine. Her name in his voice sounded more tantalizing than it should.

She turned to face him.

"Join us at the park." Water bottle in hand, he motioned in the opposite direction.

"I really just want to keep—"

"Twenty minutes. How long will it take to eat a sandwich?" He opened his arms. "You might even like the fresh air," Kavan said, raising his eyebrows.

It would be nice to sit in the park.

"Poorvi. Chalo apray saathay," Ba insisted.

Poorvi sighed and turned around, telling herself she was acquiescing because of Ba's insistence and not because Kavan's voice was as irresistible as her favorite chocolate ice cream. She ignored the smirk on Ba's face and followed them to a park across from the English Market.

The three of them sat down on a bench. Kavan attacked his sandwich with gusto, nearly moaning in delight. "It's as good as I remember."

Poorvi looked at him. "When were you here last?"

"Been a while." He shook his head while chewing. "Like twenty years. We came here after the Blarney Stone." He met her eyes.

"Your family was here." She nodded understanding.

"My mom had taken Naveen to go see something else, so my dad brought me here for a sandwich. We're both foodies." Sadness floated over him. "Or we were. It was the best part of that trip."

"Dads are great that way."

The sadness in his eyes made way for gratitude. "Yes, they are."

"Ba," she said. "What else do you have in your bag?" Poorvi raised her eyebrows, hopeful. If Ba was anything like her grandmother… Ba grinned and pulled out a couple packets of hot sauce. Score!

Poorvi gleefully opened one and added it to her sandwich. She offered the sauce to Kavan, who stared at her, his mouth full, in complete disbelief. He chewed and swallowed.

"What are you doing?" he asked as if she were defiling a sacred spot.

"Adding a bit of spice."

"It's fine as is, isn't it?" he insisted.

"But now it's desi-fied!" She waved her sandwich in front

of him as if trying to tempt him and laughed. She took a bite. "Add spice, make it desi!"

"I know what desi-fied means." He laughed. "We used to…" He shook his head.

Ba was eating slowly and with purpose. She took small bites and chewed as if she were savoring every crumb. She seemed to have forgotten that Poorvi and Kavan were there as she took in her surroundings. But the look on her face was not one of wonder so much that it was of nostalgia.

Poorvi and Kavan finished, while Ba took her time.

"I saw a coffee shop across the street. I'll get us some coffees, yeah?" Kavan left.

She nodded and watched him go. Tall, medium build. His jeans fit him perfectly. Not bad to look at at all.

She turned to find Ba grinning at her. Ba bobbed her head in happiness.

Poorvi just rolled her eyes. "Fine. He's handsome," she acquiesced. Extremely handsome. "But that doesn't mean anything."

She was still enjoying her view when her phone buzzed for the millionth time. She tore her attention away from Kavan's walk and pulled it out. Thirty texts and three missed calls. All from Bobby, her boss.

"Ba. I need to make a call," she explained in Gujarati.

"Atcha." Ba nodded her head in understanding.

Poorvi stood a few feet away, but not so far that she couldn't still see Ba, and called Bobby.

"Where have you been?" Bobby started.

"Hello to you too," she said.

"You are supposed to be at the hotel preparing for your presentation," Bobby barked into the phone.

"I texted you. My flight was rerouted. We landed in Cork," she explained blandly. She truly resented having to answer to Bobby, but here she was, and she really had no choice.

"Cork? Where the hell is that?" he demanded.

"Not far." She kept her voice neutral and her answers short.

"Great. I'll see you soon."

"No."

"What does that mean?"

She watched Ba walk around in the small park. There was something…she just couldn't place it. "It means I'll be in Dublin by Friday."

"Friday?" Bobby sounded like he was going to have a heart attack. "Your job, my job, it's all on the line here. We need time to go over your presentation. Which is Saturday. Friday will be too late."

"I am aware of what exactly is on the line here, Bobby." She refused to call him Dr. Wright. Not while he had her job. "No need to remind me." If she presented well, the lab stood to get a grant that would keep them in work for the next four years. They could potentially even hire more staff. "And I am working on it."

"I certainly hope you are aware and that you are working toward that goal."

Anger and frustration boiled inside her. This was not first time that Bobby had insinuated that her priorities may not be with the lab. "What does that mean?"

"It means that you should know that sabotaging the lab sabotages you as well." He sounded so superior. "And it's Dr. Wright."

"Why would I sabotage the lab, Bobby?"

"People talk, Poorvi. You didn't get the job, maybe you want revenge."

"You have some imagination. I, unlike some others, *care* about my work. It's the only reason I'm still there. I'll be there and I'll present." She hung up. *And when she did save the lab, Bobby could kiss her ass.* He wouldn't fire her; he needed her more than she needed him, and he knew it. She took a few deep breaths as tears of anger burned her eyes. She had to let them fall, to release the mountain of feelings inside her. She didn't mind; she was way past caring if people saw her cry. If it made them uncomfortable, that was their problem. Poorvi sat down and let her tears of anger fall for a moment. She watched Ba through her tears.

Ba was looking at the trees, smelling the flowers, looking at the sky. She walked a bit and ran her hand along one of the benches. Much like someone who was *remembering* something. She looked—pensive. Poorvi could not explain why she cared, but she did. She could not just leave Ba with Kavan and run off to Dublin. She didn't want to.

Besides, Poorvi thought with a small smile, who would drive the car?

Her anger and frustration tamed for the moment, she wiped her eyes and drank water, letting Ba have her moment.

Kavan placed a call to Naveen while he waited for their coffees. The aroma of coffee, while pleasant, wasn't what he associated with this place. His father had brought along a thermos of chai on that trip. He and his father had enjoyed piping hot, sweet and spicy milky chai after their sandwich—just the two of them. That was how they "desi-fied" their trip. He could almost smell the cardamom and clove. The coffee shop sold chai, but he didn't trust it. Coffee shop chai would never compare with the fresh chai his father made. It would never deliver the same memories he carried inside him. The ones he felt so intensely.

His brother had been blowing up his phone all day with calls and texts. Kavan had let it go because he had been focused on Poorvi.

Navigating Poorvi. That's all.

The fact that she was beautiful had no bearing. She was argumentative and seemed to have no room for spontaneity. But she had shown him kindness.

Not that he was excited about this detour either. But the only way out seemed to be through, so if they moved at a good pace, they would show Ba everything on her list and make it to Dublin by tomorrow night. Which left him plenty of time to find this P. K. Gupta and have the discussion he needed.

"It's about time," Naveen greeted him.

"Hello to you too, then," Kavan said, instantly on guard.

"I've been trying to contact you all day. I heard your flight landed in—"

"Cork."

"Great, so you should be in Dublin soon then."

"Uh…well, there's been a bit of a holdup." Kavan waited for Naveen to fire up. He was not disappointed. Naveen's next words were edged with heat.

"What do you mean? Have I not made myself clear how important it is that you get to P. K. Gupta before he presents that paper?"

"You have." Kavan sighed. "And I will be there. I just have a few things I'm taking care of." Kavan did not need to be around to navigate Poorvi. She was smart; she'd be fine. He could easily get a train to Dublin and be there in a couple hours. But he didn't want to. He was enjoying Ba's company and was intrigued by Poorvi. She was irritating and captivating all in one and he wasn't ready to leave her.

"What does that mean? Little bhai, what—"

"Sorry I've lost you." Kavan faked a poor connection. "Can't…hear…you…"

"Kavan…don't you hang up—" Naveen warned.

Kavan disconnected the call as he grabbed the coffees. He had a road trip to get back to. His brother could wait.

Chapter Ten

The driving was getting easier. Poorvi had driven them into and out of the city area with little to no incident. They were on the highway on the four-hour trek to the Cliffs of Moher. She was quite proud of the fact that she had grown more comfortable driving on the opposite side of the road.

She was even comfortable enough to sip her black coffee as she drove. Kavan had offered cream and sugar, but she liked to taste her coffee.

"Okay. Black coffee."

"Wow," she had said as he began to dress his coffee. "Having a bit of coffee with your cream and sugar?"

He narrowed his eyes at her. "There isn't a thing you don't feel the need to judge, is there?"

She stared at him a minute. "No."

Kavan and Ba were presently conversing in fairly rapid Gujarati about Ba's family. Poorvi could hear Kavan's Gujarati getting more fluid the more he spoke with Ba. The sky darkened, warning them of an impending storm. She inhaled and gripped the wheel a bit tighter.

"You okay?" Kavan snapped his head to her. It was as if he could sense her apprehension.

"I'm fine." How did he know she was suddenly nervous?

Kavan turned around in his seat and faced forward. "Looks like a storm."

"Mmm-hmm." She nodded.

"You're not liking storms, are you?" he asked her.

She side-eyed him. "No."

"And why would that be?" He was focused on her rather intently.

She shook her head. "I've just never liked them—since I was a kid."

"No childhood trauma or anything?"

"Nothing that led to a fear of storms." She chuckled.

"Same for the small spaces. I just don't like them," he said.

Poorvi glanced in the rearview mirror. Ba had fallen asleep in the back seat. They drove in silence for a few minutes. The only sound came from the rain hitting the top of the car. Considering she hated storms, the pattering of the rain was strangely comforting. Or was it that Kavan was sitting beside her?

"I was dating this psychiatrist who insisted that I must have had some childhood trauma that led to my fear of storms." She shook her head. "He would have had a field day with you. Fear of small spaces was a specialty of his."

"You dated a psychiatrist?" Kavan raised his eyebrows.

She shrugged. "Yes. Brooks."

"As in past tense?"

"As in he turned out to be a less than stellar human being."

"What happened?" Kavan's voice was calm and inviting, and she found herself wanting to tell him.

"Well, things went down at my work—bad things—and instead of standing up for me, or at the very least sticking by me, Brooks bailed." Just another betrayal in a long list of betrayals.

"Sounds like you made a near escape there."

She grinned. "Sounds about right." It was easy, talking to this man. "What about you? Any dating horrors? Or—" It suddenly occurred to her, though her stomach dropped at the thought. "Maybe you have someone right now?"

Kavan simply grinned and shook his head. "Nah."

"Really? I'd have thought you would be fighting off the women, being that handsome."

He smirked at her. "You think I'm handsome?"

"Uh…duh. Everyone thinks you're handsome." She played it off even as she flushed.

"You're not everyone," he said quietly.

Her heart thudded at the implication that her opinion weighed heavier. "You're avoiding the question," she said to avoid his statement.

Rain started falling heavily suddenly, and it was as if buckets of water were being thrown at the windshield. She slowed her speed as visibility decreased drastically.

He cleared his throat. "Well then, you would be correct. I don't have trouble getting a date. It's just they aren't usually interested in anything more than how I look." He peered out his window. "Not that it matters. Naveen feels the need to vet any serious girlfriend I might have, and they usually run screaming into the night after meeting him."

She dared a glance at him and was taken by the anger and frustration on his face. Before she could speak, he suddenly turned and glanced out the front window.

"Oh! That's our exit!" He pointed. It was the one exit that was on the right.

"Seriously?" she grumbled. He had given her no warning. Poorvi hit the gas and navigated the car quickly to the far left lane to take the exit. She made the exit but went too fast for the curve. The car skidded and veered off the road in the exact spot where there wasn't a guardrail. They were thrown forward, and then yanked back by their seat belts. The bags in the trunk thumped against one another. The car came to stop, half in and half out of a ditch.

"Ba!" Poorvi and Kavan exclaimed together, turning to the back of the car.

"I'm okay," she said, her voice shaky. "Not hurt." She looked around. "My phone?"

"Poorvi! Are you okay?" He was breathless, his concern genuine.

Poorvi looked around and saw that they were all fine. All still buckled in, even though the car was at an odd angle. The rain had let up some but was still coming down. "I'm fine. No thanks to you," she barked at him, all happy thoughts and warm feelings dissolved away.

"What? How is this my fault? You're driving."

Her mouth gaped open. "Are you saying that it's my fault we're in a ditch?"

"You're the driver."

Was he serious right now? "You were too busy chatting to do your job, which was navigating," Poorvi spat at him.

"I told you to take the exit."

"When we were on top of it."

"Array!" Ba raised her voice and they turned to her. "I can't find my phone." There was panic in her voice.

"We'll find it, Ba," Poorvi said. "It has to be in the car."

"I need my phone." The panic in Ba's voice was turning to fear. "I need my phone."

Everyone was attached to their phones, and panicked to some degree when they couldn't find it. But Ba was shaking. "Ba. It's just under a seat or something—"

Before Kavan could finish, Ba had bent over to look under the seat for her phone.

He turned to Poorvi, the question on his face. She shook her head. She had no idea why Ba's phone was all of a sudden so important.

"Ba. Nothing left the car," Poorvi said.

"We will find it. Don't bend like that, you might hurt—"

"I am perfectly fine," she snapped. "Just because I am old does not mean I will break." She glared at the two of them. "Instead of arguing, how about you get us out of here?"

"Okay." Poorvi turned back to the wheel. She started the car and tried to move forward. Nothing. Backward. Nothing. She shook her head at Kavan. "I think we're stuck. Sounds like spinning tires."

"Right." Kavan nodded at her and stepped out into the rain without a thought or his coat. Poorvi followed with an umbrella from her backpack. Kavan was soaked through by the time she reached him.

"You should have taken the umbrella. It's cold and rainy," she said. He really should have, because now his T-shirt was stuck to his very fine, very muscular chest. She could see every one of those finely formed muscles. Holy Bollywood rain scene. She did her best not to stare. "Now you're...wet." She forced her gaze to the car as if she were studying the angle.

"The front tire is stuck in the mud. We need a tow," Kavan said. She held the umbrella over him so he could call AA. "They won't be here for hours," he said after speaking with them. "A bunch of accidents are keeping them busy." He continued to study his phone. "But there's a pub only about half a kilometer away. I'll see if I can borrow a car to come get you and Ba."

"I can walk. You're soaked through and it's cold." She made an honest effort to not to look at how his T-shirt was clinging to the lean muscles of his chest and arms. She failed. Was there any part of him that wasn't gorgeous? Ah, yes. He was irritating.

"Exactly. I'm already wet. We can't leave Ba alone," he said, bending to see Ba in the car.

Made sense. "Okay." She looked at him. "Do you want the umbrella?" She couldn't keep the laughter from her voice.

He looked at her and a wide grin spread across his face as laughter escaped him. Poorvi stared at him a minute, before joining him in laughter. She hadn't been trying to be funny, it just came out. Like most things she said around him, she was just being herself. She couldn't remember the last time she had been this uninhibited around anyone besides Niki. She was freezing and she could see that he was, too. But they both laughed to the point of not being able to breathe. Together. Also something that Poorvi hadn't done in awhile.

Just then Ba cracked open her window. "It's great you think this is so funny, but I have to pee. And I still can't find my phone."

Poorvi and Kavan got hold of themselves and their laughter. Poorvi got back in the car; the bottom of her pants were soaked, but other than that she was dry. She watched Kavan jog toward the pub, but lost sight of him quickly.

Ba was silent, still patting the seats, a look of anguish on her face. Poorvi managed to climb into the back seat and bent down to look for Ba's phone. She finally found it, lodged between the seat and the door.

"I'll have to open your door to get it," Poorvi said.

"Don't let it get wet," Ba said, her eyes huge. "Please."

Poorvi nodded. "I'll do my best." She quickly opened the door a couple inches and grabbed the phone before it fell out or got rained on. She breathed relief. "I got it!" She held it up and Ba grabbed it from her.

Ba tapped it and put it to her ear. A smile came across her face as she nodded. "Perfect," she told Poorvi. "Still works."

"That's great," Poorvi said as she crawled back to sitting, but Ba's elation went beyond getting a phone back. "Was that your daughter?"

"Hmm? Yes. She left me a message." A small smirk appeared on her face. "Kavan didn't even think twice about getting out into the rain." Now that she had her phone back, Ba was back to matchmaking.

Poorvi grinned and nodded. "Yes. That was very kind of him."

"Dependable," Ba clarified. "And now he is bringing a car for you."

"He's bringing a car for you." Though the gesture was not lost on her. He was…unselfish…he cared about people. It was definitely…rare…and attractive.

"You were laughing with him," Ba accused. "In the rain." Her eyes lit up and she clasped her hands together. "Soooo Bollywood."

Poorvi simply shook her head at Ba as if she were ridiculous, but the grin on her face wouldn't go away.

"Ba." A subject change was necessary. "You looked a bit sad at that park in Cork. Is everything okay?"

Ba studied her a moment. "Nice try," she blurted out, breaking out into a smile. "But I can tell you're attracted to Kavan."

"Ba. He's a kind, thoughtful and handsome man. *Anyone* would be attracted to him. It means nothing," Poorvi explained. It was true. Just because a man was attractive and she was attracted to him did not mean that there was anything to it. Brooks was attractive and intelligent, and they had enjoyed each other's company. But when push came to shove…Brooks had bolted. "He is also very argumentative."

"Hanh." Ba grinned and bobbled her head. "He argues back at you. But you admit you are attracted to him."

A knock at her window startled her and she turned to find a soaking wet version of the man himself. Back with a car.

Chapter Eleven

Kavan had managed to borrow a car from the young bartender, Melissa, with little effort. He deposited Poorvi and Ba—and their bags, Ba had insisted—at the pub. A typical pub, the bar was wooden and took up one side of the space. On the other side were rustic wooden tables with mismatched chairs. The walls were covered with football pennants from teams and their supporters from all over Ireland and the world. The lighting was dim as there was no sun, but the owner had cranked the heat so they were warm and comfortable. Near the back was a small doorway that led back to the bed and breakfast part of the establishment.

Kavan checked his phone and found that AA would be more than a few hours.

"Might as well have a pint," he told Poorvi and Ba. "We'll be here for a bit."

Melissa, the young blonde bartender, approached them. "This is Melissa. It's her car I borrowed." He turned to her. "Thank you again." He handed her the key.

"Of course." She flushed a bit, bounced her ponytail. "Can I get you a pint, some food?"

"Um. I'm sure that we would all appreciate that."

"Of course." Melissa eyed him, a smirk on her face. "A place to freshen up?"

"If it's not too much trouble," he said with a smile as he dripped all over the pub.

"Not at all. Not for you." She tilted her head for him to follow. "Come on then." She turned to Poorvi. "My da will be by in a moment for your food order."

Poorvi wiggled her fingers at him as she raised one eyebrow. "Have a nice...whatever." She smirked.

He shook his head at her but followed Melissa through that small door in the back and then through a small maze of hallways. "This area is available if you'd like to be more comfortable." She nodded at a small sitting area that had a sofa, a plush chair, a few tables and a small bar. She continued walking and opened a door. "This room is empty for the night. You're welcome to warm up in the shower."

"Thank you." Kavan said.

Melissa lingered a moment, eyeing Kavan appreciatively. "You seem very familiar. Do I know you from somewhere?" She moved toward him.

Kavan swallowed. "I have that kind of face." He waited for her to leave so he could shower. She did not seem in a hurry to go. The room was moderately sized with a queen bed and a sofa. His phone buzzed again. AA was not going to make it today.

"Looks like I'll be needing to rent a room for the night." He looked at Melissa. "The tow won't be getting here until after midnight."

Melissa grinned and stepped closer to him. "This here is the only room I have. But my room has space for one, handsome." It was clear what her thought process was, and sadly it wasn't the first time he'd been propositioned like this. He had half a mind to tell her off, but they needed a place to stay.

"Perfect, I can send my grandmother to share with you, then. My wife and I can take this room," Kavan blurted out.

"Your wife?"

"Oh yes. My wife." Kavan smiled innocently.

"But you haven't a ring," Melissa observed.

"We…ah…couldn't afford them just yet. Only been married a few months. Taking my grandmother to see our fair country…yeah?"

Melissa stepped back and forced a smile. "Of course. Makes sense. Forgive me."

"Oh yeah." He waved it off. "Honest mistake. No ring and all."

"Well, then I'll leave you to the shower," Melissa said, all business once more.

Kavan nodded as she left. He grabbed some dry clothes from his bag and hit the shower. He was cold to the core, and the warm shower was welcome.

He changed and headed down to Poorvi and Ba. Poorvi looked like she was enjoying an Irish coffee, while Ba had hit the Guiness.

"We need to spend the night here. The tow won't arrive until later," Kavan told them.

He saw Melissa chatting with an older man, must be her da. She'd be over for his drink order any minute. "Play along with me. Just pretend we're married," he said to Poorvi in Gujarati.

Poorvi furrowed her brow. "*What? No way.*"

"We need a room for the night and I told her—" he flickered his eyes in Melissa's direction "—that we were married."

"Not my problem that you lied," Poorvi groused.

"She…she asked me to share her room," Kavan spit out.

Whatever he expected from Poorvi, it certainly wasn't rage.

"She did what?" Poorvi hissed. "Just because you're incredibly attractive does not mean she can ask… I'm going to give her a piece of my mind." Poorvi started to stand.

"Please don't. It was literally the first thing I could think of to politely refuse her." Kavan put his hand on her thigh, and she turned to look at him. She was warm and she did not push his hand away. His breathing evened out and he relaxed.

"Well, it shouldn't." Poorvi narrowed her eyes as she shifted her gaze behind him. "She's coming over."

Kavan held Poorvi's hand on the table, and it was as if they'd always held hands. She glanced at their hands and shook her head.

"Not enough." She leaned toward him, looking him in the eye. "Just kiss me," she demanded.

"What?"

"Just. Kiss me." She widened her eyes and encouraged him with a nod.

She nodded again, her dark eyes hard with determination. He was close enough to feel her breath, to catch the flower and rain scent of her. His heart gave a thud and he leaned toward her and gently pecked her lips.

"That's a kiss?" She mocked him, her lips near his. "Maybe this is why you don't have a girlfriend." Her mouth was poised in a smirk when she moved her lips back to his. She pressed her mouth against his and relaxed into him. Her mouth, so sassy, was soft and welcoming. She tasted sweet from the coffee and whiskey and he melted into her.

Kissing Poorvi felt like the most natural, but simultaneously the most wonderful sensation. He was starting to lose himself when—

"Ahem."

They startled and looked up to see the owner standing before them, a frown on his face. "I understand you are newlyweds, but this is not that kind of establishment. I believe you have rented a room from us, I expect ya to use it."

"Yes, sir, of course," Kavan said, still dazed. "Mister?"

"Every one just calls me Mr. O," said the older man.

Poorvi nodded and mumbled something, her eyes still glassy, her lips still wet from the kiss.

Still a bit off kilter, Kavan tried to slide away from Poorvi, thinking distance might set him straight, but his elbow hit Ba's pint, knocking it over. Guinness spilled everywhere, causing a commotion. "I'm so sorry!"

The owner shook his head as he mopped up the mess. "Wasting perfectly good Guinness, you are. Must have been some kiss."

"Yes, sir," Kavan said, helping to clean things off, a flush coming over him. "It certainly was." He threw a furtive glance at Poorvi, who also had a flush about her, but she was decidedly not looking at him as she chugged the remainder of her Irish coffee.

"Well now, boyo. What'll you be havin'?" asked the older man once he'd mopped up the mess.

"I'll be drinking Guinness," Kavan said. "And the soup will be fine."

"I'll have the soup as well. And another." Clearing her throat, Poorvi held up her empty glass.

Melissa put some peanuts on the table, still eyeing Kavan. "You really do look familiar."

He pulled down his ball cap. He always traveled with multiple. Those ads Naveen had him do were all over social media. He hated being recognized even more than he hated doing them.

"Ah. No. Never been to these parts," Kavan said, as he took Poorvi's hand. It was the second time he'd done that in last few minutes, but he found it grounding. And happily she did not seem to mind. "Can we not have the nuts, please? I'm allergic."

"Sure." Melissa removed the nuts and her father went to fetch their drinks and food. Poorvi released her hand from his.

He flicked his gaze to her, but she was engrossed in her cup. Of course she let go of his hand, there was no one near by they were putting on a show for. But the logic did not take away the empty feeling of not having her hand in his. "The car is stuck until at least midnight," Kavan informed them softly. "Melissa here was kind enough to allow us to rent the only room they have left, for the night. You both can share the bed and I'll take the sofa."

Melissa showed up with their beers. "Something else to eat, ma'am?" she asked Ba.

Ba shook her head. "Another Guinness to replace the one he spilled?"

"Yes, ma'am," Melissa said. She started clearing away the snacks. "So how did you all meet?"

Kavan's heart thudded in his chest, but he kept a smile on his face as Poorvi took his hand. Comfort flooded over him. "You know, the normal way." He chuckled.

Ba looked at Melissa and started telling her a story in Gujarati. Kavan was flabbergasted. He looked at Poorvi, that same smile still plastered on his face. She was also smiling, but her attention was on Ba. She translated for Melissa.

"Well. I'll tell you the truth. They met one year ago at the temple. They were immediately drawn to each other, but they weren't sure if their parents would approve. So they arranged vacations for their families—separately of course—and planned to 'accidently' meet at various locations. Hawaii, India, London, even here in Dublin." Ba was more animated than they had seen her thus far. "Until finally their families caught on. By then the families were close friends and were thrilled that the two of them wanted to be married. A wedding was planned and these two are together." Ba smiled at them with such genuine affection, Kavan was taken aback. But more importantly, Melissa was wide-eyed and smiling.

"That is just beautiful." She turned to them both. "I wish you both the best."

Poorvi nodded, but her attention was on Ba. Once Melissa left, Poorvi leaned into Ba. "That was a beautiful story."

Ba nodded.

"Is that how you and Dada met?" she asked.

Ba froze her gaze on Poorvi, her mouth pressed together. "You are very smart," she said quietly.

"As are you." Poorvi grinned.

Poorvi reached across and held Ba's hand. Kavan reached his hand out and laid it on Poorvi's.

He raised his pint to them both and sipped. "Thank you, Ba."

Poorvi raised her glass as well, to Ba and then to him. "Thanks for finding us a place to stay."

"It was the least I could do since I wasn't paying attention to the navigating." He shrugged one shoulder sheepishly.

Poorvi raised her mug to him. "No kidding." She laughed. Her phone was on the table and began to buzz. She looked at it and scowled. "I'm sorry, I need to take this." Poorvi stood and walked to the back of the pub.

Kavan watched her go, his gaze lingering a bit longer than necessary. He turned to find Ba looking at him with a huge smile on her face.

"She is beautiful," Ba said.

"Yes." But it didn't mean anything. Though if he was honest, he was still a bit dazed from that kiss.

"She's a good person," Ba added.

"She's irritating," Kavan responded, but without any real gusto.

"That doesn't mean she's not a good person," Ba said, finishing off her Guiness.

Poorvi did not return after twenty minutes had passed. And she was no longer at the back of the bar. Kavan went to find her. She was standing alone on the back porch, watching the rain.

Something about the way she stood tugged at his heart. "Poorvi?" he called out gently.

She startled. Her hands went to her face as if she were wiping away tears. "Yes. Sorry. I just—"

"Everything okay?"

"Um." She turned to face him, her eyes rimmed red. "Yes. Nothing for you to be concerned about."

"Poorvi…"

She put a hand up. "I said I was fine. You got us a room and tow for the car. Enough heroism for the day," she snapped at him.

Tears brimmed in her eyes, but she clearly did not want to share. Disappointment came over him. He had thought after the car and maybe even the kiss that maybe she was opening up to him. Clearly he had read too much.

"Right. Of course." He backtracked. "Just wanted to know if you wanted another drink. It's your turn to pay." He forced a grin for her, a poor attempt to lighten whatever upset her.

She blinked and inhaled, smiling as she moved toward him. "No, it's not, Ba stole your credit card. So yeah, I'll have another drink." She walked past him and back to the pub. "Maybe even two." She smirked at him, but there was gratitude in her watery eyes.

"What do you mean Ba stole my card?" He followed her back into the pub. Just then his phone rang with a call from his cousin and best friend, Anand. "Go ahead and order another round. I'll be there in a minute."

Poorvi furrowed her brow but continued.

"What's up?"

"Where are you?" Anand asked.

"I don't know. Near Cliffs of Moher."

"You're sightseeing?"

"It's complicated."

"Well, Naveen keeps calling me," Anand said. "He's getting on my last nerve. He thinks you're with me, avoiding the conference, and more to the point avoiding the conversation you need to have with P. K. Gupta. Which I know you are because you disagree with him, but you never stand up to him."

"I'm not avoiding. And I have told him that I disagree. That we should consider the research," Kavan explained.

"But you haven't put your foot down."

"It's not that easy. He's my big brother. I owe him—"

"You don't owe him your whole life, Kavan." Anand sighed. "Yes, he pulled you out of a tough time. But that's what family does. It does not make you beholden to them for the rest of your life." Anand chuckled. "In any case, I support you not getting to that conference until you absolutely have to. About time you had a couple days off. How'd you end up there?"

"I was—" how to explain Poorvi and Ba and the storm and the car "—detoured."

"Ah. You're hooking up." Anand snickered. "About time. I can't even remember your last girlfriend."

"Well it's been awhile, hasn't it?" Kavan always seemed to end up with the women who were more interested in his money and name more than anything. The last one, Laura, had been no different. They'd been together almost a year, when he'd found her kissing someone else. He'd been hurt by the betrayal, but he'd been more hurt by Naveen's words when he told him about the breakup. *You're too nice, Kavan. People are going to take advantage of you. Nice is not working for you. Get a backbone or keep getting your heart broken.*

"But, no. I am not hooking up."

"Well, you should."

"Goodbye, Anand."

"I'm not picking up if Naveen calls again."

"Agreed."

He ended the call with his cousin, feeling lighter. He and Anand were born a day apart, and had been best friends since birth.

He glanced outside. The rain had let up. He went back to the pub, a pep in his step, thinking about sitting next to Poorvi again.

Chapter Twelve

It was close to midnight, a few pints and a ton of delicious food later, when AA texted Kavan that they would meet him in fifteen minutes. He excused himself to go to the rental car.

Poorvi and Ba made their way to the room. No sooner had Poorvi lain down and turned off the light than Ba started snoring. Poorvi gently nudged her. It stopped. Poorvi closed her eyes and settled in just as the snoring started again.

This was not going to work. Poorvi grabbed her pillow and an extra blanket and headed for the back of the pub to the cute little sitting room where she had seen a sofa. She quietly navigated the dark inn by moonlight and found the room with the sofa in the back. She located a small lamp and turned it on. The light revealed a bookshelf. She chose a book and settled into the sofa. She wasn't waiting for Kavan to return. Not at all. She simply needed a distraction from the call earlier that day.

Her mother had called to find out how the prep was going for the conference. Poorvi had chosen that moment to be forthright and tell her mother exactly what she was doing. Mistake. Huge mistake.

"What do you mean you befriended an old lady and are taking her to see Ireland with some strange man you don't know?"

"When you say it like that, Mom, it sounds ridiculous."

"How else would I say it?"

"She's all alone. I can't just leave her."

"Beti. Your priority should be this meeting. After everything that happened at the lab, you need to redeem yourself. You need to prove yourself."

"Redeem? Mom. I did nothing wrong." She was fired up. How did you redeem yourself when you had done nothing wrong?

"Well then how did Dr. Wright get the Principal Investigator job?"

"Mom. Are you saying that you believe those...rumors?"

"Of course not but—"

"But what, Mom?"

"But you must have done something for those rumors to start. People don't just make things up," she insisted.

"Mom. I can't." Tears of frustration had built up again. "I can't keep having this conversation with you. I did nothing wrong. All I did was be a woman in a man's field. I would think you would understand that."

"I do understand that, but instead of making a stink about it, sometimes you have to roll with it."

"No. I will not." Shaking with rage, Poorvi had tapped her phone off and let the tears come. That was when Kavan had found her.

The book must have distracted her, or she was simply that exhausted, because as she was close to drifting off she felt a gentle tap on her shoulder. She heard Kavan's velvet voice saying her name.

"Poorvi?"

She turned to look up at him, slightly confused but comforted by his presence. Unbidden, the kiss that they had shared earlier came to mind and she flushed. It was supposed to be fake, but kissing Kavan had not felt real, it had felt amazing. She could not recall ever being kissed like that.

"What's going on?" He walked around and sat down next to her. He sat close enough that she could feel the heat from his body. She was immediately tempted to curl herself into that warmth and comfort, and was only able to do so by reminding herself that she had no real right to his comfort.

She closed the book. "Ba snores. She sounds like a chain saw." Poorvi grinned.

He chuckled. "Of course she does. The car is here, surprisingly no damage, so we're all set for the morning." He stood.

He was leaving? "You going to bed?" She didn't want to be alone with only her thoughts for company.

"Uh...well." He looked around. "Unless you want a drop of whiskey?"

"If you want." She shrugged like she didn't care.

He poured two whiskeys and brought them over, sitting down on the sofa. "I don't see any ice for you." He shrugged.

"This is perfect," she said. They clinked glasses and sipped. Rather he sipped, she chugged. The alcohol was warm on the way, slight burn, but she'd been drinking whiskey for years.

"Okaaaay." He raised his eyebrows and grabbed the bottle, pouring her another glass.

"Don't judge." She sipped this second glass.

"You judged my coffee." He smirked.

"You can't even taste the coffee if you put all that—"

"But that's how I like it." He raised his eyebrows at her.

She opened her mouth, then closed it. "Fine."

He sat back, grinning at her. Her eyes went directly to his mouth. She forced her gaze to his eyes. "I would never judge you."

She stared into her drink. "That call I got? My mom. Telling me I don't have my priorities straight."

"Ah." Kavan moved closer to her on the sofa and grinned. "Seeing the sites in Ireland with a strange man doesn't make your mum's priority list?" He quirked an eyebrow as he sipped. "Odd."

"No." His attempt at humor was sweet and she appreciated

it, but the tears made another showing. "She blames me for losing my promotion."

"I take it she's wrong." Kavan nodded. He turned to face her, their legs just shy of touching.

She longed to move her leg that half an inch so she could be touching him. "Yes." She nearly whispered it as if not saying out loud didn't make it true.

"What happened?"

Poorvi stared at Kavan. He had the kindest eyes, and right now he was looking at her with no judgment, no expectation.

"If you say it, you might feel better," he said softly as he took another sip of his drink.

"Or I might feel worse." She wasn't a sharer. She didn't tell anyone her personal things—by definition, they were *personal*. Even her Ba used to tell her she was a closed book. She had been since birth, but then the few times she did open up, she had gotten hurt. "Trusted" friends had told her secrets in high school, resulting in whispering behind her back, as well as comments to her face.

But right now, in this moment, she felt safe. She wanted to share with Kavan. She needed to.

He gave her a small smile, one that went all the way to his eyes. "That is a risk. But trust me. I've been told I'm a good listener."

She narrowed her eyes at him. "Yeah? By who?"

He paused and chuckled. "My mom."

Poorvi stared at him. There was no reason to laugh. His mother had faith in him. It was more than what she could say about her own mother.

"That's good enough for me." She paused and took off her glasses. "Dr. Bobby Wright and I were coinvestigators in the lab. When Dr. Steven Wang, our principal investigator, decided to move to another state to be with his wife, his job was up for grabs."

She leaned in toward Kavan. "That job was mine." She pointed at herself and paused as the anger became a lump in her throat. "When I say I'm smarter and better equipped to handle that job in every way possible, understand that that is not professional ego. That is fact. Not my opinion. Fact."

Kavan nodded. "I don't doubt it."

"Right before the announcement, Steve brought me into his office. He said things…" She shook her head, pressed her tears down and sat straight up. "He said that his boss, Dr. James Hardy, claimed that I had approached him, offering…sex…" Even now it was close to impossible to say, the notion was so ridiculous. "If he would tell Steve to pick me as the next PI."

Kavan sat up straight at this news, his eyes narrowed and brow furrowed, like he was trying to understand, but not believing what had happened. Pretty much how she had felt at the time.

"Dr. Hardy had many times over the years asked me to dinner. I had coffee with him one time when I happened to run into him in the cafeteria and he invited me to join him." She looked at Kavan; she needed him to believe her. "I never once accepted his invitations. For precisely this reason." She shivered. "He had always given me a creepy sort of vibe."

"Did you fight back?"

"With what? I had no proof that he'd asked me out. All of our interactions were verbal. I never told anyone but Niki that he asked me out. I told Steve and Bobby that Dr. Hardy was the one who pursued me. Whether they believed me or not, I don't know." Her voice became high pitched with frustration, and the tears were harder to stop.

"This Dr. Hardy, he didn't call for your outright removal from the lab for these alleged happenings?" Kavan was focused on her, his anger clearly simmering beneath the need to understand the logic.

She shook her head. "No. In fact, he even said that he didn't want to 'destroy' me by having me fired, he simply didn't think I was PI material. Like he was doing me some kind of favor." Tears of anger burned and spilled out onto her cheeks. "So I did not get promoted. And 'somehow' the rumors got out. Now the whole lab knows what Dr. Hardy said."

"Why didn't you leave?" His voice was low, a growl almost.

She fired up. "Because I shouldn't have to! My work is in that lab. All of my findings..." She shook her head. "No, I won't leave."

There. She'd told somebody and she was close to sobbing from the anger and the injustice of it all. "My mom, she thinks I should have just gone on one date, and he would have left me alone. She thinks that I must have done *something* to have lost the promotion. But I didn't. And I know how men like him operate, anyway. It wouldn't have been just one date. And anything I did with him would've become blackmail material."

She looked at him expecting to see sympathy, or kindness, or god forbid, pity. Instead, there was fury in his eyes. His jaw was clenched, and his mouth was set, his hand was fisted around his drink, which he seemed to have forgotten about.

"I'm sorry men are such assholes."

"Me, too," she said, and let loose her sobs. She couldn't help it. It was too big. Her anger at her mom, her frustration with Bobby and Steve, the power Hardy wielded, everyone in the lab second-guessing her character. Right now, it was too much for her to hold all on her own.

She wasn't sure when it happened, but Kavan's arms wrapped around her, holding her close while she sobbed into his T-shirt. She melted into the comfort she so needed, that Kavan so willingly gave. She honestly could not remember ever being held this way. Cherished.

"Wait," Kavan's voice hardened again and he pulled back a bit to look at her. "The psychiatrist?"

Fresh tears of anger filled her eyes as she nodded. "As soon as I told him, he backed away from me. He actually asked me if it was true."

"Complete dosser," Kavan grumbled.

Kavan had barely known her twenty-four hours and he had accepted her version as truth. "I don't know what that means, but it sounds exactly what like Brooks was. A dosser."

Kavan let loose a small chuckle as he wiped her tears and whispered. "You're not alone. It's a promise, yeah?"

Chapter Thirteen

Kavan held her face an extra beat as he wiped away her tears. He never could understood men like Brooks. Anger bloomed in his chest at the thought of how he had hurt Poorvi.

He said nothing, because what could he say that would change what had happened to her?

She quieted and he reached in his pocket for his handkerchief and offered it to her. "It's clean, I promise," he said.

She took it and wiped her eyes. "Who carries these anymore?"

He grinned, grateful that it was a habit for him to simply put one in his pocket always. Honestly, it was a way to remember his father. But today, it came in handy. "My dad told me and my brother to always have one on us. You can never know when one's needed."

"Well, he was right," she said. "Thank you."

"I wish I could tell him." Kavan paused.

She smiled at him, her eyes still wet from crying, grabbed her drink, and curled back up on the sofa facing him. Not in his arms, just next to him, her thigh touching his knee. His arms felt empty, but at least some part of her was touching him. "Tell me about him."

"What?"

"If you want. Tell me about your dad." She was looking at him, her full attention on him. She really wanted to know.

Kavan took a gulp of his whiskey. He didn't talk about his

dad much. No one around him ever wanted to discuss him. Naveen would merely grunt when he brought up their dad. His mother just got wistful. He looked at Poorvi.

He had gotten used to not talking about his dad, but suddenly he was excited to tell her all about him. Share all the ways in which he was a great dad. "Well, he was the one who took me to the Blarney Stone and the English Market."

"I already know that." Her eyes lit up. She had taken off her glasses, and sitting so close to her, he could see her eyes properly now. They were big and dark, dark brown, almost black. The kind of eyes that you wanted to fall into. At least he did. She narrowed them at him, pointing a finger. "Something else."

Kavan just looked at her. "He used to coach my football— soccer—teams when I was very little, like five or six. Back when we lived in the States."

Poorvi smiled all the way to her eyes.

"Then after, no matter how well or poorly we played, he'd take us to an ice cream truck and get every one of us an ice cream treat. Naveen had asked him why he did that even if we played badly." Kavan shook his head. A mix of sadness and pride filled him. "And my da would say that soccer should be fun, and he wanted us to always remember that playing should be fun."

Poorvi was gazing at him, her eyes glassy. "He sounds like an amazing dad."

Kavan nodded, a sense of peace coming over him. "He really was." Silence sat between them, comfortable and quiet.

"What ice cream did you get? From the truck."

Kavan grinned wide. "Same thing. Every time." His eyes went distant. "Well, almost every time. Oreo ice cream sandwich."

Poorvi's eyes bugged out. "Me too! My hands-down favorite."

Kavan focused on her a minute. Her dark eyes sparkled, her

smile was animated, she looked as happy as a little girl with an Oreo ice cream sandwich.

Huh. Something niggled in the back of his mind. Like a thread of memory he couldn't quite grasp.

"Tell me more about him," she said, sipping her drink.

"Well, he would have liked you."

"Why is that?" She was smiling.

"Because he loved a strong, feisty, irritating woman."

She laughed and it was a beautiful thing, the way her face lit up and her eyes crinkled. "I do my best," she said as she raised her glass. "So, your mom. She's feisty?"

He shook his head. "Not anymore," he said quietly. "She changed when he died."

Poorvi pursed her lips and nodded. "I hear you. My mom and dad are like this." She crossed her fingers. "I hate to think what would happen if…"

"Sounds like they're happy," he said.

She shrugged.

"And what do you think of that?"

"Of getting married?" She shrugged. "I have my work. My mom of course would love for me to be married, but she really doesn't nag me about it. Though it would be nice to share your life with someone. To have that companion in life." She turned and crossed her legs, facing him fully. It meant her legs were no longer touching his and he felt it like a loss. "Not just anyone, though. The right person. You know what I mean?"

He nodded as he sipped his drink. "I do know."

"So, what happened when your dad died? How come Naveen raised you?" She leaned in toward him.

He drew his gaze over her. Was she really interested or just passing the time? He shrugged. He wanted to share with her. "My brother kind of took over when our dad died. He was eighteen. I was fifteen.

"Grief hit my mom hard. So Naveen was the one feeding

us, making sure we got to school, all that. Then after some time, I was getting myself mixed up with the wrong crowd. It was Naveen who pulled me away from all that. He saved me." Kavan gulped his whiskey. "Of course, he's never let me forget it."

"Sorry. He probably feels like he doesn't want to lose you as well as your dad." Poorvi looked him in the eye.

Silence floated between them as he considered this possibility.

She grinned at him. "Your American accent comes out every so often."

He nodded. "I was born in the States, we moved here when I six or seven?" He shrugged. "In any case I fluctuate depending on who I'm talking to. The American is coming out because I'm sitting here with you."

She nodded. More silence, but Kavan did not feel the pressure to fill it as he usually did.

Kavan believed that relationships took time to build. So maybe it was the whiskey, or the storm or the way Poorvi's dark wavy hair framed her face. Or maybe it was because they were being honest with each other, but the idea of an instant connection with someone was so incredibly unbelievable, he never would have given it any credence if it weren't for how he felt right then.

"You know, I noticed you at the airport," he said softly.

"Yeah. You took my outlet," she taunted him, smiling.

"I got there first." He chuckled softly, taking in her sassy smile, tousled hair and red-rimmed eyes. "But before that. I saw you."

She met his gaze as she sipped her whiskey, narrowing her eyes at him. "So when you took my outlet, that was your way of hitting on me…?"

"No. I would say it was the biggest mistake I'd ever made, but here we are anyway."

She locked his eyes with his. They had been leaning toward each other as he spoke.

"Here we are," she said softly. Her gaze dipped to his mouth. He leaned toward her, eager to taste the whiskey on her lips, eager to kiss her again. Once had most definitely not been enough.

Her movement was minute, but she did move toward him. Their breath mingled in the small space between them.

It did not matter that twenty-four hours ago he hadn't even known that she existed. It didn't matter that twenty hours ago, he thought she was the most irritating woman on the planet. What mattered was the connection he felt to her. It was beyond any connection he'd ever felt before. The time was irrelevant. He leaned down to taste her.

Ka-boom! Thunder rolled and Poorvi jumped up and away from him. The moment was gone. Kavan was flustered, his heart rapidly pounding.

Flustered, she stood. "I should go to bed. Try to get some sleep." She did not make a move to go upstairs.

So close to what must be heaven. He nodded and stood as well. "Right. Long day tomorrow."

"Right." She turned to go. "You know, Ba's snoring is really bad. One more whiskey might help." She picked up her glass.

"Makes sense." Anything for her not to go. He moved to get the bottle. When he turned back, Poorvi was right behind him. Their bodies grazed each other.

"I noticed you, too. At the airport." She spoke softly, but her words were sure. "But then you stole my outlet."

"Not my finest moment."

She shook her head. "No. So make up for it now. Kiss me."

Kavan did not need to be asked twice. Bottle in one hand and empty glass in the other, he lowered his mouth to hers, intending to gently place his mouth on hers. But that was impossible. He'd had a taste a few hours ago, which meant that as soon as his lips touched hers, he wanted more. The bottle and glass slipped from his hands and landed with a crash.

He barely noticed the whiskey that had splashed on him.

She did not move.

She kissed him back with want and need that matched his own. He brought one of his free hands to her face and the other to her waist as he nipped and tasted. She stood on her toes and deepened their kiss as he pulled her closer.

It was as if there had never been a time when he hadn't known her. She always been here with him; he simply hadn't realized it until she showed up.

"Oi!"

They jumped away from each other and found Mr. O in a nightshirt taking in the mess they'd made.

"What's goin' on here?"

"Oh, so sorry, Mr. O," Poorvi said. "We'll clean it up. Not sure what happened."

"Looks like you dropped a bottle of whiskey trying to kiss each other." He scowled at them. "Newlyweds. Keep spilling things in m' pub."

"Yep. That's us. Newlyweds." Poorvi smiled at Mr. O.

"We'll pay for it, sir. Apologies," Kavan said, finally finding his voice.

"Yeah. Well, all right then. Wasn't the good stuff anyway." He turned to go. "Clean up, then carry on."

Poorvi looked at Kavan, amusement in her eyes, biting her bottom lip trying to hold back laughter. Kavan met her eyes, overcome with the thought that he would give anything to bite that lip.

Chapter Fourteen

Poorvi woke to the sun shining down on her face, warm and yellow. She didn't open her eyes, not wanting the dream to end. She dreamed that she'd had the sexiest make-out session with Kavan last night.

"Hanh."

She opened her eyes. She looked to where the sound had come from. Ba.

She sat bolt upright. "Ba." No Kavan. Had she really dreamed it? It had seemed so real. How much whiskey had she had? Had she slept here on the sofa?

Though if she *had* dreamed it, that was for the better. She really didn't need to be kissing random men she'd only just met. Too risky, no matter what.

Ba narrowed her eyes, then tilted her head at her. She felt like Ba knew what she had been thinking. What did it matter? Ba wasn't even her real grandmother.

"You slept down here?" Ba asked.

"You snore, Ba," Poorvi said matter-of-factly.

"Ah." Ba nodded. "Next time I will get my own room."

"Where is—"

"There's no next time, Ba," Kavan said from behind her. Poorvi turned to find Kavan standing there, looking down-right delectable in a fresh long-sleeved, fitted green T-shirt and jeans, his wet hair sticking out from under his ball cap. He grazed his eyes over her, and her heart pounded in her chest.

It hadn't been a dream.

He seemed unable to make eye contact. Of course. Look at him, he probably made out with random women all the time. She didn't really believe that.

She quickly brushed aside the disappointment that started to build. Disappointment that she had felt something, and he had not. Disappointment that she allowed herself to consider that they might have some sort of…connection. She'd barely known him a day. What kind of feelings could they really have beyond simple lust?

"We're finishing your list and getting to Dublin tonight." He was still addressing Ba, as if Poorvi weren't even there.

"I'll just go grab a shower," she said, putting as much ice in her voice as she could muster. She brushed past him and to their room.

She had quite literally cried in his arms. And then told him all about work—what an idiot. Must have been the whiskey.

But he had shown no signs of wanting to be anywhere but with her.

Anger at her mother popped up as she recalled their conversation yesterday. She squelched it down. She could only deal with one thing at a time. Right now, her focus had to be getting to Dublin. Once she presented her paper, she could return to her lab, where she would simply focus on work. Rumors be damned.

Science. Numbers. Facts. All were dependable. People. Feelings. Kissing. Not dependable.

She finished her shower, then wrapped a towel around herself before stepping back into the room, just as the door opened and Kavan entered the room. He stopped when he saw her. For an instant she forgot she was only clad in a towel. The way he was looking at her—eyes darkened with desire, mouth slightly open like he wanted her not only then and there, but to be *his*.

"Hey! What the hell are you doing here?" she shouted, tightening the towel around her. It was simple lust in his eyes. She should stop making more of things than they actually were.

"I came to get my computer," Kavan said as he grabbed her computer.

"That's *my* computer," she barked as she squeezed her arms tight around her. He wouldn't even look at her.

He looked down at what he had grabbed and dropped it on the bed, glancing around the room, presumably for his computer. "Uh… About last night…"

"What about it?" She glared at him, daring him to say anything. A spark of hope shot through her at the idea that he might really want something with her.

"I'm sorry."

Her eyebrows shot up. That spark of hope extinguished immediately. Anything but that. "You're…sorry?"

"We had a lot of whiskey…"

Any hope she might have had, any wish that they had some kind of connection, withered away, leaving a trail of disappointment. Heat rose to her face as mortification took over her and she realized she was standing alone in a roon wearing nothing but a towel with a man who would rather NOT have kissed her last night. Talk about about missing the message.

She should have known better. Brooks had taught her that lesson the hard way, and she had still let her guard down. That kind of thing only happened in books. Not real life.

"Right. Too much alcohol," she confirmed.

"Mmm-hmm." He bobbed his head.

"Okay then." She was short with him.

"Okay then." He started to leave.

"Your computer is over there." She pointed with her chin.

"Right." He walked over and picked it up, took one more glance at her and left, bumping into the door on his way out.

She threw herself on the bed. Seriously? She was an idiot. At least she knew who he was now before she was even more invested. Before she caught real feelings and had to get over him.

The thing was, she might already be too late.

Chapter Fifteen

Kavan did not need his computer. He'd used that as an excuse to see Poorvi. To talk about the amazing kiss they'd shared last night. Well, really, to kiss her again. To tell her there was simply no way he could ever get enough of her. Seeing her in nothing but a towel caught him off guard, in the best possible way, except that it had rendered him speechless. So he had acted like a complete dork. He burned with embarrassment.

But it was probably just as well. Because clearly, the kiss had meant very little to her.

Just a drunken kiss.

Except that he had not been drunk. He hadn't really thought she was, either.

No matter. He should know better than to believe that real connections could be made in twenty-four hours.

He made his way to the kitchen and found Ba teaching Mr. O and Melanie how to make tepla. She had a few going and they smelled fabulous. He also caught a whiff of cardamom, cinnamon, clove.

"Ba. Did you make chai?" he asked.

She nodded toward a teapot. "I strained it into there."

Fantastic. He poured himself a mug of the milky chai and settled down at the bar with the round spicy thin flatbread Ba was rolling out with a rolling pin and then roasting with oil on a flat pan. He was adding sugar to his chai when Poorvi arrived, her dark hair still damp on her shoulders. He tried not to stare at how great she looked in jeans, a pink blouse and matching pink-framed glasses.

"Smells fabulous, Ba," she said, a wide smile on her face, her voice light and breezy, as if she hadn't a care in the world. She poured herself some chai and sat down a couple stools away not even acknowledging him. She added sugar to her chai as Ba placed a plate with tepla in front of her.

Ba shifted her gaze between them, while Poorvi made conversation with their hosts. Mr. O kept shooting him confused looks like he was trying to process what he had seen last night with what was going on right now.

If he figured it out, Kavan would have loved his insight.

"You've lived in Ireland all your life and you have never been to the Cliffs of Moher?" Ba asked as Kavan loaded their bags into the car.

"Poorvi. I need your bag," he called out, unsuccessful in his attempt to hide his irritation. The sun was out today, adding some much-appreciated warmth to the air, but all he felt was the chill from Poorvi as she stomped over to him with her bag.

"I'll do it." She stepped up next to him, her jaw set.

"I'm happy to load the car." He glared at her.

"Just because you're a man doesn't mean that you have to put my bag in the car," she snapped.

"It's not because I'm a man." He spoke slowly. "It's because you're doing all the driving. I'm just trying to pull my weight."

"Fine. Whatever." She left the bag and sat down in the driver's seat.

"Fine," he snapped back. Probably better that there was no connection between them.

"You didn't answer my question," Ba said once they got on the road.

"We didn't travel much when I was younger." He shot a glance at Poorvi. "And now I never seem to have the time."

"Make time," Ba said. "You don't know how much you have."

"That is very true, Ba," he said softly. "But we're busy."

"What are you busy with? What are your jobs?" Ba asked them.

"Oh, well, I'm an—" He spotted the sign for the next exit. "You're going to need to be in the far-left lane, the exit is coming up," Kavan told Poorvi.

"Thank you." Her voice was polite, formal even. Like they'd just met. Except when they had just met, she was definitely not this polite. Not to mention the phenomenal kissing session they'd shared just hours ago. He side-eyed her so she wouldn't see him looking. She was completely focused in front of her, as if he weren't even there.

"Did your family travel, beti?" Ba asked.

"We traveled some. But my mom and dad work a lot, so it was hard," she answered.

"So you both have the world left to see. How wonderful!" Ba clapped her hands together as if this were something fabulous they had in common.

"I suppose," Poorvi answered.

Silence prevailed for the next hour or so. They were getting close when Kavan felt a thunk on the outside of the car. He snapped his head to Poorvi. She snapped her head to him in the same instant.

"Not good," they said in unison.

"Pull over! Pull over!" he cried.

"Really? You think I should pull over? Brilliant," she snarked, but she pulled over within a few seconds. They both jumped out of the car.

"Ba, stay put." Again they were in unison.

They glared at each other.

Sure enough, they had a flat tire.

"I thought you said there was no damage to the car," Poorvi snapped at him.

"There wasn't," Kavan told her between gritted teeth.

"Then what the hell is this?" she yelled.

"How is this anywhere near my fault? Flat tires happen all the time. Maybe you hit a nail or something."

"Oh, so now it's my fault?" she groused at him.

"I'm not saying that. But I am tiring of you blaming every little bit on me, yeah?" he growled at her.

"So, you're clearly not taking responsibility," she threw at him.

He inhaled deeply and stared at her. "Sometimes things just happen and they're nobody's fault."

"That doesn't even make sense." But he caught the confusion in her eyes. She rolled up her sleeves and opened the trunk. "Where's the spare? Must be under...ah, here it is." She grunted as she slowly lifted the spare out. Kavan knew better than to interfere, so he rolled up his sleeves and pulled out the jack and the lug wrench. He placed the jack under the car and began cranking it.

"I can do that," she grumbled.

"I got it," he mumbled.

She picked up the lug wrench and started to unscrew the bolts. He was shocked she didn't fight with him to do it all herself. This must be her way of accepting help. Not that he needed to be learning anything new about her.

Once they were loose, he knelt beside her. He put his hands on the part of the tire that was closest to him, she put out her hands on the side closest to her. They looked at each other and nodded. Then they pulled. The tire popped off.

He stole a glance at her. Her face was fixed in a scowl and she was focused on the tire. They were both sweating in the sun.

He picked up the spare and lined it up with the nuts and Poorvi tightened the bolts with the wrench. They worked side by side, each anticipating the other's moves, saying very little. In short time, they were functional again.

He put the flat tire back in the car. The physical activity had syphoned off some of his earlier angst with her. "We make a good team," he said, leaning against the car. He wiped his hands on a towel.

"I could have done that by myself," she said.

"I have no doubt. But you didn't have to," he said pleasantly. The more pleasant he was, the more irritated she seemed to get. He liked that.

"I didn't need help." She was firm.

He shrugged. "Maybe so, but we changed that tire together, like a team. There's no shame in that." He had enjoyed that moment of them being in sync.

Poorvi narrowed her eyes at him and huffed back into the car.

He inhaled and sat down in the passenger seat.

Chapter Sixteen

Poorvi was silent the rest of the journey. She was still worked up about their kiss and the fact that Kavan seemed to think it was okay to accept help. Against her natural tendencies, she was starting to see his point.

Not to mention that they had worked in tandem, and that had felt good. To know that he was going to work with her as a partner to change out that tire.

They arrived at the Cliffs of Moher without further incident. Poorvi pulled into the lot and calmly parked the car. The three of them exited the car without a word. The air was cool and misty, but the sun offered some warmth. People were milling about, or walking toward the trail that ran along the edge of the cliffs.

Ba looked from one to the other. "You two are boring today. I'm going to see the cliffs on my own." With that Ba walked away, her handbag hooked on her arm.

Poorvi gaped at Ba as she watched her walk away. "Nicely done." She turned on Kavan.

"You're blaming this on me, too?" He had the audacity to appear shocked, but more amused than irritated.

"Well, yes. *You* are clearly the extrovert here. Why didn't you talk to her?" Poorvi shook her head at him in disappointment. Wasn't that the point of extroverted people? To talk so introverts didn't have to?

"Why didn't you? Just because you're the introvert doesn't mean you can't make small talk with a sweet old lady," he shot back. "It's good to exercise those small talk muscles."

She stared at him. He did not back down from her—ever. Annoyance built in her throat. She hadn't made small talk with Ba because she had been preoccupied thinking about him.

Not to mention that he was clearly fighting a grin that indicated he knew that. While he was winning that battle, he could not hide the clear amusement in his eyes. Which was actually more irksome.

"Let's just go see the cliffs," she snapped. "We need to find a garage as well. Because the spare is not meant for long distances."

"Fine." Kavan extended his arm out. "After you."

"How polite," she sneered.

"I am, yes. As a matter of fact."

She rolled her eyes and led the way up the short hill to the edge of the cliffs where people were gathered. She approached an open spot and stopped. The sun was still out and had burned away the fog, so the view was clear. She had seen pictures and wondered what all the hubbub was. The cliffs just dropped into the ocean, the water smashed against the sides, relentlessly, patiently wearing down the rock. Smaller structures dotted the ocean, poking up from the water like giant triangles. She had never seen anything so frighteningly beautiful. She took in the sound of the water crashing into the cliffs, over and over, insistent in its effort to take down stone and earth. This was an experience without equal. The sheer persistence was inspiring.

Her irritation melted away. Kavan was standing behind her, silent and steady. His chest a mere inch from her back. She felt his body relax as hers did. She had the urge to lean back into that strong chest, to feel the comfort of his arms around her. She fought it.

"It's hard. Me asking for help," she said softly, her irritation with Kavan gone. She took off her glasses as they were getting sprayed with mist.

He said nothing so she turned to look at him. He was staring out at the cliffs, a small smile on his face. He was calm, a look of reverence on his face. "I know."

"I just never know—"

"When someone who seems like they're helping you is really trying to hurt you," Kavan finished her sentence, his eyes never leaving the sight before them.

"Yes," she answered, tears of gratitude building behind her eyes at having been seen. No one had ever understood her like that before.

He looked down at her. "I will never do that."

Poorvi's heart pounded in her chest, but more than that, a feeling of peace came over her that she hadn't ever experienced. She believed him, completely. She nodded and turned back to face the mighty ocean.

"My dad used to talk about this place all the time." He spoke softly so only she could hear. It was intimate and familiar, like he didn't talk this way with anyone else. "Among other beautiful places in the world—many of them in India." He sounded a bit sad. "His father—my grandfather—had taken them everywhere. All over India, Ireland, the States." He waved a hand to indicate there were more places. "But it had been the cliffs that stuck with my dad." He sighed. "We never made it here, Naveen and I. Not with him, anyway."

She took his hand in hers. The movement was instinctual. No thought involved. Even though the action was to comfort him, it was a risk she was taking, and her stomach filled with butterflies the instant she did it. She had no reason for concern however, because he immediately threaded his fingers through hers. "I'm sorry."

He nodded without looking at her. "Let's walk."

They walked the perimeter of the cliffs, gravel crunching beneath their shoes as they quietly enjoyed the magnificent view from different angles, never tiring of the sounds of the ocean. This silence between them was companionable, not fraught with the tension from the car. Poorvi thoroughly enjoyed the physical touch of threading her fingers with his. His hand was warm and strong, with a few rough spots. He didn't try to remove his hand from hers, either. They walked with their joined hands between them, arms entwined, leaning toward each other. They paused every so often to appreciate a certain angle or view.

Kavan stopped where they could see the cliffs and water crashing behind them. "We should take a picture," he said.

"We aren't really traveling together," she said.

"Except that we are," he said softly. "Come on. One selfie. What could it hurt?"

She shook her head at him and made a show of rolling her eyes. "Fiiiine. If it'll make you happy."

He beamed at her. "It really will." He removed his hat, held out the phone and glanced at her. "Closer."

She moved closer to him and looked up at the phone.

"You're going to have to move closer so we can get the waves," he insisted.

She inhaled and moved yet closer. There was almost no distance now between his body and hers. If it weren't for their coats, their bodies would be touching. She put the thought out of her head. No matter that they were getting along right now, she didn't want to expect more if it wasn't available to her.

He clicked and they looked at it together. Not bad.

"Nice," he said.

A group of middle-aged women passed them by, but then one of them did a double take and came back.

"You look familiar," she said to Kavan, eyes narrowed. "Can't place it, but I feel like I've seen your face before."

He quickly replaced his ball cap, pulling it low over his head. "I just have one of those faces, I suppose."

"Would you mind taking a picture of us?" another asked, smiling and quite literally batting her eyelashes. Poorvi rolled her eyes, even as a hint of jealousy hit her heart.

"Of course." Kavan took the woman's phone and took their photo with the cliffs in the back.

"We can take one of you two." A different woman offered. "For your kindness."

"Um. Sure." Kavan handed her his phone and stood next to Poorvi.

She turned to look at him and found him watching her from underneath his hat. She wasn't sure what he saw, but he was smiling, and she didn't think anyone had ever looked at her quite that way. Her heart gave a solid thud so loud she was sure he had heard it. She smiled at him and then turned to face the woman.

"There you go. Beautiful." She kept clicking. "Always lovely to see a young couple in love, yeah?"

Poorvi's jaw dropped and her eyes flashed as she flushed. "Oh we're not in—I mean we're not a couple—we just met yesterday." She stepped away from him, clamping her lips together.

The woman handed Kavan's phone back.

"Well, that don't mean a thing, does it now? What matters is the connection. And you two have it. Anyone with eyes can see it," the first woman said.

"Well, thank you," Kavan said, indicating his phone. "Enjoy your day." One of the women lingered a bit, looking at Kavan as if trying to place him.

Kavan put his hand at the small of Poorvi's back and gently steered her in the opposite direction of the women. Even through her coat, Poorvi had to admit she did not mind his hand there at all, his strength guiding her away from an uncomfortable situation. Kavan's phone buzzed a few times. He just kept sending it to voice mail.

"Is that your brother?"

He nodded.

"You're not answering."

"He's trying to get me to Dublin faster." He paused and looked at her, his hand still comfortably on her. "To be honest, I'm no longer in a huge hurry to get there. I need to be there by Friday. And I will be." He fixed his gaze on her. Something passed between them. Something intense and hot.

"What happens on Friday?" Poorvi tried to break the spell. It worked.

"Oh uh—I'm meeting—a colleague."

"Ah, there you are." Ba approached them, slightly out of breath. "Let's go to Doolin for lunch and a drink."

Kavan returned his hand to his pocket. Poorvi felt a chill. "Sure. I could eat."

Poorvi drove them the few minutes into Doolin, a small town next to the Cliffs of Moher. The Aran Islands (next on the list) was accessible via ferry from Doolin as well.

She felt his eyes on her while she drove. She didn't hate it.

"Left! Left! Left!" he called out loudly. He'd been paying more attention to her than to her driving.

"I got it," she called back. "I'm good."

"No. You were not! These roads are narrow, you have to stay left," he insisted.

"You're not the one driving!" she snapped. "The 'road' is only wide enough for one car!"

"There's a garage." Kavan pointed. "Just down from that pub."

She nodded and pulled into the garage. Kavan got out and turned back to her. "Mind if I do the talking?"

Poorvi rolled her eyes but nodded. While Kavan spoke with the young mechanic, Poorvi took in the small garage. Clearly it was privately owned—there seemed to be only the one bay, though car parts seemed scattered everywhere, but what did she know? She didn't know much beyond changing tires.

The mechanic was a young petite blonde woman, her hair

back in a braid. She wore a jumpsuit that bore her business logo. *Marlene's Garage.*

She listened to Kavan and nodded. She squinted at the car, and then looked at the tires.

"I don't stock these, normally. But I can get you one in a couple hours, if that suits you," she told them.

"Seriously?" Poorvi looked excited. "I thought for sure we were going to have to spend the night here."

"Not unless you'll be wanting to. Doolin's a great little town. Lots of good music, good food and Guiness."

"We're on a bit of a schedule," he answered quickly. "A few hours is perfect. We'll just be going to the islands, then." He nodded at her and walked out.

"Well, at least there's a pub." Ba started walking toward it.

Poorvi met his eyes and they both chuckled as they followed her. He could use a drink.

The three of them found themselves in a crowded pub. They seated themselves at the bar. Ba and Kavan ordered a Guinness, but Poorvi had fallen for Irish coffee. They clinked glasses and drank.

Ba put her Guinness down and smiled at the bartender. "I was here, fifty-three years ago, on my honeymoon," Ba told him.

Kavan snapped his head toward Ba at the same time as Poorvi. They made eye contact with wide eyes.

Ba had just spoken in English.

Really good English.

"In this very bar, with my new husband. I had never had a Guinness, and he got me my first one." Ba grinned at the bartender. "To this day, I only drink Guinness in Ireland."

The bartender chuckled. "Anywhere else, it's not really Guinness now, is it?"

"No, sir, it's not," Ba agreed.

Kavan was still speechless. She could speak English this whole time?

"Um, Ba—you speak English?" Poorvi asked.

Ba widened her eyes as if now just realizing what she had revealed. Then she grinned. "What of it?"

"We thought you were—" Kavan started.

"Old. Feeble?"

"Um. Well… No…" Poorvi started.

"No. We thought you did not speak English," Kavan told her.

"You let us believe it," Poorvi added.

Ba opened her mouth as if she were going to argue, but she shut her mouth. "Yes. I did let you believe it." She went back to her beer.

"Ba!" they both cried in unison.

"What?" she asked, annoyed, as if they were the ones hiding a secret.

"Why did you let us think you didn't speak English?" Kavan asked gently.

"Because both of you need help with your Gujarati," Ba shot back, but she didn't look at them.

"Ba," Poorvi said softly. "You've been to *all* these places before, haven't you, not just the cliffs?"

Ba looked at them both and nodded, sadness coming over her. She went back to speaking in Gujarati. She was obviously more comfortable doing so. "My husband died just over one year ago." She sighed. "I miss him terribly. He and I used to bicker the way you two do." She chuckled. "But I would not have had it any other way. That man was rock-solid and he drove me crazy, but I loved him with everything I had." Ba paused, tears in her eyes. Poorvi reached out and put her hand on Ba's.

"You needed someone to bring you here." Kavan sighed.

Ba nodded at him.

Poorvi furrowed her brow. "But why not ask your daughter, Devi?"

Ba waved a dismissive hand. "My children keep telling me to 'move on,' 'Dad is gone,' 'go on with your life.' How can I go on with my life when my life's partner is gone? I don't want to move on." Ba raised her voice and had gathered a bit of an audience. She lowered it now. "I don't want to forget him." She looked at them, apprehension in her eyes. "Sometimes…sometimes… I forget how his voice sounded." She widened her eyes, true fear mingled with the guilt that she might let that happen.

"Your phone—" Poorvi said.

"You have his voice on there," Kavan finished.

Ba nodded. "We made a pact to grow old and die together. I am not ready to die—I have grandchildren I love—but he is supposed to be here with me." She pounded a fist on the bar. "He left me here before he was supposed to and sometimes…" She pressed her lips together as if she were afraid to finish that thought.

"Sometimes you get really angry at him for leaving you here." Kavan completed her sentence.

She nodded. "Isn't that terrible?"

Kavan shook his head. "I used to get mad at my father for dying and leaving my mum and me and Naveen. Our family has never been the same. We were all angry in our own way." He paused. "Maybe we still are." He remembered what Poorvi had said about Naveen being controlling because he was afraid to lose another person. "I think it's normal to be angry for a bit, when someone you love leaves us too soon, yeah?"

"All we had dreamed about after our children were married was spoiling our grandchildren until our children got mad at us." Teary laughter as she shook her head. "Now I have to do that all on my own. But worst of all. I have no one to bicker with anymore."

Tears filled her eyes. Kavan moved on instinct and wrapped his arms around her. Poorvi did the same. "We can bicker with you, Ba," she said.

They were rewarded with a cackle from Ba. She and Kavan pulled away from the older woman. "You two are amateurs. You'll get better after you've been together for a while."

Poorvi gaped at her. "We're not together."

Kavan's heart sank again. That was a quick answer.

"Well, you weren't yesterday. But now you've spent some time together." Ba wiped her eyes and cackled. "Are you sure?"

Kavan glanced at Poorvi. "Yes."

"You're both wrong." Ba shook her head.

"Ba!" they both said in unison.

She rolled her eyes. "You know, Dada and I did not meet at the temple. We met at Clerys' clock."

"You didn't." Kavan broke out into a smile.

"We did." Ba nodded.

"What's Clerys' clock?" Poorvi looked from Ba to Kavan.

"It's outside Clerys department store in Dublin. People arrange to meet under Clerys' clock for various things. It's an icon. There's a newer building next to it, Clery's Quarter, that has a bar and restaurant," Kavan explained. "We—you should check it out when you get there." He turned back to Ba. "Go on, tell us."

"Well, my friend had set me up with her boyfriend's friend. My parents, of course, back then, knew nothing of this. She had arranged for me and this young man to meet under Clerys' clock." Ba chuckled. "Well, ten, then fifteen minutes, then twenty minutes passes and the young man had not yet arrived." She closed her eyes a moment. "We did not have cell phones, see? There was this very handsome man who was also waiting for someone who he said was also late. He was very smooth and charming and we started chatting, as you do. We waited over thirty minutes for these two and neither person came! He had tickets for a movie, and asked if I would like to join him." Ba shrugged. "I was ready to join him when the man I was supposed to meet arrived. He was a mess. Out of breath from running, hair tousled." Ba shook her head.

"What happened?" Kavan asked.

"It seemed he had been held up with a last-minute assignment at his job. But I did not believe him." She chuckled. "He became rather cross with me and asked why he would lie."

"I did not have an answer, so he asked for another chance." She sighed. "Something about him—" she shook her head "—I don't know. But something about him, made me give him another chance. I let him take me to dinner, and by the end of that meal, I knew I had made the right choice."

Poorvi was looking at Ba with pure joy on her face. "You gave him another chance—" she snapped her fingers "—just like that?"

"Like I said, something about him…but it was the best risk I ever took." Ba finished her beer and stood. "Time for the Aran Islands."

Chapter Seventeen

They called an Uber to take them to the dock. It was much too early in the season to go to all three of the Aran Islands, so they were going to settle with going to the closest one. Ba seemed disappointed but didn't argue.

"Ba." Poorvi approached the older woman as they waited for the ferry. "Tell me what you love about the Aran Islands."

"Oh, they are rugged and beautiful. The one we are going to has castle remains and nice pubs. The views are very beautiful." Ba paused and looked out at the ocean. "Take the carriage for a quick tour, or just walk to the castle remains—you can't go wrong."

Poorvi squeezed Ba's hand. The older woman's hand was soft but strong when she squeezed back. "Will do. Thanks."

The ferry was large, with a viewing deck as well as an underdeck. Poorvi, Kavan and Ba stood on the viewing deck. No actual decision was made, they all just ended up there, taking in the view of the islands as well as the ocean. No one minded that the wind was cold.

They were on the ferry for about ten minutes when Poorvi grabbed Kavan's arm. She was pale and sweaty. Her eyes were huge. "Motion." She shook her head.

She was going to be sick. Ba pulled out a motion sickness bag that she must have gotten from the plane and handed it to him.

He raised an eyebrow at her. She shrugged. "You never know when you will need it." She nodded at Poorvi.

"You have something for your hair?" he asked Poorvi as he handed her the bag. She held out her wrist, and he took the hair tie and tied her hair back into a messy bun. She looked awful but somehow did not vomit.

Then it hit him. The turbulence. Motion sickness. "Why didn't you say anything?"

"I was hoping it wouldn't happen," Poorvi said. "I made it through the turbulence. I thought I could make it through this." She held up the bag. "I'm going to hold on to this."

They disembarked from the ferry with Kavan holding Poorvi's hand. This was beginning to feel natural to him, but he wasn't sure if that was a good thing or not. She didn't seem to mind holding his hand, but then she also yelled at him a lot. From the dock, the castle ruins were easily visible atop of a large hill, surrounded by green grass.

No sooner did their feet touch ground than Ba waved them off. "I will be back in time to catch the boat back to Doolin," she said. "I have things…I need to do."

Kavan waited with Poorvi on a small bench until she was okay to walk. He took her hand again and they trekked up the steep walkway to the castle ruins. The path wound around plots of land. They passed a beached shipwreck that was hundreds of years old. Once they reached the castle ruins, they were able to explore the parts of the castle that still remained. Kavan enjoyed every minute of finally being able to see the country he grew up in, and it was that much more precious because Poorvi never let go of his hand and they chatted like they'd known each other for years.

They sat next to each other for a bit on the grass in front of the castle. Their legs touched and the added warmth was welcome in the cold wind. The electric zing he felt was a bonus.

They could see much of the island and the ocean around it. The view was breathtaking.

"Thank you," Poorvi said softly.

"For what?" Kavan was thoroughly enjoying the view of the ocean, but he gladly turned away from it to look at Poorvi. Her hair was tousled in the wind and she still appeared a bit pale, but her eyes were alert and her smile was beautiful.

"For the boat." She scrunched up her nose. "My hair and the bag."

He shrugged it off. "I also owe you some thanks, not to mention, an apology," he said to her.

"I'm sure you do," she said, smiling. "But what specifically are you talking about?"

"The bathroom on the plane. Thanks for opening the door—" He looked away.

"You don't like small spaces," she said quickly.

He shook his head. "You were trying to help."

"You were embarrassed."

He nodded. "Come on. There's another pub near the dock. I'll buy you a Guinness." He stood and took her hand. "Or a soda."

Chapter Eighteen

Kavan ordered them both another round. They'd been in the pub for a while; Poorvi'd had some soda to settle her stomach, but now she was ready for whiskey. And Ba would not be back for a while.

"Good call," she said as she raised her Irish coffee to him. "More whiskey is needed after our revelation this afternoon." She grinned. They were sitting side by side on a bench at a rustic wood table in the corner with a view of the ocean from a window across from them. The pub was slow at the moment; the bartender was cleaning glasses. They weren't touching, but the space between them was definitely charged. "I'd like to be Ba when I grow up. She's amazing."

Kavan tapped his pint to her glass. "I'll drink to that." He drank deeply and stared ahead for a moment. "Why do you think people wait until they're older to do what they want?"

Poorvi shrugged. "Older people know that time runs out and they want to do what they want to do."

Kavan took a gulp of his Guinness and then stared at the glass. "You know why I don't drive manual?"

"Too lazy to learn." She grinned. "You have a driver. You have a fear of shifters." She bumped her shoulder to his, and he thrilled at the intimacy of that gesture. Maybe she was done yelling at him. "I have a ton of them. I can go on."

He chuckled. "No, but thanks for that." He paused. "My dad's car was a manual. Naveen tried to teach me."

She raised her eyebrows and widened her eyes in mock surprise.

"My dad had taught Naveen," Kavan said. "He'd promised to teach me, but something always got in the way. And then he was gone.

"I was fifteen and I wanted to learn." He looked at her and she was focused on him, her eyes watching him intensely. "Naveen had learned in one day—or so he said. I was having a hard time coordinating the gas and the clutch and the shifter. Needless to say, Naveen's patience ran thin." Kavan paused, tears of anger and frustration burning at the back of his eyes. "We argued. I told him that Mom was in charge and he had to teach me until I learned."

Kavan turned to Poorvi. "The truth was that Mom was not in charge at that time. She barely got out of bed. Naveen had taken over. Bought groceries, cooked food, went to school— you name it." Kavan looked at his fingers. "I don't think he ever really grieved, you know?"

He paused and then Poorvi's hand was on his. "It's hard. And you were just kids. Both of you."

Kavan cleared his throat. "I tried the clutch and gas a few more times but kept stalling the car, grinding the gears. Naveen had about all he could take, I suppose. He yelled at me that I would never learn and that he had to go to work. So he left. And he took Dad's car." Kavan's voice cracked. "He told me I could just drive Mom's car, and he never bothered trying to teach me again.

"Truth is, I actually never bothered to ask." A tear escaped his eye and he wiped it away, the humiliation as fresh right now as it had been in that moment.

He looked out the window at the ocean, Poorvi's hand in his, grounding him. "I watched him drive my dad's car every day. It was a clear reminder that I had disappointed not only Naveen but my father as well." He had never voiced those words out loud. He almost did not want to look at Poorvi. To see the disappointment in her face.

"You know. You might think your brother is the hard-ass, but isn't it possible that he's just afraid of what would happen if he couldn't control everything? Maybe someone else would die," Poorvi said.

"That's what you got from that story?" Kavan turned to her, agitation coming off him in waves.

"No, that's what I got from the way you talk about him." Poorvi put down her drink and looked him in the eye. "I'm not saying it's okay for him to treat you that way, it's not." She squeezed his hand, and his irritation melted away. "He could learn a thing or two from you, about kindness and doing what needs to be done, without hurting anyone in the process."

Kavan scoffed. "Yeah, right. He'll not be learning anything from me, not ever. He'd have to admit there was something he didn't know now, wouldn't he?" Kavan looked at her, frustration in his eyes. "And that, he will never do."

Ba walked in the pub door an hour later. The last ferry back to Doolin was coming up. They got on and within minutes, Poorvi felt nauseous again. Honestly, she was all done with boats.

"Whiskey was not a great idea," she managed, as she sat on the bench with her head in her hands. Kavan rested his hand on her back and made small soothing circles.

Her stomach was in knots and exhaustion had set in. The drive to Dublin was a solid three hours.

They took an Uber to the mechanic who thankfully had put a new tire on the car for them.

"Thank you," Kavan said as she handed him the keys.

"Anytime." The mechanic smiled at him.

Kavan started to hand Poorvi the keys. She tilted her head at him. "How drunk are you?"

"Not at all."

"Good." She nodded at the keys. "Keep them. You'll need them to drive."

"What the— Poorvi?" His eyes nearly bugged out his head, but a small grin had started forming on his mouth.

"Get in the car. You're a grown-ass man. This is as good a time as any to learn to drive a stick shift." She grinned at him. "Besides. Consider this me asking for help. My stomach is a mess." He broke out into what can only be described as a little-boy grin, he was so excited.

"Seriously?"

"You must be joking!" Ba exclaimed.

"I am not joking, Ba. He'll be great," she said to Ba. She sat down in the car. "Let's go, Kavan."

Chapter Nineteen

Kavan had learned to step back and let Naveen run things.

He stepped back when he went to uni. He stepped back when choosing his specialty. He stepped back when Naveen wanted to open the clinic. He let Naveen schedule photo shoots for him and use his image to sell surgery.

Maybe…maybe he did not have to step back. Maybe he could do what he wanted.

He got in the car.

"Okay, first…" Poorvi went into what Kavan could only call "teacher mode." He kind of liked it, authoritative, but kind. "The right is the gas pedal, and the far left is the clutch. The brake is the one in the middle. Every time you shift gears—" she put her hand on the gearshift "—press the clutch all the way, and ease on the gas. The key is the balance between the gas and clutch."

Sounded easy enough.

"It sounds simple, but it can take a bit to get used to," Poorvi said.

He nodded at her. It clearly hadn't been that easy when Naveen had tried to teach him.

"Start the car."

He did.

"Ease off the clutch and give some gas." She sounded confident, not at all wary.

He did as she said. The car lurched, he slammed the brake and the car stalled.

"Hai Ram!" Ba had pulled out her prayer beads again.

"Ba? Seriously? We're in a parking lot." Poorvi smiled. "Ignore her," she said gently. "Maybe not so much gas."

He nodded and started over. And he stalled the car again. This time grating the gears. He stiffened for a reprimand. All he heard was Ba's murmuring of prayers. Instead, Poorvi laid her hand on his over the gearshift. "Take your time. It's a finesse thing."

He nodded.

She grinned. "Try again."

He did and this time, the car rolled some feet before stalling out again. He let out a breath.

"You're making progress. There's a learning curve here, as there is in most things." She sipped some water. "Try again."

It took some time, but finally Kavan was on the road, driving.

"Now just shift up."

He did.

"Again."

He did.

"Again."

He did. He was driving a stick-shift car! If Naveen could see him now! He would say it was about time and probably insinuate that Poorvi was some kind of miracle worker. If his dad could see him, he would say that he knew Kavan could do it all along.

"Great." Poorvi beamed at him, her smile broad. "That's fabulous! I've never taught anyone that. You're my first pupil."

"You are not my first teacher for this, but you are the most successful." And the most beautiful. He kept those words to himself. Poorvi had made it clear how she felt about last night.

But he didn't want the angst of that to interfere with his moment now. "Thank you."

"Don't thank me yet, now you have to drive."

"Where to?" He would take her anywhere she wanted to go.

"Let's just drive around Doolin for practice. Then we'll head for Dublin," Poorvi said.

Kavan drove them around Doolin, which was a quaint if not touristy small town. She didn't know much about Ireland, but the green hills that went on forever seemed to be plucked from a movie.

She left her hand on his because not touching him was not acceptable. She told herself it was so she could cue him in to which gear he needed to be in, but it was really so she could just have an excuse. He was rubbing small circles on her hand with his thumb, and she let herself fall into the intimacy.

They were enjoying their little trek around Doolin when Bobby called. She had already let one call go to voice mail. He would just keep blowing up her phone if she didn't answer. But she was not about to have this call with an audience. "Hey, I need to take this. It's my boss." She pressed her lips together. "Do you mind pulling over?"

Kavan threw her a furtive look and proceeded to stall the car. "Oh shoot. Sorry."

"It's fine. Just start her up and then pull over up there." The countryside was a lush green with no other cars at the moment, and the ocean could be seen from here.

Kavan did exactly that.

"Perfect." She beamed at him. "I'll be right back." She got out of the car and called Bobby.

"Are you in Dublin yet?" His clipped voice grated her ears.

He really needed some basic phone manners. "'Hey, Poorvi. How are you? Good? Okay, great to hear. By the way, when are you getting to Dublin?' That's how you talk on the phone, Bobby."

"Dr. Wright," he said, and she knew he had gritted his teeth. "Whatever."

"I have the ability to fire you," Bobby threatened.

"True. But you won't."

"Why? Why wouldn't I? You've been nothing but a thorn in my side since I got this job."

"Two reasons. One. Only I can present this paper properly, and the lab needs the grant. And two. I'm smarter than you and you know it." She paused. "Why did you call?"

"I heard that the Shashane brothers are going to try to convince you not to present your findings."

"Who are the Shashane brothers?"

"They run Shashane Eye Clinic just outside of Dublin. They do more C-MORE than any other clinic," Bobby informed her. "At least in Ireland. Though their numbers are competitive in the States."

Huh. "Well. Whatever. Numbers don't lie. And the numbers are on my side. And I'm not telling them to stop forever—just until we get more data."

"Just giving you a heads-up to expect some pushback from them," Bobby said.

"Fine." She blew air from her mouth. What could they possibly do? They could try to talk her out of presenting, but that would never happen, so whatever. "I can't worry about all that."

"You're welcome," Bobby said into the phone.

"I didn't thank you," Poorvi retorted. The day she thanked Bobby Wright—well, she never would. He used to be her friend. But when she had needed him, when she could have used his support, he had kept his mouth shut.

"I'll be there by Friday, Bobby, to go over my presentation before I give it on Saturday." She heard him say "Dr. Wright" as she tapped off the phone.

She walked back to the car to find Kavan also on the phone.

She opened the door, but started to back away to give him privacy. He motioned for her to sit down.

"I'll find him. Don't worry." He tapped off his phone.

"Everything okay?" she asked.

"Let's not talk about work," he said, beaming at her. "We have this gorgeous countryside and I just learned how to drive this thing." He grinned at her like a little boy, and it was the happiest thing she'd seen in a while.

"Let's do it. Let's see Doolin." She laughed.

Chapter Twenty

After about an hour of practice, Poorvi guided him to the highway toward Dublin. Ba was still praying in the back seat, but her outbursts to God were fewer and further between. Poorvi seemed a bit less green, and she was doing a fine job of navigating them in the general direction of Dublin.

"Ba. I'm going to need Devi's address," Poorvi called to the back.

"Give me your phone. I'll enter an address." Ba held out her hand.

Poorvi handed her phone back. They followed the new directions, but they were being taken off the highway and into the countryside.

"Ba," Kavan said. "This is the long way around. We aren't closer to Dublin. And the signs say that Dublin is still at least an hour away. Ba?"

"She's asleep," Poorvi said.

They took a few more turns; the navigation indicated that they were close to the destination, but they were clearly not in Dublin. Kavan glanced at Poorvi, and she nodded her head. Ba had pulled another one over on them.

The sun was just setting when they drove up to the address. Kavan was about to wake Ba and verify the address when he took a final turn and a true Irish castle loomed before them.

Stone walls and turrets, ivy growing up the side, lights in all the windows gave the castle a majestic feeling.

"I don't think this is where Devi lives," Kavan said to Poorvi.

"It's not," Ba said as she bounded of the car. "But this is where we stay tonight."

"Are you kidding, Ba? You weren't even really sleeping," Poorvi said as she got out as well. Kavan could tell that her heart wasn't in it. She was gazing up at the castle in awe.

"No. And I got three rooms." She ran a disappointed gaze over them. "Come on."

The valet came for the car and the bellman for the bags. Kavan eyed Ba. "You paid for this?"

She smirked. "I have some money. And I spend it how I like."

"I will pay you back for the rooms."

"Yes, Ba," Poorvi chimed in.

"You most certainly will not. I can spend my money on my children if I so choose," Ba scolded them.

"Ba—" Kavan began his protest, though he warmed at the idea that Ba considered him and Poorvi her children. A glance at the soft look on Poorvi's face confirmed that she felt the same way.

"Stop arguing with me and come see. The pictures were beautiful." Ba started toward the door, the bellman in tow. The inside was as magnificent as the exterior promised. High ceilings, regal decor, massive chandeliers. Kavan took it all in, but he found himself watching Poorvi as she slowly realized the awesome beauty and splendor of her surroundings.

"Ba. This is…too much!" She focused back on Ba. "We can't let you pay for all this."

Ba turned to her. "Of course you can." She came close to them. "It's beautiful, nah?"

They both nodded.

"Dada and I had dreamed of staying here." Ba drew her gaze

over the paintings, the red-carpeted double staircase and all the trimmings. "But something was always more important." She sighed. "We never made it." She looked from him to Poorvi. "Don't waste time. Don't save the good things for later."

Ba moved to the check-in desk. Kavan caught Poorvi's eye. She shrugged. *Might as well.* He was still stuck on the fact that she had said "we" like the two of them were a team, like they were…together.

Ba checked them in and handed them each a key. "The restaurant here is gorgeous. Have a fabulous dinner. Enjoy. I will take my dinner in my room." She grinned at them. "Think of it as payment since I held you hostage for two days. I promise, tomorrow we will be in Dublin." She nodded at the bellman and headed for the elevator.

Kavan turned to Poorvi. "I could eat. Up for having dinner with me?"

She narrowed her eyes as if she were thinking about it. She looked all around them, her face literally glowing. "I could eat." She grinned at him. "You got any fancy clothes in that bag of yours?"

Poorvi wasn't sure what had come over her. Maybe it was this castle. Maybe it was Ba's confession. Niki had insisted she pack one dress that was fun, and she had acquiesced at the last minute. This seemed to be the perfect time to wear it.

Not that she was trying to impress anyone or anything.

The three of them had rooms next to each other. Each just as gorgeous as the next. She took a few pictures and sent them to her sister. She was in an actual castle! Her sister was going to be so jealous. The setting was quite romantic. She needed to put herself in check.

Maybe dinner with handsome and kind Kavan was not a wise choice. What was the point in entertaining anything with him, anyway? They irritated each other constantly and he lived in Ireland. She did not.

But the way he'd held her hand in the car… She sighed.

She pulled out the dress from her bag. A simple black above-the-knee fitted cocktail dress with bell sleeves and rhinestone edging. She was rethinking the dress and reaching into her bag for her jeans and a nice top when the phone rang. Face-Time call from Niki.

She inhaled and answered. "Hey!"

"Where are you?" Niki asked. "That room is gorgeous! Please tell me you will be making proper use of that room to-night?"

"If you mean sleeping, then yes."

"Didi! Come on! Do something fun—or at least do *some-one* fun!"

Poorvi bit her bottom lip. "I have…sort of…met somebody."

Niki's squeal was nearly deafening. "That's perfect. Who is he? What does he look like? Are you sharing this room with him?"

"His name is Kavan. Very handsome. And no."

"You *like* him!" It was an accusation more than anything.

"I mean…he's nice." And thoughtful and patient, and damn let's not forget hot.

"Oh my God! You really like him! You never say anyone is nice."

"It's complicated."

"Why? You have this gorgeous room in a castle! Enjoy your-self for once," Niki said.

"I already kissed him."

Niki squealed. "Perfect! So what's the problem?"

"The next day he acted like it was a mistake."

"He acted like it was a mistake, or you acted like it was a mistake?" Niki quirked an eyebrow. That was the thing about Niki, she knew Poorvi inside out. There was no hiding any-thing from her.

"Him, I…think." How *had* that gone down?

"Go to dinner tonight and find out. You deserve to have a fun night out. All you do is work. This doesn't have to be serious. You're allowed to just have fun. Especially after everything that happened at the lab. And with that jerk Brooks."

Tears sprang to her eyes at the thought of the lab. The place she loved had become a minefield. She was afraid to interact with people, not knowing how it would be interpreted, worrying that something she said (or didn't say) would be used against her in the future. When she realized that people were believing the lies despite having known her for years, she became angry. Anger turned to frustration, turned to fear. Then when Brooks, who was supposed to be her *boyfriend* basically ghosted her, she shut down.

"Come on, Didi. You don't always have to be responsible. Just let loose. Everything will be okay. Have a one-night stand if you want. It's fine."

"I don't...let loose. I'm not even sure I know how."

"There's a first time for everything." Niki's hazel eyes danced with amusement. "What's the worst that could happen?"

Poorvi stared at her sister. After everything in the lab, along with Brooks's behaviour, if she put herself out there with Kavan and he didn't... She tried to mask her face. She failed.

Niki looked at her, her brow furrowed, and in the next instant, her mouth gaped open. "Didi." Her voice was gentle now. "You *really* like him—like you have *feelings*."

Poorvi swallowed hard. "I don't know what I have." Or what he had, either. "It's been less than two days. It takes longer to have a *real* connection."

"Says who?" Niki smiled like Poorvi was a child. "All the more reason to find out. He could have feelings, he could not. It's better to find out, don't you think? Take the risk, either way, you'll be fine."

Niki was right. Life could not be lived only in the lab. "Okay, fine." She exaggerated an eye roll for Niki's benefit. "If you say so." Maybe one night of carefree fun was what she needed.

"I want a report tomorrow." Niki giggled.

"Bye, Niki." Poorvi tapped the phone off and hopped in the shower. Bobby was going to have a fit when she didn't show up tomorrow morning. Right now, she did not care. Her sister was right. Poorvi never did anything for herself. Tonight, she was going to have a lovely dinner with a handsome and kind man in a gorgeous castle. She would be at the meeting in time to present her paper. But tonight, she was going to enjoy herself.

Kavan did indeed have nice clothes in his bag. These conferences always had cocktail parties and usually one formal event. He pulled out black dress slacks and a pink button-down. He located an iron. Took a shower. Did something with his hair. He eyed his ball cap. Not tonight. Applied cologne. He was going on a date with Poorvi...huh, he didn't even have her last name. Didn't matter.

His phone buzzed somewhere. It was his mom's ring, so he looked for it. He had already ignored a couple calls from Naveen.

Kavan located his phone in his coat. FaceTime. Huh. "Mum."

"Hi, beta. Why is your brother constantly calling me?" She sighed heavily. She'd had it rough after their father died, but Veena Shashane had pulled herself together, gone to therapy and then gone back to school to become a therapist. She looked at least ten years younger than she was and she took care of herself. Right now, her hair was tied in a low bun, and she was in the kitchen, likely cooking for herself and a few friends.

"Maybe he misses you." Kavan chuckled to himself. Naveen would never allow himself to have such feelings. Everything he did was duty and obligation. He didn't doubt that his brother loved their mother. But missing her would likely not even occur to him.

His mother rolled her eyes. He'd been told more than once that he had his mother's eyes. She always said he had his father's everything else. "He is complaining that you are not doing what he asked."

Kavan sighed. "He wants me to convince another doctor not to present findings from a study that might make patients wary about having C-MORE done."

"You disagree?"

"I do."

"So, tell him, beta." She was stirring something.

"You know how that goes, Mum."

She sighed and put down her spoon, focusing her attention on him. "You're all dressed up. I thought you weren't in Dublin yet."

"I'm not, Mum."

"Where are you?"

"Just a couple hours away."

She narrowed her eyes at him. "You're acting strange. And the room behind you looks like—"

He sighed and stepped aside.

Her eyes widened and she gasped. "The inside of a castle." She focused her attention on him. "Kavan Shashane. You tell me what is going on."

He flushed and sighed. "I might have met someone."

"And you're going to propose at that castle!" She clasped her hands together in joy.

He furrowed his brow. "What? No, Mum. You haven't even met her—"

"I get to meet her?" She looked around her kitchen. "I will have to make something spectacular to impress her. How about dahi vada? Mine are very good. And I have been practicing jalebi—"

"Mum. Mum. No." Kavan inhaled. "What I'm meaning is

131

that I would never propose before introducing her to you, yeah? But I'm not proposing to anyone. It's just dinner."

"You're having dinner with a woman?" His mother was as excited about the dinner as she had been about his potential proposal.

He sighed. "In a way."

"In a way? What does that mean? You either are or are not having dinner."

"I am having dinner with her, but I don't really know how she feels about it, do I?" He paused. "About me."

His mother smiled. "Is she smart?"

"Very."

"Tell me about her." His mother sighed like he was the exasperating one.

"I met her at the airport."

"You've known her two days?" Her voice went from excited to cautious.

"Yes."

"She likes you?"

He laughed. "I really have no idea. She argues with everything I say and I find her to be quite irritating at times, you see?"

His mother chuckled. "She keeps you on your toes."

"Yes, but she's also sweet and kind and accepting." His thoughts drifted to his driving lessons today. "She taught me how to drive a manual shift car."

"Well, it is about time."

"I know, but Naveen wouldn't teach me—"

"No. I mean it's about time you found someone you really liked. You deserve to be happy, beta." She grinned.

"Mom—don't get your hopes up. I don't even know what this is. We're just having dinner—"

"Does she know who you are?"

"No. She's American. She doesn't know who the Shashanes are." Thank God.

"Perfect. Then you know she really likes you. And not the money or the name."

"Mum." He started to protest, but she wasn't wrong. More than once he had been taken in by a woman who was only interested in the Shashane name or money.

"Beta, I haven't seen that smile on your face in a very long time. You work so hard all the time. There is more to life than just work."

"I know, Mum."

"Have a wonderful evening. I can't wait to meet her!"

"Mum!" But she had ended the call.

Chapter Twenty-One

Poorvi squeezed herself into the fitted dress, put on some lipstick and eyeliner, and took the time to blow out her hair. She started to don a brand new chic black pair of glasses, but then she put them down. She slipped on her heels and knocked on Kavan's door.

Butterflies fluttered around in her stomach as she waited for him to open the door. Ridiculous. This was Kavan, whom she'd spent the last two days sparring with. Kavan, whose kiss had melted her.

He didn't answer. He must be waiting in the restaurant. She walked down the hallway in her fitted cocktail dress and high heels and started down the first set of stairs. She saw him at the bottom of the stairs, his hands in his pockets, facing away from her, leaning against the railing.

He had on black dress pants and a light pink collared shirt that hugged his broad shoulders and grazed the muscles in his arms. He had left the ball cap behind, and he paced away from the steps. As she watched, he nearly bumped into a bellman, seemingly surprised that the bellman was there to begin with.

A smile came to her face. She started down the steps, her gaze fixed on him. As if he could feel her eyes on him, he turned toward her. She knew the instant he saw her because his eyes lit up, then his lips parted and stretched until his cheeks flushed and created the dimples she'd only seen once. As if his eyes had a direct link to the cells in her body, a thrill shot through her and she smiled back, stopping on the step before the bottom, now eye level with him.

"Wow," he said softly, a small smirk on his lips. "I thought you were going to dress up."

She shook her head, unable to stop smiling. "What?"

"That dress is hideous." He raised his eyebrows in mock disgust and wrinkled his nose as he slowly and deliberately passed his gaze over her, heating every inch of her. "But on you, this dress is transformed."

Poorvi's insides were turning to mush, and he hadn't even touched her yet. She rolled her eyes. "Let me guess. You can't believe how amazing I look in this dress."

He shook his head. "No. I can absolutely believe how beautiful you are in that dress. Because you are beautiful in everything." Heat simmered in his eyes as he dropped his gaze to her mouth.

Her heart pounded in anticipation of feeling his lips on hers again, of melting into him and forgetting the world. She leaned toward him.

"Hey!" a woman shouted near them. "It's him."

Kavan pulled back and turned around. He reached for his cap as if to pull it over his head, but it wasn't there.

"It's you, right? From those ads." She scrunched up her face. "I can't remember the ad, but I wouldn't forget that face." Her friends had come closer.

"I'm sorry. I believe you have me mistaken for someone else," Kavan said softly, but he kept his head ducked as if hiding.

"No. I would never forget your face." She grinned.

"Well, sorry." He took Poorvi's hand and tried to walk away. "We have dinner plans."

"Wait. Can't we have a selfie?" The woman started to follow them.

"No." Poorvi turned toward the woman. "My husband and I are trying celebrate our wedding anniversary, we would like some privacy," she snapped. "He said you were mistaken, so you were mistaken." Poorvi drew herself up to her full five foot two—five foot five in the heels—and stared the woman in the eye, daring her to contradict Kavan again.

"Oh! I'm sorry. Uh…happy anniversary," the woman said, awkwardly forcing a smile and retreating.

"Thank you," Poorvi said kindly. Kavan tugged on her hand, and she turned to him and smiled as they walked to the restaurant. He settled his hand on the small of her back and leaned toward her ear.

"How long have we been married?" He chuckled.

"Not nearly long enough," she said.

Kavan sat down across from Poorvi as the sommelier poured them each a glass of wine. He raised his glass to her. "To quick thinking."

She laughed and clinked his glass. "Anytime. Anything to help a friend."

His sipped his wine and put the glass down. "Is that what we are? Friends?"

She shrugged. "Aren't we?"

"Well, yes. We are friends. But is that all we are?"

"I mean don't diminish friendship here like 'that's all we are.'" She waved her hands a bit, obviously trying not to answer him.

"Poorvi."

She put her hands down. "I don't know."

"You don't know?" He felt like a stone had fallen into his stomach.

"I mean can't we just have fun?" She looked him in the eye, like this was the most logical thing.

He stared at her. She just wanted to have fun. His heart thudded in his chest. Sure, he could absolutely have fun with her. Why not? They could have an amazing evening, and possibly even a fantastic night together. One night...that would be incredible. One night...that would quite possibly ruin him.

Kavan wanted more, much more, but he was starting to realize that he would be willing to take any part of Poorvi that she was willing to give. He did his best to mask the disappointment that bloomed like an ache in his heart.

"Not to mention, are you some kind of celebrity?" she asked.

"Celebrity? Why would you think that?"

"People recognize you. Like everywhere we go." She shook her head like he was dense.

"Oh, that's because I do ads for our family business." He shrugged.

"What's the family business?"

He waved a hand. He did not want to talk about Shashane Eye right now. And he certainly did not want to talk about the pictures Naveen had taken. "You really just want to have fun?"

She stared at him. "Yes. That's all I can do right now."

He nodded. Okay. He could do this. They could just have fun. He downed his wine, and the sommelier quickly refilled his glass as well as Poorvi's. "Then let's not talk about anything else. Fun it is."

They finished that bottle and then the next while they enjoyed a fabulous coursed-out meal. Poorvi ate her share and a decent portion of his as he had lost his appetite, despite the talent of the chef. Clearly "just having fun" with Poorvi was not sitting as easily as he thought it might.

The wine, however, was going down quite smoothly. It made it easier for him imagine Poorvi as simply someone he had met at the airport. As someone he had developed a *friendship* with, as opposed to someone who made his heart rate exceed normal and his palms sweat. Or someone he wanted to kiss senseless. The memory of her in a towel popped into his head and he envisioned untying it and letting it fall.

"Kavan?"

Kavan extinguished that image and looked at Poorvi. She was standing. "I think it's time to turn in. Long day tomorrow."

"Right." He stood. Of course. Tomorrow, they would be in Dublin.

They walked side by side, comfortable in their silence. They reached Poorvi's door first. His was right next door. With an adjoining door, he recalled. She stopped and turned to him. "Thank you for a fabulous evening."

"Anything for my wife on our anniversary." He chuckled.

"What would you do for your wife on an anniversary?" she asked. "Like your real wife. If you got married."

"Oh, uh, that would depend on my wife."

"What do you mean?"

"Well, does she like dinners out like this? Or would she rather order a pizza and stay in and watch a movie? Does she want to hike? Or maybe charter a boat?" He opened his mouth and stopped himself. *Or just stay in bed all day.* "You get the idea."

"Anything."

He nodded. "Anything that makes her happy."

She nodded as if she approved of his answer and light flooded inside him knowing he had made *her* happy. They were close enough that their bodies grazed each other. He inhaled the scent of flowers in the rain from her. Surely her lips would taste like the wine they'd been drinking. If he kissed her right now, he wouldn't stop. He could kiss her now, and he would have tonight. He leaned down, his mouth hovering millimeters from hers.

"Kavan." She whispered his name, her voice thick with desire and need. For him.

Just for tonight. *Just for fun.*

Tomorrow, everything would go back to where it was right now. She would go her own way, and he, his. She was happy being *friends*.

No.

With nothing less than sheer willpower and the need to protect his own heart, he pulled back and stepped toward his door. "Good night, then."

She looked confused and she shook her head. "Yes. Good night."

His door clicked shut and she stood in the hallway feeling like an idiot.

What the hell just happened?

She had been sure he wanted to kiss her. That he had been ready to spend the night with her. She certainly had been ready.

Had she read it wrong? Taking it slow, as friends, seemed to be the wisest way to go. She had been simply trying to follow Niki's advice to have fun. He had agreed. She opened her door just as Niki called. She answered.

"Why are you answering?" Niki chided.

"You called."

"I was hoping you would be otherwise preoccupied."

"Well, I am not. But I have had quite a bit of wine. So I'm going to bed."

"Did you at least have a good time?"

Poorvi grinned. "I did. We talked nonstop and joked and laughed—I don't even know where the time went."

"You should see your face. You sooo like this guy."

Poorvi shrugged. "Well, I must have read it wrong. Because he is not interested in anything more." Or even just one night.

"Well. All right." Niki yawned. "Bedtime."

"Good night, sis," Poorvi said as she disconnected. She stared at the door that divided their rooms. That first kiss must have been a mistake.

Chapter Twenty-Two

Poorvi woke the next morning with a grand headache. She ordered breakfast to her room so she could lie in bed a few extra minutes. It certainly wasn't because she vaguely remembered putting the moves on Kavan and him turning her down. She was a strong, modern woman—it was his loss if he didn't take what was offered. Right?

She flopped on the bed. Her head hammered and her stomach felt queasy. She was mortified. She had put her herself out there to him and he had turned her down. She glanced at the tray of food. She inhaled and sat up. Enough of that. She would simply act like she was fine with the fact that he hadn't wanted to have sex. All she had wanted was one night anyway, so *whatever*.

She was forcing down some toast and eggs when there was a loud knock at her door. Her ridiculous heart did a flip, hoping it was Kavan. But a second later, Ba walked into her room.

"Jai Shree Krishna, Ba." The greeting just fell out of her like it had whenever she had seen her own grandmother. It was still an ache she had from time to time, missing her grandmother. Like when she smelled jasmine hair oil or delicious fried masala puri.

Ba didn't miss a beat. "Jai Shree Krishna, beti." She looked around, taking in the bed and Poorvi's open bag, the dress from last night laid neatly over the chair. "Where is he?"

"Who?" Poorvi furrowed her brow and stuffed some muffin in her mouth, even though she knew exactly which "he" Ba was referring to.

"Kavan. Who else?" Ba looked at her with impatience.

"He has his own room." Poorvi worked to add irritation in her voice so her disappointment would not show through.

Ba stared at her, eyebrows almost lost, she raised them so high. "Really?"

"Really."

"I thought you both had dinner last night." Ba was now piercing her with narrow eyes and walking closer. "Together."

"We did."

Ba stopped short. "That's it?"

"That's it."

Ba stared at her a moment. Then she shook her head at her and started speaking in rapid Gujarati to God, the gist of which was: *What was she supposed to do with these children? They cannot even see what is in front of them!* She ranted like this for a moment. Then throwing Poorvi one last glare, she left. Poorvi ran for the door that divided her room from Kavan's and listened while Ba knocked on Kavan's door.

Kavan greeted Ba with a Jai Shree Krishna as well. Poorvi smiled. Huh. Then she stopped smiling. She needed to not find more things about him that she liked. Ba proceeded to rant at him for a few minutes about not seeing what was right in front of him.

After which there was silence.

"Come both of you. We have the Holi party at Devi's today."

"Yes, Ba," she heard him say.

"Poorvi?" Ba called.

She poked her head out the door. "Coming, Ba." She looked over and saw Kavan in his doorway. He glanced at her. And instead of the warm smile she had become accustomed to, he pressed his lips together and gave her a curt nod as a greeting.

She stared at him, not responding. Then she went back into her room without saying a word. What was his problem? *He* had turned *her* down last night. Fine. He just made it easier for her to ignore him. She hopped in the shower, then donned jeans and her blue blouse with her blue glasses. She barely looked at the dress as she packed it up. Better to just give it to Niki. She'd get more use out of it.

Poorvi strutted right out to the car to find Kavan already leaning against it.

He was scrolling his phone, sunglasses on, completely oblivious to her.

She approached. "You have the keys?"

He glanced at her over his glasses, his mouth set. "You didn't have breakfast." His voice was low and slow. He smelled amazing, like soap and rain.

"I had it sent to my room," she said as blandly as possible. Now that she was near him and could see and smell and hear him, a vise seemed to clamp over her heart. Also, her stomach was still unhappy with her alcohol choices from the night before, and her breakfast choices from this morning.

He just watched her over his sunglasses.

"Keys?" she asked, this time putting her hand out.

"I have them."

"So, open the trunk," she said, annoyed. What was he looking at?

Kavan stepped back and opened the trunk. She placed her bag in and walked around to the driver's seat.

"What are you doing?" he asked. She seemed annoyed, though he had no idea why. *She was the one who only wanted to be friends. Only wanted to have fun.*

"I'm driving," she said, as if it were obvious.

"No. I am." He corrected her as he walked over to the driver's seat. She was adorable in those blue glasses. Those might be his favorite. They were the same ones she'd had on in the airport when he first saw her. A lifetime ago, but only two days.

"Aren't you hungover?" he asked, trying to keep his voice neutral, like he didn't care one way or the other.

"I'm fine," she snapped, clearly irritated about something. He glanced at her, and she suddenly went pale. Poorvi bent over and vomited on the ground next to his feet.

"Yep." He grabbed her hair just in time, twisting it around his hand to keep it out of her way. With his other hand, he rubbed her back. "Get it out. You'll feel better."

He stood there like that until she finished. "Hold up." He went in and got her some water. She took the glass from him and simply looked up at him, clearly embarrassed.

"Drink this." He was more curt than he needed to be, but it was the only way to keep his feelings in check. Feelings that made him want to sweep her up and kiss her senseless, take her up to his room and undress her slowly so he could simply worship her.

"Thank you."

He just nodded. The sooner they parted ways, the better for him. He had paced the door between their rooms second-guessing his choices half the night. The other half he spent dreaming about her. Even right now, his instinct was to hold her until she felt better.

All thoughts of Dublin and finding P. K. Gupta had fallen from him. All he cared about right now was the fact that in a matter of hours, he would never see her again. Two days with her and his heart was going to break, and he'd only kissed her twice.

She took the water and sipped.

"You sleep in the back," he said. "I'll drive."

"Whatever." She wouldn't even look at him. She stood and went to the back seat. Ba sat in the front and shot him a glare as she handed him Devi's address.

He looked back at Poorvi. "You okay back there?"

"Fine," she said, but the edge was gone from her voice.

"Dublin, then."

She nodded. "Dublin." She leaned her head back and closed her eyes.

He put the car in gear and got on the road.

Chapter Twenty-Three

The sun had come out and was warming the air around them by the time they arrived at Devi's house.

Poorvi stepped out of the car and her mouth dropped open. Devi lived in a mini castle. At least her house was big enough, and the structure looked like a castle. Stone walls with a small turret and large wooden doors, and iron accents.

"Ba! This is gorgeous. Your daughter lives here?" Poorvi walked around with her head tilted up.

Ba nodded. "Come. There is much to do before the party."

"Oh. No. Ba, we have to go—" Kavan started looking at Poorvi.

Poorvi nodded. Sitting with him alone in the car was going to be uncomfortable, but she'd manage. Bobby might be angry she wasn't there this morning, but if she didn't show at all? "He's right. I'm already late for—"

"No." Ba was firm. "You both stay. This is Holi."

"Ba—" Kavan started.

"No!" she said. "This is the celebration of color and spring." She paused and narrowed her eyes at them. "Of love." She threw her arm out and pointed to the front door.

"You better listen to her. She's stubborn." A woman's voice chimed in, and they all turned to it.

"Devi!" Ba turned away from them and opened her arms. Her daughter rushed to hug her. Devi's long hair was in a ponytail, and she was about Poorvi's height. Her smile was the same as her mother's. Two small children trailed behind Devi and flung their arms around their grandmother.

"Where is Yash?" Ba asked, looking around.

"He has gone to get the colored powder for the Holi party." Devi answered. "Who are these people, Ma?" Devi narrowed her eyes at her mother. "You said you were with a tour group."

Ba shrugged. "Is that what I said?"

"Ma!" Devi's eyes widened. "Is this how you 'toured' Ireland?" She covered her face with her hands. "Oh my goodness." She looked at Poorvi and Kavan. "I'm so sorry. She told me she joined a bus tour… I should have known. I should have just come out to Cork and picked her up. She insisted she was fine."

Kavan broke out in laughter. Poorvi could not help but to follow. "Ba!"

Ba shrugged.

"You must both stay for the party—we have a ton of food, the community comes out, and it's a lot of fun. I insist. It's the least I can do for…taking care of my mother." She shook her head at her mother. "I promise I'll let you leave in the morning and get back to your jobs." Peering at Kavan, Devi did a double take. "Have we met? You look familiar."

Kavan shook his head as if he had no idea what she was talking about. Poorvi furrowed her brow. Why didn't he just say that he did ads for their family business?

Devi started walking toward the house. "I will not take no for an answer. My stubborn streak comes from her."

Kavan met Poorvi's eyes. She shrugged and nodded at the car. She was right. They really had no choice. Pretty much the story of the past couple days. Kavan sighed and got the bags from the trunk. Poorvi grabbed hers and Ba's.

"I can get all that," he told her.

She shrugged. "Not a problem," she said as she rolled both

bags to follow Ba and Devi into the small castle. He needed to get away from Poorvi, but that was not going to happen.

He locked up the car and caught up with Poorvi, taking Ba's suitcase from her.

"I said I could get it," she hissed at him.

"I got it," he hissed back.

"Just because I'm a woman does not mean I can't get things like luggage."

"I never said it was because you're a woman. I'm just trying to help, to be nice."

"No one asked you to be 'nice.'"

"That's the point of it. No one has to ask."

They had raised their voices without realizing it and now they turned to find four pairs of eyes watching them. Devi had a smirk on her face and looked at her mother. She nodded at her mother. "Ah ha."

Ba nodded. "See?"

A look passed between mother and daughter.

"So, I have some staff here today. They can take your bags up." She nodded behind them. "Liam."

Kavan turned to see a young man behind them. Liam stepped up and took the bags from them and disappeared.

"Come, I have lunch ready. The festivities will start late afternoon," Devi said.

The children looked up at him. "You are very tall," the young girl said. She was maybe five years old.

"He's too tall," her brother stated as they craned their little necks to see him. "What does everything look like from up there?"

"I could pick you up and show you," Kavan said to the little boy.

Kavan glanced at Devi. "May I?"

She nodded.

The boy narrowed his eyes in doubt and Kavan was immediately reminded of Ba. "You don't even know my name."

"Right, I'm Kavan. What's your name?"

"Dharmesh. But everyone calls me Dharm." He continued to eye Kavan with suspicion.

"Oh my God. He looks just like Ba right now," Poorvi said softly. Kavan turned to her and they shared a glance. He quickly turned back to the child.

The little boy raised his arms and Kavan picked him up and put him on his shoulders. He had a vague memory of his dad doing the same. Dharm squealed with delight.

"This is awesome!" Dharm determined. His sister was clamoring for her turn. "I'm Mira," she told him as she lifted her arms to him. Kavan gently returned Dharm to the ground and picked up Mira, who squealed with pure delight.

The children continued bombarding him with questions as they ate the spectacular but simple spread of chutney sandwiches and mango that Devi had made for lunch.

Kavan turned to Poorvi. "How's that on your belly?" he asked softly.

"Fine. I'm fine." She softened a bit but was far from the woman he'd had dinner with last night.

He had to remind himself that they would not be more than friends.

"Thank you for lunch, Devi, but we must be going," he said, this time not bothering to look Poorvi's way.

"He's right. Besides, we don't really have clothes for Holi…"

"Nonsense. We have plenty of white clothes," Devi insisted. "Yash will return shortly with the colored powder—"

"Then we'll throw the powder on each other to celebrate spring." Mira's eyes widened. "Plus we made water balloons filled with colored water, too!"

"You can't go." Dharm joined in. "We have to throw colors on you!"

Devi laughed. "Her aim is deadly."

Ba pierced them with a look. "Are you going to disappoint small children, now?"

Poorvi glanced at him and shrugged, as she reached for her phone.

Kavan grinned at the kids. "I'm pretty good at this Holi thing."

They cackled with glee.

Chapter Twenty-Four

Poorvi donned the white salwar kameez Devi had lent her, and washed up in what looked like a shared Jack and Jill bathroom. The family was wonderful, the kids were adorable, but she was struggling with Kavan. At times supersweet, at times cold, she didn't know what was happening.

He had turned her down.

Right? So why was he so angry?

Music and the call of the dhol interrupted her thoughts and she found her way to the back to enjoy the festivities. Devi had set up the colored powder under a tent in her spacious backyard. Somehow the sun was their companion today, so it was perfect weather. Poorvi took out her white frames that transitioned into sunglasses in the sun.

She had texted Bobby that she would be at the conference by tomorrow and that there was really no need for them to go over her presentation, because she was going to say what she was going to say regardless of what his input was.

Then she muted him.

By the time Poorvi got to the tent, many of the neighboring families had arrived. She squinted in the sunlight. She had forgotten her glasses in the room. The children had armed themselves with water balloons and water shooters filled with colored water and were attacking people indiscriminately. Kavan was already covered with purple, blue and yellow powder. She watched as the children stalked him and then soaked him through with water.

His white kurta was soaked through and stuck to his skin. She should look away. But she did not. She was so distracted that she wasn't paying attention when the children and their friends sneaked up on her—Poorvi was balloon-bombed before she knew it. The water was cold and a shock to her body. She froze for a second.

The sound of Kavan's laughter got her moving. She grabbed fistfuls of colored powder and tossed it in the air above the children. The colors landed on them, dusting them with yellow, green and pink. She grabbed another fistful and threw it (as much as one can throw powder) in Kavan's direction, dusting him again in purple and green. She cackled and then attempted to run as Kavan came toward her, a fistful of powder in one hand. He was too fast, and the children had her surrounded. He approached and came close, tossing the powder in the air above her, dusting her in yellow and red. She had stopped as he came close. He made eye contact; his breath was coming hard.

"Poorvi." There was a glint in his eye. He lifted a fist as if to throw the color up again, but instead, he opened that hand and rubbed it on her cheek. "Gotcha!" He laughed and tried to step away as her hand came up.

He was too slow, and she placed both of her hands on his face. "Right back at you." She laughed.

They played until everyone was soaked through. Poorvi could not remember the last time she had laughed this hard or had this much fun.

Kavan hadn't played Holi since he was kid, maybe no older than Devi's son. He leaned against a table under the tent and attempted to remove as much of the powder as possible before entering the house for a shower.

Poorvi was standing two tables away, doing the same and

talking to Devi. She was soaked as badly as he was. Watching her laugh and relax the past half hour was a highlight for him. He had been told more than once that any woman he wanted, would surely want him back. He had never really believed it and at the moment, it seemed as though the one woman he did want did not want him.

Someone started the dhol beat and then the band picked up the tempo. The children came to get him for some dancing. He saw Devi and Poorvi hit the makeshift dance floor as well.

He watched for a moment as Poorvi started dancing, slowly at first to match the beat and then faster as the tempo increased. They were doing the traditional folk dancing, garba, a kind of line dance in a circle. Almost every Gujarati kid grew up learning garba and Poorvi was no exception. For that matter, neither was he. He waited for her to come around in the circle and then joined in beside her.

Who would have thought that Kavan could dance like that? Poorvi switched up the garba step to yet another complicated pattern and Kavan kept up. The music sped up and Kavan changed the pattern of steps. Poorvi kept up. The two of them twirled and clapped and stepped until the last beat.

Out of breath, they both stopped when the music stopped. "Impressive," Poorvi told him.

He nodded as he caught his breath. "You, too."

"Well, Niki and I have always loved dancing." She shrugged.

"My dad was a huge fan. Always took us to Navaratri." He shrugged. "Naveen used to be really good. He doesn't go anymore."

"Maybe it's too painful."

Kavan looked her in the eye. "I understand that."

Before she could question him further, the music started again. "Come on. If we're first, we get to pick the step." He grabbed her hand and took her to the dance floor as a slow beat garba started. Ba joined them for the simple step. Poorvi was going to miss them both.

They danced and ate until the sun set. Then tired and dirty and full, the guests began to leave, and Poorvi headed to her room. Kavan had disappeared. He must still be playing with the children.

She found her way back to the beautiful room with the attached bathroom Devi had shown her earlier so she could change her clothes. She gathered her shampoo and a towel and entered the bathroom to find Kavan standing there with nothing but a towel around his waist. Like low on his waist. Very low. Her reaction was slower than it should have been.

"Ah! What are you doing in my bathroom?" She was harsher than she had meant to be.

"This is the bathroom attached to my room," he said and made no move to leave.

She nodded, unable to keep her eyes off of him. Kavan with his clothes stuck to his muscles was one thing, but Kavan in nothing but a towel was breathtaking. She was quite unable to speak. "It's attached to my room, too." She tried to snap, but her words came out sounding as dazed as she felt.

"You okay?" he asked, leaning against the counter, his gaze running the length of her body. She became aware that her clothes were sopping wet and stuck to her as well.

"Yes. Sure. Except for seeing you in a towel. Wow." What was she saying? Stop talking. She clamped her lips together. She should leave. Just turn around and walk out of the bathroom that currently held one extremely sweet and excessively attractive man in nothing but a towel smelling like...lemon soap.

She didn't move.

Kavan tensed and stood. "Don't."

"Don't what?" She had no idea what he was talking about, although her brain wasn't fully functioning with him standing there, half-naked.

"Don't act like you want something more from me when all you want is to be friends," he growled at her.

"Friends is good though, right?" What was she saying? She was not having any friend-like thoughts right now, nor was she having them last night.

"I do not want to be friends with you, Poorvi." He shook his head.

"What do you want?"

"The question is what do you want?" he said.

"I wanted you last night. You walked away." She pursed her lips, challenging him to deny it.

"I wanted you like you wouldn't believe." Kavan's voice became low, intimate and more irresistible.

"Then why…?"

"Because according to you, that would've been it. One night."

"Are you saying you want more?" her breath hitched on her words.

He looked at her, his jaw clenched, his eyes on fire. Everything he felt was right there on his face. She knew his answer before he said it.

"Yes." He moved toward her and turned facing her, so he had a hand on either side of her, caging her with his body. It was not unpleasant. With him so close, the scent of lemon soap intensified. Which conjured images of him using said soap on his body. Her body heated.

"I'm saying that I've never known anyone like you. You drive me crazy, but I can't get enough of you." He moved even closer. "I'm saying all I can think about is how amazing it felt to kiss you two nights ago. And how badly I wanted to kiss you last night." He paused. "I didn't want to stop there." He leaned down toward her neck and inhaled deeply. "Flowers. In the rain," he whispered. "Every. Time."

Poorvi's heart pounded in her chest. He was so close and

the things he was saying were things she had wanted to hear. "You said kissing me was a drunken mistake."

"*You* said kissing me was a drunken mistake. I came back to the room that morning to kiss you again, to tell you—" He stopped and raked his gaze over her. Her body electrified by his gaze, she nearly held her breath waiting for him to reveal what he had wanted to tell her.

"To tell me what?"

He studied her face for a moment. She saw the instant he decided to tell her everything, to be vulnerable, his heart be damned. "To tell you that I was attracted to you. To tell you that I feel that connection between us. I know it seems impossible after such a short time...but I know what I feel."

She turned and caught his eye, his breath mingling with hers. "Why didn't you say any of that?"

He flushed and chuckled. "Because you were wearing nothing but a towel and you were shouting at me."

"Seriously? You're going with 'I couldn't control my words around a half-naked woman'?" She swallowed again. Damn, he was getting closer to her. She might just melt right there.

"I certainly was not able to control my words around a half-naked *you*." He leaned down to her ear. "You are deliciously tantalizing in nothing but a towel."

She glanced down past his taut, bare chest and stomach and bit her bottom lip. "Right back at you."

He pulled back an inch and grinned at her. "I know it's only been a few days." He met her eyes with his, his voice earnest and beseeching. "I *know* I don't want to be without you." He tilted his head so she had to look into his eyes. "I don't want there to be any doubt like after that first kiss."

She nodded. He was so very close. "I'm not foggy now." She took off her glasses and dropped them. She wanted nothing between her and Kavan.

When Poorvi's lips touched his ever so gently, Kavan

thought he would lose his mind. He was desperate for her, and there was no hiding that now. The heat from her body was a beacon to his hands. He lifted her damp salwar over her head and untied the drawstring on the bottoms, letting them pool at her feet.

"I don't want to be friends with you," he growled.

"Who needs friends?" she whispered, her breath grazing his bare chest.

He grinned at her and placed his hand on her cheek. "Have you seen you?" His voice was low and intimate. He bent down, his eyes focused on her mouth. "Your mouth, for example, is exquisite." He gently touched his lips to hers. She gasped and he relished it.

"Your eyes." He continued in that same voice as he kissed each of her closed lids. "I would gladly fall into." He trailed kisses down her cheek. "This dimple, right here—" he licked it with his tongue "—deepens when you're angry." She groaned and moved closer to him, her body pressed against his.

He continued down to her neck. An almost feral animal sound built in her throat, which he felt rather than heard. "If kissing your neck elicits those sounds, I never want to stop."

"Poorvi."

"Hmmm," she groaned under him.

"The towel."

Chapter Twenty-Five

Poorvi woke in Kavan's arms, their bodies tangled together in the most pleasant way. The scent of that lemon soap was everywhere, mostly because they'd ended up in the shower together at some point. The sun had not yet risen, but the partially open blinds told her that dawn was upon them. Her phone was blowing up.

So was Kavan's.

"Hey." She kissed his shoulder, then sat up. Hmm. It may have been the one spot on his body that her lips had not touched last night. "Your phone."

Kavan groaned and gently tugged her back to him. She did not resist. She settled back into his arms. There were good men out there. Kavan was one of them. She didn't know what was happening between them, but this most certainly was not a hookup. Not for either of them.

Her phone rang. She groaned and turned it over to see who it was. *Bobby.* Again. She sent it to voice mail. Before she even settled back, it rang again. Mom. This time she sat up and answered. Kavan's phone was ringing, too. He finally rolled over and away from her to get his phone.

"What's up, Mom?" she said.

"What the heck are you doing over there?" Her mother sounded accusatory.

"What do you mean?" How could she possibly know she'd just had sex?

"I mean. I saw that post." Now she was accusatory and irritated.

"What post?"

"Instagram. Facebook, you name it."

"I don't know what you're talking about. Hold on." She sat up properly and put her mom on speaker to open her Instagram account. Kavan had stepped away to the other side of the room to deal with whoever he was talking to. A glance at his face told her that his conversation was no more pleasant than hers.

Funny. He looked like he was opening an app on his phone, too.

She apparently had over ninety notifications for every platform. Odd. Her heart started hammering. Her texts from Bobby and Niki were fifty deep. Bobby's face popped up on her screen again, but she sent it to voice mail. Poorvi finally opened her Instagram and there it was.

A picture of her and Kavan at the Cliffs of Moher. They were looking at each other and the attraction was obvious. She swiped and saw the selfie they had taken. Swiped again and saw a picture of her wide-eyed and looking annoyed. It was when she had told the woman that they were not together. Behind her, Kavan was looking—devastated. She hadn't seen that.

These were all pictures from his phone. He must have posted them, but he didn't really seem the social media type.

"Yeah, Mom. I met a guy—" She stopped as she read the caption. "I told Niki, but I was going to tell you when…"

Her voice trailed off as the meaning of the caption hit—and so did reality.

@pkguptamd and @kshashane together at the @cliffsofmoher before the @ICO meeting where Dr. Gupta is set to present her paper on the hazards of C-MORE. @Shashaneeye is the leading performer of that procedure. Wonder what recommendations she will make now that her fling with @kshashane looks to be over? This on the heels of the rumors that Dr. Gupta lost the position of principal investigator because of an alleged affair with her boss's boss.

Maybe this is how Dr. Gupta softens the blow? Or maybe @ kshashane is hoping that he can influence her recommendations?

"Mom, I gotta go." She tapped off the phone and turned to Kavan, glaring.

"You're last name is Shashane?" She hopped out of the bed, grabbing the sheets to cover her, suddenly aware of how naked she was.

"You're P. K. Gupta?" He grabbed his pants, pulling them up as he stood and faced her.

"It's you! You and your brother. You're the ones who are trying to get me to present only certain facts, so that you can still do C-MORE no matter how questionable. All this time…" She shook her head at him. "Was this your plan?" She found her underwear and attempted to put it on without dropping the sheet. She ended up sitting on the floor to do it. "Did you think sleeping with me would change my professional opnion? Do you have any idea how bad those pictures are for my job future—especially given everything that had already gone down? I *trusted* you!" She paused for breath. "And you gave him these pictures and he posted them—or he gave them to someone to post."

"I did not give any pictures to anyone and I certainly did not post anything," Kavan shouted back at her.

A light went on. She glared at him from the floor. "This is about money. If I make my recommendations in line with my numbers, you stand to lose money."

"No. I mean yes, that's true. I didn't know who you were! But that's not—"

"I'm supposed to believe that?" She found a pair of jeans

and a T-shirt that seemed clean and tossed them on. "You could Google me—it's a little too convenient, isn't it? You've been lying to me this whole time." Once she dressed, she tossed the remainder of her clothes and toiletries into her bag.

"Poorvi. Listen. Please…it's not like—"

"Stop talking." She nearly screamed at him as she rolled her suitcase to the door and stopped. "You don't care about me." The words caught in her throat. She was so angry she could hardly breathe. Tears threatened, but she refused to cry in front of him. "There's no 'connection.' That was all bullshit." She inhaled back her tears of fury. "I opened up to you. I didn't want to, I was afraid, but I let you into my…heart."

Her voice cracked. The tears were going to fall; she could do nothing about it. "I'll give you this much, you had me. I believed you were falling for me. Though it seems unnecessary to have gone through all this since you already had the photos. But I guess you got a good lay out of it."

Kavan flinched as if she had slapped him; she registered pain in his eyes. Her rage boiled inside her, but she didn't care. "I told you all of it, how I had trusted my colleagues and they stayed silent, how I had leaned into Brooks and he ghosted me. I don't know how you did it, but—*bravo*—" she smirked at him "—you made me trust you, when I trust no one." She never should have let him into her heart, but it had been too hard to fight it. "This was the best you could do? Try to discredit my reputation by painting me as a 'woman scorned'? At least have the balls to do it intellectually. At least fight me on the same turf. This—" she raised her eyebrows "—this is low, desperate."

She left without another word.

Chapter Twenty-Six

Poorvi called an Uber and waited on Devi's porch swing, facing out toward the road. She squeezed her eyes against the memory of what they had shared the past three days and nights. Falling asleep next to him last night had felt like a new beginning.

What the hell did she know? She knew the lab. She knew numbers. She did not know men. Her history with them was proof.

She felt someone come and sit next to her. She knew it wasn't Kavan before she opened her eyes. She already knew how his body felt next to hers. And no lemon soap.

"Beti." The voice was soft and sweet and filled with love. Ba.

She opened her eyes. Ba placed a comforting hand on top of Poorvi's and Poorvi was visited by a round of grief for her own grandmother. "I'm sorry I lied to you."

Poorvi shook her head. "Ba. It's strange but I get it. You needed to do something, you went after it." She leaned over and hugged Ba. "I'm glad we met."

She saw her Uber approaching. She squeezed Ba's hand one more time and got up.

"Beti. Listen. I don't know what happened between you two, and maybe I'm just an old busybody, but you have both built a bond in just a few days. Imagine your bond if you stay together and work at it. Love isn't easy. Trusting people and being vulnerable is scary. But it is worth it."

"Would you do it again, knowing what you know now?" Poorvi side-eyed Ba.

"Without hesitation, beti."

Poorvi sighed and picked up her bag. "It's complicated, Ba."

Ba nodded. "I know. But just remember, just because we fight with men, does not mean we have to fight like men." She got a glint in her eye. "We are women."

Poorvi stared at Ba and shook her head. "Okay."

"Text me when you get there."

Poorvi had to chuckle.

Ba frowned. "I'm serious."

"Okay." Poorvi opened the door of the car. She felt eyes on her and found Kavan watching her from the door of the house. Her heart thudded in her chest. She froze for a moment. Then she got in the car and left.

He was in love with P. K. Gupta.

And that's what it was. He knew it when he woke up this morning with her in his arms. He knew it last night when she walked in on him in the bathroom. What he felt was more than a connection.

He loved her.

He had stood frozen for a moment while the bedroom door closed behind her. Then he grabbed a T-shirt and ran after her while trying to put it on. But he couldn't find the arms and it got stuck on his head. He paused in the middle of the hallway, fixed the T-shirt and then continued his chase.

She could not have gone far. She'd probably called an Uber. He headed for what he thought was the front of the house and ended up in the back where the tent was being taken down. He turned around and ran back inside. Kavan entered the kitchen and, to his luck, found Dharm having cereal with his sister.

"Hey, Dharm. I need your help." Kavan was out of breath.

"It'll cost you." Dharm eyed him.

"What?" Where was the sweet kid from last night?

"You need something, I have it. It'll cost you," Dharm repeated.

"Fine, whatever." Kavan was not going to argue with an eight-year-old. "I need to find that auntie I was with yesterday."

"Your girlfriend?"

"Well, she's not really... It's complicated."

"Do you like her?" Dharm sighed.

"Yes. Very much."

"Does she like you?"

"I think so, but she's gone mad at me, see. So I need to find her before she leaves, yeah?"

Dharm hopped off his chair. "Basically, you want her to be your girlfriend, yeah? And she's mad." He folded his arms in front of him. "It'll cost you extra."

"Fine. Okay," Kavan said.

"She's probably on the front porch."

Kavan grinned. "Right. And which way is that?"

"What did you do?"

"What do you mean?"

"I mean what did you do to make her mad?"

"Well... I... I mean she thinks that I... Look, it's complicated, and if she leaves, I'm done. Help a guy out, eh? Which way is the porch?"

Dharm eyed him and then huffed. "All right then. Follow me."

Kavan sighed and followed the young boy, who did indeed lead him to the front porch.

Just in time to see Poorvi getting into her Uber. She turned and saw him standing there. Her expression was wounded, hurt. She thought she was a master at hiding her feelings, but he could read her. Right then, her face and body begged him to stay away, she clearly wanted nothing to do with him. So he had stood there, frozen, unable to move, while she turned away from him. He did not move, even when the car drove away, taking his heart and soul with it.

Ba saw him and walked over. She smacked him on the arm.

"Ow. Ba!" He rubbed his arm and furrowed his brow at her. "What was that for?"

"Why are you standing here, watching her leave?" Ba barked at him. "You love her, don't you?"

"Yes."

"Go get yourself together and go after her."

"No. Ba. It's over." He shook his head. "She deserves—I treated her no better than every other man in her life."

"You must try." This time Ba was not shouting or scolding him. He looked at her. Tears brimmed in her eyes. "There is never enough time with our loved ones. Go. People make mistakes. That's how we learn and grow. Apologize for whatever you have done. And *be* with her." A tear escaped Ba's eye.

"Ba, don't." He wiped the tear away. He much preferred being smacked on the arm.

"If you love her, you have to fight for her!" Ba was adamant. "That connection—it is rare. You may never find it again. What do you have to lose?"

She wasn't wrong. He would never get over her. He would never find anyone like her again. "You're right, Ba. I'll go fight." He knew exactly where Poorvi was going.

Chapter Twenty-Seven

The city was a bit of a shock after three days of small towns, cozy and simple B and Bs, castles and local pubs. Dublin hustled and bustled like any other city. But if she looked closely, she saw the corner pubs, the cozy bakeries and the Irish hospitality she had enjoyed for the past few days. True, she was just a tourist.

She hurriedly exited the Uber and was approached by a bellman.

"Help wit' your luggage, ma'am?"

"No thank you. It's just the one bag." She forced a smile.

He nodded and opened the door for her. "Check-in is just up the stairs and to your right."

"Thank you," she said, and made her way to check-in. The hotel was gorgeous; she had splurged to stay in the same hotel as the conference. She had just been handed her room key card when a familiar voice called to her.

"Poorvi! It's about time."

She turned to see Bobby hurrying toward her. "Where have you been?"

"On my way. I told you I was held up."

He looked around and stepped closer to her. "Come with me." She followed him toward the large conference room. "They changed the schedule. You present in an hour," he said as they walked. They arrived at the conference room, which was more of a ballroom. She peeked at the crowd. There were hundreds of ophthalmologists here. Bobby led her around the corner of the staging area to a small alcove.

"Listen." He lowered his voice. "We need this grant. What the heck are you doing, fraternizing with the enemy?"

"Fraternizing with? What do you…?"

"Don't play dumb with me. You hooked up with Kavan Shashane and now they're going to use that to discredit our work. Maybe think about who you sleep with," Bobby spat at her.

"You know what, the hell with you. You've never had my back. Not before you were promoted and certainly not since you were promoted."

"What does that mean?"

"That means that you knew that James Hardy had asked me out multiple times and you knew that I turned him down, multiple times. We were friends—at the very least we were coworkers—and not once did you stand by me when all the accusations came down." She fumed at him. "Now I have my colleagues believing that my research and my recommendations, which existed long before I ever laid eyes on Kavan Shashane, will be affected by a supposed 'broken relationship.'" She was fired up. "And by the way, let's be clear. That work is not 'ours,' it's *mine*."

Bobby glared at her. "You may lay claim to the work, but where would you be without the lab? You just get up there and say whatever you must. The Shashane Brothers are having a panel discussion in favor of C-MORE, immediately following your presentation. We can't have people believing them over you, we'll lose that grant. You have an hour."

Poorvi was tired of her work being put second to whatever her personal life was. She worked hard and she was the smartest person in that lab. She knew it and she did not need Bobby—or anyone else—to tell her that.

Her phone dinged. Text from Ba. Did you arrive?!

Crap. She forgot. Yes, Ba.

Now she needed a shower.

Chapter Twenty-Eight

Kavan showered quickly and put on his suit. He threw his things in a bag and said hasty goodbyes to his hosts. Dharm gave him a hug after Kavan paid him.

It was Ba who stopped him. She was shaking her head at him. He could feel her disappointment. "I'll fix it, Ba. I promise."

"Uh-huh." She pursed her lips, but she hugged him. "Text me when you get there."

"Ba."

"Text. Me."

"Okay," he assured her, and got back in the car. So focused was he on what he needed to do, he drove the manual car without a thought. Anand called.

"What's this Instagram post?"

"It's Naveen," Kavan growled. "He did it."

"Who's the woman?"

"It says right there."

"No, brother. I mean, *who is she*?"

"She's The One." Kavan said. "She's *the one* and I messed it up."

"So make it right."

"I don't know if I can ever make it totally right. But I'm absolutely having words with Naveen."

"About time. If she's the reason you're finally standing up to Naveen, I like her already," Anand said. "Good luck."

Luck? He didn't need luck. Naveen had pushed him too far this time.

Kavan drove up to the hotel and valeted the car. He entered the lobby and texted Ba. Then he texted Naveen that he was here. Almost immediately, Naveen texted back. Meet me in my room.

Kavan took the elevator up to Naveen's room. He didn't even need to prep what he was going to say. He had a sense of calm within him that he had never experienced. He barged into Naveen's room.

"How could you do this?" He held up his phone to Naveen.

"You're welcome." Naveen said, with the ultra calm of someone who was confident in his every action. "I did your job for you."

"Bull, Naveen. You can't just make things up about people and post it. How did you even get the pictures?"

"We share the same cloud," Naveen said coolly, like Kavan was an idiot. Maybe he was. "Are you 'with' her?"

"No." Not after this.

"Were you?"

"Yes."

"Then it's not made up." Naveen grinned at him.

"Naveen. It's wrong. You're using her personal life to discredit her work. That's slimy and unethical! No more, Naveen. I'm done." Kavan was firm. "I'm not your lap dog anymore, Bhai. I will not blindly do whatever you want, are you hearing me?"

"I saved you." Naveen narrowed his eyes, his tone going cold. It was an old tactic he had used many times. Kavan had always given in. Not today.

Kavan sighed and paced the room. "That you did, yeah." he said with more calm than he felt. "Just like a good brother should. And I will forever be grateful to you for that." He stopped pacing and fixed his own gaze on his brother and hardened his tone. "That doesn't mean you own me."

Naveen stood and faced him. "I guided you away from those blokes in high school, to university, then medical college—"

"All true." Kavan did not move away but stood firm. He had never stood up to Naveen like this before. Kavan had seen the possibility of true happiness with Poorvi. Not only had Naveen used him to hurt the woman he loved, he had destroyed that possibility Poorvi would never forgive him, but Kavan no longer had to be at Naveen's beck and call. "What you fail to acknowledge is that once I got there, I did the work. I got the grades and skills that were necessary to be where I am today," Kavan said.

"So now that you have everything, you're not needing your older brother, is that it? You got what you wanted and now you can do whatever you want? You can walk away?" Naveen glared at him.

"I'm not walking away, Naveen. I want to be my own person. Decide what I want to do. I've been trying to tell you for years that I want to add a research aspect to my clinical work and you literally wave me off as if I'm a child. I'm not a child." Kavan shook his head at him.

"Is that what this has been about all these years? That I would have to need you?" Kavan softened. He recalled Poorvi's assessment of Naveen. *He's afraid of losing you.* "You're my brother, I will always need you. What I don't need is you running my life." Kavan walked away a few steps, then turned back around. "You took over after dad died. You were barely eighteen. That's hard on anybody. But you don't have to be that hard-ass, driven, success-at-any-cost person. You never needed to be and you don't now. It's time for you to let things go, Bhai."

"Where is all this coming from, all of a sudden?" Naveen shook his head at him. "Her?"

"It's not sudden, Naveen," Kavan said. "And yes. She opened my eyes to a lot of things…"

Naveen's eyes popped open. "You think you're in love with her." He snapped his fingers. "Of course."

"Bhai, I *am* in love with her, but that has nothing to do with you and me," Kavan tried to explain.

"Before you say anything you're going to regret, let me stop you right there, little brother. Before you stand by a woman who is about to destroy you. Her lab needs a grant for further research, to survive. So don't think for one bloody minute that she won't do whatever is necessary—include damage your reputation—to get it."

"She can do whatever she needs to do to survive. If that means discrediting us, then it's well deserved."

"You can't do that, Kavan. I'm your family." Naveen was fuming.

"Then act like it." Kavan stormed out of the room and went down to hear Poorvi's presentation.

Chapter Twenty-Nine

Poorvi showered and donned her black dress pants, crisp white shirt and black blazer. Her black dress from the other night was scrunched in a ball on one side of her suitcase from where she had tossed it into her bag. Was that just the night before last? Seemed like a lifetime ago that she and Kavan had had their "date." Her heart ached at the thought of it. Of how she had allowed herself to be part of a scandal once again. The post had not come from Kavan's account, but the pictures were from his phone. It didn't matter. The damage was done.

She started to don her red-framed glasses but thought twice and left them behind. It was time to stop hiding.

Poorvi waited in the wings while she was introduced, and Ba's words came back to her. *Just because we are fighting men, does not mean we have to fight like men. We are women.*

We are women.

She took the podium to a murmuring in the crowd. "Good afternoon." She glanced around as everyone fell silent. The seats were all full and people were standing two deep in the back. People loved a good scandal, and doctors were people, too.

"This is an exceptional turnout for a paper on refractive surgery," she said without humor. Some of the crowd chuckled.

Poorvi waited for silence. Then she spoke with authority. "My research on C-MORE has been ongoing for the past three years, and I will show that further research is necessary before we can safely continue this procedure in a clinical setting. Please focus your attention on my first slide." Methodically, Poorvi walked them through her research and her findings along with how she reached her conclusions.

"Based on these side effects, and the long-term implications of the procedure, I *do* recommend a halt to the C-MORE procedure until we have further study that can guide us toward the most positive clinical outcome." She looked around. "I understand that the numbers simply indicate caution, but it is my professional opinion that C-MORE be halted for the near future. Thank you for your time. I will take questions now."

"Aren't you just coming down on C-MORE to hurt Kavan Shashane?" someone called out. "Everyone knows the Shashane Clinic does more C-MORE than anyone else."

"Well. Thank you for asking." She squinted into the crowd. "Who asked that? It's an excellent point that should be addressed."

A man in the front stood, a smirk on his face.

"I'm sure you're not the only one who requires an answer to this question, am I right, Doctor?" Poorvi was cordial to the point of being over-polite.

A round of applause was her answer. She nodded her head and scanned the room.

"My answer to you all is, shame on you. Shame on those of you who came here today looking for drama instead of knowledge. Shame on you for judging your fellow women colleagues, not on their intelligence or character, but on who they may or may not be sleeping with. This is 2023 and women make up 30 percent of the eye care specialists in the world. Shame on you."

A hush fell over the room.

She paused. "Now I am happy to take questions that pertain to my work."

"You did not answer the question," the doctor up front insisted.

"Nor will she." A woman stood and faced him. "Unless you, too would like to tell us how your relationships—such that they are—affect your professional decisions."

"All I'm saying is that we are all going to lose money based on her recommendations. And she's only saying that because Shashane dumped her," Dr. Lewis fumed.

"Jeez, Lewis, did you listen to the presentation? I'm sure even a graduate of whatever school you hail from can do the simple math. This research has been going on for years. Dr. Gupta has been making this recommendation for over a year. Shut up and sit down, Lewis."

Dr. Lewis blanched and sat down.

The woman, who Poorvi recognized as a pioneer in refractive surgery, Dr. Jahigan, looked at her and smiled. "Continue."

The remaining questions did indeed refer to her presentation, and Poorvi happily and easily answered them.

"That's all the time I have. Please enjoy the rest of the meeting."

Everyone applauded and then started leaving the room.

Bobby was waiting for her when she exited the podium. "I've already received emails from the board. The grant is as good as ours."

She stared at him.

"Thank you."

She continued to stare at him.

"You're right. I saw an opportunity and I said nothing," Bobby told her. "I'm sorry."

Poorvi nodded at him. "Let's see." She started to walk away.

Bobby caught up and walked beside her. "You're incredible. You handled that crowd better than I ever could have."

"You know why, *Dr. Wright*?" She glanced his way and raised an eyebrow.

Bobby appeared confused. "Why?"

"Because I am *excellent* at my job." Poorvi grinned.

Chapter Thirty

Kavan exited the room full of pride. Poorvi had been amazing. Lewis was begging for a punch in the mouth. But other than that, Kavan felt as good as he possibly could, despite knowing that he and Poorvi could have had something, and he messed it up. He made his way to the panel discussion Naveen had set up. A very large crowd had already formed in the room.

"Dr. Shashane. Dr. Shashane, do you have anything to say regarding that post of you and Dr. Gupta?" people were asking as he approached the stage.

He took his seat on the panel which consisted of Naveen as well as two other colleagues who performed high numbers of C-MORE.

"Yes, as a matter of fact I do. Dr. Gupta and I ended up at the Cliffs of Moher with a close friend. Neither of us had ever been, so we took some photos. It's that simple. The caption was written to have you believe what the narrator wanted you to believe. It wasn't posted from my account," Kavan said. "I agree with Dr. Gupta's sentiment. Shame on you for making her personal life an issue."

"What about her recommendations?" another doctor asked.

"If you are referring to Dr. Gupta's recommendation that C-MORE not be performed until further research is complete, I have to say that I also agree with her on that."

Murmuring flooded through the crowd. He met Naveen's

eyes, the anger in them real and deep. The message was clear. *What the hell, Kavan?*

"And that," Kavan said clearly, "is my professional opinion."

"You agree? But your clinic does C-MORE almost regularly."

"That is true," Kavan said calmly. "But I do not."

Surprised murmuring floated in the crowd. "What do you mean?" one of the doctors spoke up.

"I mean, I have followed the research on C-MORE for years. Not just Dr. Gupta's, although hers is the most extensive. And I have collected data from the C-MORE procedures done in our office as well. The research indicates that there are long-term effects that need further study. Read the studies yourselves, doctors. You'll see that Dr. Gupta's recommendations are sound. And should be followed, regardless of financial cost."

"How about you, Dr. Shashane?" They turned to Naveen. "You do the procedure."

It was the first time that Kavan had ever really gone against his brother. The first time he had been his own man. Naveen plastered a smile on his face and turned to his colleagues. "Well, I did until today." He chuckled. "Dr. Gupta makes some excellent points, as does my brother. At Shashane Eye, our focus is always what is best for the patient. In the case of C-MORE, it appears that it is best to discontinue the procedure until we have more information." Naveen nodded at him. Kavan had forced his hand.

It was about time.

Kavan was elated and heartbroken all in the moment.

He had Poorvi to thank for that. He looked out into the crowd and saw her in the back, leaning against the door, her arms folded across her chest. Her mouth pursed and brow furrowed. She'd heard everything. She met his gaze for a moment, and hope ran free through his body. He smiled at her.

She pressed her lips together in a tight smile and dipped her chin at him. In the next instant, she turned and left.

He'd never felt so free yet so alone.

Chapter Thirty-One

Two weeks later

Poorvi collapsed onto her sofa, exhausted.

"You need to eat." Niki sighed and stood.

"I ate," Poorvi said, her eyes closed. The lab was extra busy now; they were hiring some staff and gathering data from clinicians all over the world. Her research had hit a nerve, and everyone wanted answers.

"Probably out of the vending machine," Niki said as she placed a plate of shaak and a rotli in front of her.

"It was hummus from the vending machine." Poorvi defended herself. But Niki's food smelled amazing. Poorvi had not bothered to learn how to cook, always finding something more interesting to do than mixing spices and kneading dough. But Niki had loved learning at their mother's side and as a result, Niki was an amazing cook. Just one of many reasons having your sister as a roommate was not at all a bad idea.

"Oh…you had hummus? So you don't need rotli shaak." Niki started to take the plate away.

"I didn't say that." Poorvi sat up and took the dish from Niki. She scooped some of the potato and spinach with a piece of the flatbread. "This is fabulous. Thank you. What would I do without you?"

"Wither away into nothingness," Niki said, sitting down and diving into her own plate.

Poorvi's phone dinged and she eyed it.

"You know it's him," Niki said.

"Whatever." Poorvi went back to her amazing meal, though she no longer had an appetite for it.

The phone dinged again.

Kavan had been texting her since she got back. Not every day, just…whenever. Things like he'd been to Clerys' clock and thought of her and Ba. Or Ba had made him tepla. Or he was babysitting Dharm and Mira. Random things. She never responded. Every so often he would throw in a "can we please talk?"

She grabbed the phone.

"What does he say now?"

She furrowed her brow. "It's not him. It's Ba." She ignored the disappointment that washed over her. She had to ignore it. She should not be looking forward to Kavan's texts. But she had to control herself from jumping at her phone when it dinged.

"You could call him, you know," Niki said. "Nothing wrong with having feelings."

"Now you sound like Ba." Poorvi grinned at her sister. "She texts me the same thing every other day. Besides, he…"

"He what? Fell in love with you?"

"I'm just scared, that's all."

"Fine." Niki raised her hands in surrender.

Poorvi's phone dinged again. Another text from Ba. She was coming stateside to see her son and wanted to see Poorvi. Well, that sounded fun.

Poorvi texted back. Sounds wonderful. When?

Ba: Tomorrow. Can you meet me here? She left an address. For lunch.

Poorvi: Can't wait to see you.

A bit of lightness filled Poorvi at the thought of meeting Ba. And it was only partly because she knew that Ba kept in touch with Kavan as well.

Chapter Thirty-Two

"Why haven't you even called Poorvi?" Ba was on a roll. Devi's house was not too far from his, so he stopped by to visit every few days. Naveen was still mad at him, but Kavan found that while he wasn't a fan of that, he was okay. He was still mad at Naveen as well.

Naveen did have a brotherly attachment to him that was generally expressed in being bossy and telling Kavan what to do, but he'd come up with something more palatable, soon enough.

The office wasn't suffering quite as much as Naveen had predicted. It turns out that patients like ethical doctors who will look out for them, so when Shashane Eye put out an official statement that they would be doing the tried-and-true refractive methods for a while, the patients responded well.

The bottom line moved but not too much, so Naveen's argument fell flat. Naveen had taken the photos from their shared cloud and turned them over to their social media person "to do something." For this Kavan still fumed. Naveen might have admitted it wasn't the best way to do business, but the reality was that Kavan was finding it difficult to forgive Naveen for hurting Poorvi in that way.

The panel discussion had gone viral. Kavan was looking into teaching and research positions. He wanted a break from the clinic.

"I've been busy. With work. Besides, I did text her. And she never responded," he said as he sipped Ba's excellent chai and ate a piece of her tepla.

Ba waved at him, her expression disappointed. "You're afraid."

It was true. He had texted her a few times when she had left. Things like "we need to talk." She never responded. He switched up the content of the texts to refer to things he was doing. Clerys' clock for example, or meeting Ba, etc. He hadn't even had a chance to explain about the post. She never responded, so it would have been easy to assume that she didn't care.

But with Poorvi, she would have responded if she didn't care so much. The fact that she did care was the reason she was so hurt and therefore the reason she was unable to answer. He just stared at the older woman.

He knew that because he loved her. What he didn't know was how to reach her.

"I thought you had changed," Ba said, shrugging. "I thought you were the kind of man who went after what he wanted." Ba glared at him. "You sold your half of Shashane Eye to Naveen. That was brave. Be more brave. Text her again."

"Fine." He sipped more chai. Ba stared at him. "What? Now?"

Ba didn't budge.

He inhaled. Fine. He pulled out his phone. His thumbs hovered over the screen. Nothing came to him. How could it? What he was feeling could not be done over text. He stared at his phone.

Having chai with Ba.

Ba picked up his phone and looked at it. She rolled her eyes into the back of her head, like a teenager. He looked at Ba. "Where did you learn the eye roll, Ba?"

She grinned. "It is good, right?"

"It's great," Kavan deadpanned.

"Dharm taught me."

Of course he did.

She shook her head at him in disappointment. His heart was broken. He needed to repair it. There was only one thing for it. "No more texting, Ba."

Chapter Thirty-Three

"I'm meeting someone for lunch. I'll come by after," Poorvi said to Bobby. "About an hour or two."

"Two hours?" Bobby's eyes widened. "Do you know how much work—?"

"Bobby." She met his eyes and was firm. "I'm taking the time. The lab—and you—will be fine." She grabbed her backpack and left. She texted Ba. On my way.

Ba responded instantly. Okay I'm here.

Poorvi hurried downstairs and quickly walked the few blocks to the café where she was meeting Ba. Late March was being kind, allowing them this day of gorgeous spring weather. She scanned the area for little old ladies in saris and came up empty. She scanned again and froze. Ba was not there.

But there was no denying the ball cap and the movie-star shades. He was pacing next to an empty table and, in the few seconds she watched him, nearly bumped into two waitstaff. The second motioned for Kavan to sit down. Poorvi had to press away her smile. He was wearing what she imagined him in whenever she thought about him—which was all the time— jeans and a long sleeve T-shirt. He rolled up his sleeves just as someone came up beside her.

Ba.

"Don't just stand here. Go," Ba said softly.

Poorvi could not believe her eyes. "Ba?"

"Just go. He came all this way." Ba nudged her. "Just say hi."

Her stomach filled with butterflies as she walked toward him. He was turned away from her, so he didn't see her approach. She came close and removed his hat as a greeting.

"Still hiding?" she asked as he turned to see who had accosted him. He ran his hand through his hair as he smiled at her. Still handsome as ever.

"Hi."

"Hi." She watched him watch her. "You're getting old ladies to do your dirty work are you, now?"

"Guilty. You didn't respond to my texts, so drastic measures were needed."

"Well, when someone doesn't respond, it usually means they don't want to interact with you." Poorvi explained.

He pursed his lips and nodded. "Not you." Kavan sighed and spoke softly. "If you didn't want to interact with me, you would have texted me to eff off on day one. You would have dusted your hands off and moved on. You didn't do that because you were hurt."

She stared at him, her heart thudding in her chest. He was right, of course. She sat down next to him, careful to leave some distance. She took off her glasses.

"So why are you here?"

He took off his sunglasses. The eyes that she had become so familiar with in such a short a time were bloodshot and… sad. And you didn't even need to be an ophthalmologist to see that. "I came for two reasons."

He nodded to where Ba was still standing behind her. Poorvi expected to hear Ba's footsteps behind her, instead she heard dress shoes hitting the concrete. As she turned, the owner of said dress shoes came into view.

Naveen Shashane. Not quite as tall as Kavan, but easily just as fit. He was quite handsome, but not in the movie star way that Kavan was. Naveen wore an expensive suit with expensive dress shoes and carried himself as if he were better than everyone around him.

"Hello," he said to her. It was obvious that this was not his idea. Yet here he was.

"Sit down, Bhai," Kavan said.

Naveen pressed his lips together as he looked at his brother. Poorvi was about to get up. She had no interest in what Naveen Shashane had to say. She glanced at him to tell him so when she saw something soft flit over Naveen's face as he looked at his brother. He really cared about Kavan. It was only that look that kept Poorvi in her seat.

"Baltimore isn't…" He looked around as he took a seat next to his brother, facing Poorvi.

"Isn't what?" Poorvi asked.

Naveen looked at her and forced a smile. "It isn't Dublin."

She glanced at Kavan. *What the hell was going on here?*

Kavan looked at his brother. "Naveen."

"Of course." He inhaled and looked at Poorvi. "I am here to tell you that it was I who took those pictures from our shared cloud and had them posted on social media."

Poorvi looked at Kavan. "Is this true?"

"If you were going to believe him, there was really no need for me fly over here now, was there?" He sighed. "Of course, it's true. Kavan is too *good*. He's not capable of such…manipulation. But you already know that." He nodded at her. "I told our social media person that I wanted to…make you look bad. And he did." Naveen gave a small shrug. "He's very good at his job, you see—in any case. It was me, not Kavan." He paused and glanced at Kavan before looking back at her. His next words were likely the most sincere she'd heard yet. "All of that explanation to say that I am truly sorry for hurting you."

"You are?" Poorvi could not believe her ears. She harumphed.

Naveen glanced at Kavan. "I see what you mean, brother.

She's not trusting. She's skeptical." He grinned. "I like that. She would be good for you." He leaned toward Poorvi. "Kavan is too trusting, don't you think?"

She stared at Naveen. Unbelievable. But still, he had flown here to apologize in person. Not to mention, Naveen wasn't wrong. Kavan was very trusting. A smile played at her lips but she fought it. She wasn't ready to be friendly with Naveen Shashane.

"I would also like to add that I found it quite interesting that you did not out us publicly when you had the chance. I don't know if I was impressed or relieved." Naveen looked at her with what she could only discern was—respect. Huh.

Poorvi simply looked at him for a moment. "I appreciate what you have said."

Naveen went wide-eyed. "Is that all? Appreciate?" He chuckled. "Oh, she is a tough one, little brother." Naveen pushed his chair back and looked at Kavan with a question on his face. Kavan nodded and Naveen stood. "Dr. Gupta." He turned to her. "My brother has been an absolute mess since you left. He doesn't come to clinic, even on his new part-time schedule, and it is starting to…be upsetting…for our mother." He paused. "Very well then, I will go occupy myself until it is time for my flight." He nodded at Poorvi and squeezed his brother's shoulder as he left.

Poorvi stared at Kavan. "You stood up to your brother." She grinned at him, impressed and proud. "That's fabulous."

Kavan nodded at her.

"What was the second thing?"

He leaned toward her, not close enough to touch, but close enough that she caught his scent. "I wanted to give you a chance to yell at me." There was no smirk. No cocked eyebrow. Just his heart open for her to see, to do with what she wanted. "And I needed to see you."

"I'm not going to yell," Poorvi said. Naveen was right. Kavan was not capable of that sort of manipulation.

"I left Shashane Eye Clinic," he told her. "Rather, I sold my half and work there a couple times a week, and I'll leave when I figure out what I want to do."

This was huge. "What did Naveen say?"

Kavan shrugged like it didn't matter. "Naveen does not get to say anything about my life anymore. I'm considering my options. I have a few offers to teach, some offers to aid in clinical trials, that kind of thing. But mostly, I'm going to travel. I've started with Ireland. Trying to see all the things my father used to talk about. India is next up." He grinned and there was a peace about him that hadn't been there before.

"It must have been hard, breaking free of Naveen," she said.

"Not as hard as I would have thought. He's my brother, but it's way past time that I do my own thing." Kavan continued to watch her.

"You're in the States, traveling with Ba?" Sounded like fun.

"No. I just got off the plane. Ba is here to see her son. Naveen and I are going back in a few hours."

"You came all this way to apologize?" Who does that?

"Yes." Kavan looked at her in earnest. "There is just one more thing." He paused and looked her in the eye. "I was not making anything up in Ireland. I made Naveen come here and apologize in person because I was appalled at the way he treated the woman I love."

He paused and her heartbeat accelerated.

"I love you. I think I knew I loved you when I took your outlet." He chuckled. "But I definitely knew I loved you the last night we spent together. You can say all you want about how we don't know each other, it's too fast, whatever. It makes not one bit of difference to me. I know we have a connection. I know how I feel. I love bickering with you. I love laughing with you. I love being challenged by you." He paused and touched her hand. It was as if electricity coursed through her body. "I love loving you."

She heard him.

"I know you might be too angry to ever consider having me in your life, to consider trusting me again. But I do know you have feelings for me."

She stared at him, her heart racing, her palms sweaty. "You're pretty cocky to say that you know I have feelings for you."

"It's not cockiness." He chuckled. "Not really." He looked at her smiling. "You took off your glasses around me the last few times we were together. And today too." He nodded at her glasses on the table.

She shrugged. "So?" How could he possibly know?

"There's no prescription in them. You only wear them to put a barrier between you and the world. It helps you focus and assess." He said it as if it were obvious.

Her mouth gaped open.

He shrugged. "We were only in each other's company a short time, but I pay attention. You like your coffee hot and black, but you want your chai sweet and milky. You don't let people in very easily, but once they're in, they live in your heart," he said softly. "If your glasses are off, you're comfortable, and you don't need that barrier." He nodded at them again.

"They're off." He leaned toward her, and she caught the scent of lemon soap. Not fair. But she inhaled deeply anyway. He spoke softly near her ear, sending chills to that side of her body. "If you ever want to give us a chance, if you ever want to even try and see what we could be, I'll be waiting for you."

He stood, put on his cap, and walked out.

Chapter Thirty-Four

Kavan's phone dinged as he finished up his emails for the day. He grabbed his phone, hope running eternal through him. But it wasn't Poorvi. It was Ba.

Ba: Meet for dinner in Dublin? Clerys. Today is the day.

Kavan: Sure.

Ba: I'm bringing the family. Bring yours.

Kavan: Okay.

If Ba wanted to celebrate the day she met Dada at Clerys' clock, then that's what they would do.

"Naveen," Kavan called out in the empty clinic.

He heard footsteps and then Naveen was at his door. "Why shout? I'm two doors down. Just get up and walk."

Kavan just stared at him.

"What is it you want?"

"Dinner tonight with Ba at Clerys. Mom too."

"Are you serious?" Naveen looked at his phone. "I have calls to make."

"You have to eat," Kavan insisted. "You're coming. Calls can wait one hour."

"Fine." Naveen was less than thrilled, but he had been quite cooperative since they returned from the States two days ago. "Any word?"

Kavan turned back to his computer. "No." Two days. And nothing. At least she hadn't officially dismissed him. And she didn't seem the type to ghost. He called his mother. She was thrilled to join them.

He went home and changed from his suit into dress pants and a shirt. He bypassed the pink one he had worn on his date with Poorvi and chose a blue one instead.

Ba texted. Reservation at 7:30 sharp!

Ya. Okay.

Kavan and his family arrived at Clerys by 7:20 p.m. It was easy enough to spot Ba and her family once they entered the restaurant. Dharm came running over from their table by the front window. Ba loved a view. Devi and Yash were there with their daughter, Mira, and a woman he did not know. She seemed familiar.

Dharm hugged Kavan's legs, nearly knocking him over.

"Whoa. Hey, bud." Kavan hugged him back.

"Kavan Uncle, wait 'til you hear what we have been doing in school." Dharm was overexcited as usual. "Learning about eyes!"

"That sounds absolutely fascinating," Naveen said. "You must tell me more."

Dharm started to tell Naveen all that he knew about eyes as they walked over to the table. Before Kavan could sit down, Ba tugged on his sleeve.

"Come out with me." She jutted her chin toward the outside. "To see the clock."

"Of course." Kavan followed Ba as she made her way outside. The building was white with columns, and the clock protruded out about half the way up. Black with a green face and golden roman numerals, Clerys' clock was a distinctive meeting place for many people. Including many couples—like it had been for Ba and her husband.

"This is where we met." She grinned as they stood under it.

"That's fantastic, Ba." Kavan could see the joy on her face.

"But I lied. Today is not the day." Ba grinned.

"What do you mean?" Honestly, Ba was always full of surprises; he had just started to go with it.

"I mean today is not the day that Dada and I met. But today is your day." Ba's eyes brimmed with tears.

"My day?" Kavan was confused. "What—?"

"Hey, Kavan." Poorvi's voice floated from behind him. Or that's what he thought he heard. He stared at Ba.

"Did you hear that, Ba?" He didn't want to turn around if it was his mind playing tricks on him.

Ba raised her eyebrows and turned to go back inside.

"Kavan?"

He turned and sure enough, Poorvi Karina Gupta was standing there, looking more beautiful than his memory could possibly do justice to. Of course, she had an eyebrow raised.

"Did you not hear me?" her eyes sparkled as she playfully chided him.

He broke out in a huge grin. "I heard you."

She sighed and shook her head at him. "You like your coffee *and* your chai sweet and milky. You're left-handed, but you eat with your right. You don't hide how you feel, and even if you get hurt, you still open yourself to people." She stepped closer to him. "I pay attention, too."

"So you do." His fingers ached with the need to touch her, but he waited. He moved closer to her. She couldn't have come all this way to turn him down.

"You said that you would be waiting," she said softly, taking a step toward him.

"I did." He nodded. "It's only been two days, but I did say I would wait, and I will."

She moved yet closer. He smelled flowers in the rain and— "Lemon soap."

She flushed and looked up at him. She was close enough to graze his body with hers. He ached with longing to touch her.

"I wasn't looking for a connection with anyone—especially not you. I didn't think I needed that. I was my own person." She stood straight and met his eyes.

"You are your own person, Poorvi." He agreed.

"But I felt it, too," she said softly. "I felt that...connection." Kavan held his breath.

"I'm not easy," she blurted out.

"I know." He grazed her bare arm with his fingers; his heart thudded in his chest.

"I like to get my way," she said.

"I know." He trailed his touch to her upper arm.

"I love my work."

"As do I." He reached her shoulder.

"I'm nerdy."

"It's what I love most about you." He let his hand rest over her heart.

"Love?" He felt her heart thud in her chest. For him.

"I told you that two days ago. Love is a feeling, Poorvi Karina Gupta. And I love you." He nudged closer to her.

"I don't know about love," she said softly. "It scares me."

"That's okay. Just give us a chance." His leaned down so his mouth was millimeters from hers. He would certainly burst if he couldn't taste her soon. "You didn't come here smelling like lemon soap to break my heart, now did you?"

"No. I came here to tell you I had feelings for you." She cocked a smile. "The lemon soap is just a bonus."

"Feelings, huh?" He kissed her cheek, his lips just grazing her skin. She sighed into him.

She closed her eyes and made that soft humming sound he craved. "Mmm. A feeling like…"

"Like…what?" He pressed his lips gently on one eye then the other. She moaned and pressed closer to him.

"Like love." She lifted her chin and pressed her lips to his, tenderly. "I love you, Kavan Shashane. And I always will."

It was like coming home.

"I was hoping you would say that," he said on a low growl. He pulled her close and kissed her like she was his.

Epilogue

Twenty-seven years ago

The ice cream truck jingle had all the children at the playground dashing for their respective adults.

Around the perimeter of the playground, their adults stood with a collective sigh and reached for cash. The price of outdoor play in any city in America.

Poorvi's mother handed her money for both her and her sister. "You got that, Poorvi?" her mother asked.

"Poorvi's fine," her father said, laughing. "She's a big girl now."

Poorvi beamed at her father's praise. She was six years old now, after all. She took Niki's hand. "Come on. Let's go." Both girls ran hand in hand and joined the line at the ice cream truck. A couple boys were in front of them. The taller one was reading out the list to his brother.

"Ice cream sandwich. Ooh! Choco Taco! Oreo ice cream sandwich! How about that, Kavan?"

"Oreo! It's my favorite!" the smaller boy said.

"Ha! That's my favorite, too!" squealed Niki.

Kavan turned to Niki and high-fived her. He looked at Poorvi. "What's your favorite?"

"I don't have a favorite," Poorvi answered, not really looking at the boy.

"Everyone has a favorite," insisted Kavan.

"No, they don't." Poorvi was firm. She turned to him to make a face, but he was looking at her so wide-eyed, she simply pursed her lips.

"Well, they have a favorite they love from the truck," he insisted.

Poorvi rolled her eyes. "Not so."

The boy looked at the list and seemed to study it. "Rocket pop?"

Poorvi sighed. "No."

"King Cone?" He grinned.

"Nope."

They moved closer; it was the boys' turn next. A lot of kids were walking away with Oreo ice cream sandwiches.

The boy looked at Poorvi for minute. She tried to ignore him as she watched all the Oreo ice cream sandwiches go by.

The boy's jaw dropped. "Your favorite is Oreo ice cream sandwich, too."

Poorvi just shrugged her shoulders. It was, but she hadn't wanted to say, because sometimes they ran out, and she wanted Niki to have what she wanted.

The boys gave their order. "One Choco Taco and one Oreo ice cream sandwich," the older boy said. They took their ice creams and paid. The older one tucked into his Choco Taco with gusto. Kavan hung back while Poorvi ordered.

"Two Oreo ice cream sandwiches, please," she said.

"I'm sorry, sweetheart, we only have one left," the ice cream man said.

"Then I'll take that one, and I'll get…" She let her gaze wander over the pictures. The first one to catch her eye was the Choco Taco, and she pointed. "That one."

"All right." The man took her money and gave out the ice cream.

The boy named Kavan came up to her. "Actually, my favorite is that." He pointed to her Choco Taco.

"No, it's not. You said it was Oreo ice cream sandwich," Poorvi said.

"I didn't mean it. Really. Want to trade?"

"Really?" She looked at the foil-wrapped ice cream in his hand hopefully.

"Sure! It's win-win," Kavan said.

"Well, if you mean it," Poorvi said.

"I do."

Poorvi handed over her Choco Taco and took the Oreo cookie sandwich he passed to her, a smile coming to her face. "Thank you."

"You're welcome," Kavan said.

Poorvi and Niki ran back to their parents to enjoy their ice cream.

"You can't eat that," Naveen said to Kavan. "You're allergic to peanuts."

"I know." Kavan handed it to his brother. "You get two today."

"Why did you do that, then?" Naveen sounded irritated.

"She looked so sad. And now she looks happy." Kavan shrugged as he watched Poorvi from afar.

After they finished their ice creams, Poorvi went over to the boy called Kavan. "My parents say we have to go now. But we might be back tomorrow."

Kavan lit up. "Maybe we can play together tomorrow."

Poorvi grinned. "Maybe."

Kavan nodded. "I'll be waiting."

* * * * *

Read on for a brand-new novella,
Detour to the Gingerbread Inn,
from Mona Shroff!

And don't miss the previous titles in
Mona's Once Upon a Wedding series:

Their Accidental Honeymoon
The Business Between Them
No Rings Attached
Matched by Masala
The Five-Day Reunion

Available now!

DETOUR TO THE GINGERBREAD INN

Chapter One

"It's snowing harder," Naina Goel said as she pursed her lips and stared straight ahead from the passenger seat. Tiny white flakes were falling in front of them in a sheet of white. They were never going to make it to the wedding on time if this weather kept up.

"I have eyes," her husband growled, his nearly perfect jaw clenched, clearly at the end of his patience with her. Which was saying something. For all his faults (and there were many), Jais Patel was quite a patient man.

Naina narrowed her eyes at him and let out an audible "Hmph." She could list any number of times that he couldn't find something that was sitting right in front of him, making her question whether he actually used his eyes.

"Why do you always try to see how far you can push me?" he snapped at her. Another new thing. Jais did not get riled up. He was perpetually in a good mood.

It had always been irritating.

She rolled her eyes. "All I'm saying is that we need to get to that wedding," she said innocently, though she was completely aware of what she was doing. Everybody had their own way of syphoning off steam, especially when forced to navigate a snowstorm on the way to a family wedding with their currently estranged spouse.

Well, her family, anyway. Her cousin was marrying Jais's best friend.

Which he was, since he had moved out six months ago.

"No kidding," Jais grumbled, shaking his head at her.

He kept his gaze fixed on the road (and snow) in front of them, leaning one arm on the door. Naina also had her body facing forward, and leaned toward her own door.

They used to lean toward each other.

Not that it mattered. The car was so small, they were barely a couple feet from each other. She could even catch a whiff of his leather and spice scent every so often.

"All I'm saying is that I don't think that we will be able to continue driving for much longer," she said as evenly as possible. "Especially in this car."

"I was trying to save gas. The forecast didn't call for snow."

"You didn't think there might be snow three days before Christmas in New England?" Naina raised her eyebrows.

Jais turned away from her, seemingly back to concentrating on the road. Naina turned her attention to her phone.

"Take this next exit—there's a hotel or something," Naina commanded. Visibility was near impossible as the unpredicted blizzard bore down on them. There was already at least six inches on the ground, their small *Mini Cooper* was barely moving. "We can spend the night and continue to the wedding tomorrow, once the storm stops. We won't miss anything."

"Says you," Jais grumbled.

"What? We're going a day early anyway. The first official event is the mehndi night tomorrow. All this—" she waved her hand at the window "—will be cleared by tomorrow, and we'll be there in no time."

"I'm the best man. Kaden and I were doing bachelor things tonight." Jais continued looking forward, his eyes on the road. "Who gets married on Christmas weekend anyway?"

"I'm the maid of honor. I had things today as well. But

there's no way we're making it there in this mess. I'll text them both." She texted the bride, who was her cousin Savita, and Kaden, the groom, in a group text with Jais about their situation. "And to answer your question… Indian people who need three or four days to have a wedding—that's who gets married on Christmas weekend."

Jais was silent and pressed his mouth together, but he took the exit.

That was another thing about Jais. He'd never had any problem leaning into her strengths. Navigation was one of them. He'd always been proud of her ability to find any place anywhere. Seeing pride for her in his eyes had always warmed her. There was no pride right now. He simply took the turn.

"What did you tell your family?" he asked softly, his voice taking on that familiar tone of intimacy that existed between two people who had promised themselves to each other.

Naina squirmed slightly in her seat. They did need to get their stories right, after all. She forced lightness into her voice. "Nothing. You and I had a deal, right? We don't tell anyone we're separated unless we have to."

"You didn't even tell Savita?" He quickly glanced her way. She caught the doubt in his hazel eyes, which was fair.

She sighed. She should fess up. "Well, I did tell Savita." She confessed, glancing at him. She could tell something was… off. "What did you say?"

Jais looked at her for a split second, his brow furrowed, before focusing back on the road, a sigh escaping him. "Kaden knows."

She pressed her lips together and nodded. Of course he told his best friend. She'd told hers. "Anyone else?"

"No. You?"

She shook her head. "I guess we both broke the deal, then, huh?"

Jais shrugged one shoulder. "The deal was your—" The car

skidded at that moment, and Jais diverted his attention back to the road. His arm flew out in front of her, pressing her into the seat.

"Whoa." Naina braced herself against the seat, Jais's strong forearm pinned firmly against her chest as he held her in place while trying to regain control of the car. The car wiggled, tossing them both back and forth. Naina's heart raced as Jais deftly avoiding hitting anything and straightened the car.

"You okay?" Jais turned to her, eyes wide with concern. His arm still pinned to her chest, where her heart thudded rapidly. Keeping her safe. He looked slightly pale and his breath was coming fast. "Naina!" He demanded an answer when there was only silence for a moment.

"I'm fine," she managed, nodding her head. "I'm fine."

Jais pulled his arm back as if only now noticing where it was. She felt its absence as if her own arm were missing.

In another lifetime, Jais would have taken her hand and brought it to his lips, kissing her, thankful she was unharmed. She calmed her breathing. "All good." She swallowed. "You?"

"I'm fine," he said as he gave his full attention back to the road.

She nodded. "Good. That was nice driving."

He glanced at her, as if skeptical that she would say something nice. "I'm being serious," she said softly, trying to hide her hurt that he would be wary of any nice thing she said.

She watched him for a moment. Chiseled jaw, deep brown skin, slight scruff, tapered hair. Jais Patel was handsome. And not just to her. She'd seen plenty of women bat their eyelashes at him, but he never seemed to notice.

"According to this, the hotel should be on the right just a bit ahead," Naina said. They were clearly in a rural part of the state, so there weren't really any landmarks. Naina squinted out of her window and caught sight of some red-and-green strands of light in the white mist. "There. Where the lights are." She pointed.

Jais slowed down just as they caught sight of a large house with lights around the doorway and a partly covered circular driveway in front of it. He turned toward the driveway. The house was dark red brick with many windows and a huge double door that became visible as Jai pulled up into the carport. Closer inspection revealed that many of the light bulbs were missing or just dead. Christmas greenery was haphazardly adorned around the door, and two small, sparse evergreen trees stood on either side. The small trees had Christmas ornaments on them that looked like they would drag the branches to the ground.

"Well?" Jais looked directly at her sending a jolt through her.

She glanced at her phone and at the entrance. The picture on the phone made it look better than what she was currently looking at. Maybe it was an older picture. "This is the place." She shrugged. "The Gingerbread Inn," she read from her phone. Though the sign over the doorway read *T Gin read nn*.

A man in a faded, once possibly maroon uniform came to Jais's window. He opened it.

"Welcome to The Gingerbread Inn. Will you be using valet services?"

"Well, we don't have a reservation, but we need a place for the night—"

"No problem, sir. We can watch the car while you and your wife talk to Mr. and Mrs. Vijaya." The man opened the door.

"Um. Yeah, okay." Jais looked at her. She shrugged. They really had no choice. They really just needed a place to spend the night and ride out the storm. They both got out as another bellman opened Naina's door.

"Let's go see what they have." She donned her coat against the frigid air and led the way through the large front doors and into the lobby.

Christmas was everywhere. But it was more like leftover, almost dead Christmas. Trees, holly and pumped-in cinnamon and pine scents overpowered them as they entered. But the trees were dying, the scent was cloying and ornaments were scattered and shattered on the ground.

She stole a glance at Jais. His mouth was set as he glanced around with a wary eye. Was he remembering their Christmas?

She quickly focused in front of her before he caught her looking. Christmas had been their thing. But that was all in the past now. In any case, this was not the version of Christmas they'd shared together.

Besides, it wasn't as if they had a choice. It was one night. She approached the desk with Jais close behind her.

"It's a lot of Christmas," he murmured and she felt the rumble of his voice in her ear, momentarily diverting her attention to how close he walked behind her and the fact that his hand was at her lower back.

A bespectacled older man with wrinkled brown skin, a salt-and-pepper beard and generous belly chuckled at them from behind the desk. "Shant Vijaya." He bowed his head. "At your service."

Naina glanced at Jais and read her thoughts in his face. Brown Santa? Seriously? "Shant? As in calm?"

"Yes," the man continued. "Most people stand right there just trying to take it all in. You can't. I promise you that. My wife starts putting up all this—" he waved both arms around "—right after Halloween." He leaned into them. "It's *layered*!"

A woman with shoulder-length white hair, medium brown skin and round glasses playfully smacked his shoulder. "I have to start at Halloween because he doesn't help me." She shook her head and grinned. "Look around. How could one person create all of this glamour themselves?"

"My wife, Shanta." Mr. Vijaya grinned at her.

Naina clamped her mouth shut so she would not remark on

how *unglamorous* the Christmas decor appeared. She felt Jais look at her and turned to him, a small smile at her lips. He widened his eyes. She shot him a glance that said *IKR?*

Jais leaned toward Brown Santa. "Shant Uncle," Jais smirked conspiratorially as he tilted his head toward her, "she's the same. Never enough Christmas decorations." He chuckled softly.

When Naina turned to look at him, sadness flitted across his face. He glanced at her, but upon seeing her looking at him, he turned back to the old man. "Any chance you have a room available for the night?" He thumbed toward the front door. "That snow surprised us. We'll be gone in the morning. Promise."

"The tiny car he rented will never make it in this weather," Naina added. "We're heading to a wedding that's only about three hours away, but our flight was cancelled and we've been driving all day, and now the snow—"

"No car could make it in this," Jais mumbled.

"A truck. A truck could have made it."

"Well, let me see…" said the old man as he tapped away on his computer. "Where are you headed?"

"Portland, Maine," they said together.

"My college roommate is marrying her cousin," Jais said. He was doing his thing—turning on the charm in the hopes that this man would work harder to find them a room. Naina smiled to herself. Half the time, it wasn't even intentional. Jais was honestly interested in people, and people responded to that curiosity. "Quite a place you have here." His smile today looked a bit forced. Like he knew they needed this room, but he really wasn't feeling especially talkative. "Very homey."

"We like it," Uncle said.

"How long have you owned this place?" Jais asked while Uncle typed away.

Naina did an internal eye roll but said nothing, as Jais continued hs conversation with Shant Uncle, learning all about how he and his wife came to own this inn. A glance out the door confirmed that the snow was still coming down in curtains. There was no leaving. They truly did need to stay here tonight.

Uncle typed into the computer while Auntie waited on another couple who was checking in. One of the men was tall, quite muscular and clean-shaven. His blond hair was perfectly tousled, likely from the hat he'd just removed, but it was his eyes that stopped Naina. And not just that they were a brilliant color blue, but the way he looked at his husband—complete adoration, as if there were nothing else around them. His husband was slightly shorter with leaner muscles, brownish skin and a shock of dark hair. Naina could hear their conversation.

The dark-haired man spoke first. "My, what a lovely place you have here. And the decor—so beautiful and festive." He looked at the blond man, his face filled with the same adoration. "We should consider some of this in our home—don't you think, Robbie?"

"Derek—" the blond man squeezed his husband's hand "—you do equally gorgeous Christmas decorations, but I do love the candles," Robbie replied with enthusiasm. "So unique."

"You are very kind." Shanta Auntie smiled at them. "Here is your key, and your room is on the second floor. We will have your things sent up."

Naina stole a glance at the candles Robbie had mentioned and had to quelch her gasp. They were dusty and half-used, the glitter chipping away. Those candles had seen better days for sure. She caught a glance of the young couple as they held hands walking up the steps. Their love was palpable. A pang hit Naina in the heart. She remembered a time when Jais looked at her like that.

Naina wandered a few feet away, taking a look at a gingerbread house that was clearly a depiction of the property. There was the main building, from which three covered walkways extended a bit, each to a small private cabin.

She went back to the front desk, where Jais had successfully charmed Shant Uncle.

"Well…" Shant Uncle glanced at them over his spectacles. His accent was slight. "You are in luck. The couple who had reserved the honeymoon cabin cancelled this morning due to weather. So, it can be yours."

"How many rooms in that cabin?" Naina asked.

Uncle narrowed his eyes at her. "Well, as it is the honeymoon cabin, there is one bedroom and a living area." He glanced from her to Jais and back. He gestured to Jais's wedding ring. "You are married, correct?"

They both nodded. "Yes, of course," Naina said. "We're married." It was technically true. She felt Jais's eyes land on her. But when she looked at him, he was smiling at Uncle and signing something.

"Rudy will park your car and bring your luggage," Auntie said as she led them to the cabin. She tossed on a heavy cape at the doorway. "This cabin is stocked with enough things for a light meal, but we usually serve dinner in this main building every evening at seven. Tea at 4:00 p.m. and cocktail hour at 6:00 p.m. We are sending the staff home early because of the storm, but I will ask the chef to make you something before he leaves. You must be hungry."

She opened the door to the cabin and let them in, hitting the switch for the light. The lights flickered and then went out. "Strange," Auntie said. "It was fine this morning." She walked into the dark cabin, and Naina heard drawers opening and closing and then there was a flicker of candlelight. "This will last you until my husband can look at the breaker." She sent a text. "Should be any minute."

She grabbed the fat candle and led them around the cabin. "The fireplace works—there are logs right next to it. There is another fireplace in the bedroom." She continued to go over the amenities. Naina drowned her out and looked around best she could. The cabin was a Christmas extension of the lobby. A nearly dead tree drooped in the corner, its ornaments nearly falling from it. The holly on the mantle looked dry. Naina shuddered at the chill in the house.

A sudden whoosh and the lights turned on. The clanking and chugging sound of a heater doing its best to provide heat reached them.

"Ah, much better," their host said.

Their bags were already there. What the hell? Naina caught Jais's eye. He had noticed, too.

"Wow," he said forcing a chuckle. "I never even saw our things arrive."

"Oh. Well. The staff is well trained to be…ah, what is the word?" She mimed walking on her toes and looking behind her.

"Stealthy?" Jais offered.

"Yes." Auntie snapped her fingers. "The staff is stealthy and quiet as mice."

Naina pressed her lips together. Was that a good thing?

"I'll send Rudy with your food shortly," Auntie continued. "Please let us know if you need anything else. The room is available for a few days, if you need." Shanta Auntie left. "Just let me know."

Jais looked at Naina, disbelief on his face. "You see it, right?"

"The rundown decor?" she asked as she continued to digest their surroundings. "The dead tree? The lumpy sofa and the cobwebs? The dust?" She sneezed.

He nodded. "Lucky it's just the one night."

"But that other couple in the lobby just raved about it!"

"I know, right?" Jais furrowed his brow. "I suppose everyone has their own taste. I need a shower. You want to go first?"

"No, you go ahead."

He shrugged and went to the bathroom.

Chapter Two

Even the bedroom looked like Christmas had thrown up—
and not in a good way. All the decor was old, broken, dusty.
A rocking chair in the corner had seen better days. As had the
bed. He wasn't sure what the Vijayas were going for here, but
at this point he didn't really care.

He needed some space between him and Naina. It was physi-
cally painful to be in her presence and not be able to touch her.

The bedroom was fairly large with a fireplace and sitting
area complete with overstuffed love seat, which also looked
like it had seen better days. Fake snow withered on every end
table alongside half-used fake candles colored like candy canes
and, of course, small, chipped figurines of Santa, Rudolph or
Frosty. The sconces alongside the fireplace dripped with plastic greenery and plastic Christmas-tree balls.

It went on. The Christmas-tree candy dish with mini candy
canes that looked like they were probably inedible. The old
red-and-green comforter on the bed, as well as the pillows with
Santa's face on them. It was slightly off-putting.

The best thing in the room was the wall of floor-to-ceiling
windows that currently gave a view of rapidly accumulating
snow. He put Naina's bag on her side of the bed and his on the
other side.

He needed to get to Kaden's wedding and then get home
to New York. It was bad enough that he had to pretend to still

be in a relationship with Naina after she had kicked him out six months ago—it was another thing to have to pretend to be happily married in this honeymoon cabin. Though they would be pretending at the wedding as well. Naina had insisted that they keep their separation as quiet as possible until the wedding was over. He was fine with that, but it was harder than he'd thought, being here with her.

Especially at Christmas.

Jais had been relatively indifferent to Christmas growing up. Sure, he'd liked getting presents like every other kid. Even after he'd lost his parents, his grandparents had put up a tree and decorated it every year. They'd exchanged gifts and Santa had come every year. Jais and his sister, Jyoti, had continued this with their grandparents long after they'd stopped believing in Santa Claus. The Christmas traditions, along with Diwali, Holi and Rakshabandan all compiled together, had grounded them all. After they'd lost their grandparents, Jais had called anywhere Jyoti had been home.

But as much as he'd kept up the traditions since his childhood, he hadn't truly loved Christmas until he'd met Naina.

Jais showered and threw on sweatpants and a T-shirt before exiting the bedroom with his bag. "You can go."

"Thanks." Naina passed him to get to the bathroom.

He nodded as she left the room, trying not to think about the fact that there'd been a time—many a Christmastime, in fact—when he and Naina would warm up in the shower together. There would be no such invitation tonight.

Not that he would say yes.

That was a lie.

Of course he would say yes.

He opened the fridge and found a bottle of wine and some beers. He opened the wine and poured a glass just as someone knocked on the door.

He answered it to find the red-haired valet standing there

with two stacks of small round stainless steel containers, each held together with a stainless steel handle. He grinned. Legit tiffins. Filled with food.

"Mr. Patel." Rudy nodded at him and passed by him to the kitchen.

He set both tiffins on the small island and went over what was in each. Dhal. Rice. Shaak. And rotli.

"Rudy." Jais beamed. "Tell me the shaak is potatos and peas."

"Yes, sir." Rudy nodded.

"And the dhal?"

"Gujarati-style lentil soup, spicy with a hint of sweetness. Shanta Auntie's secret recipe." Rudy grinned as if he had cooked the meal. "And of course, freshly rolled and hand-roasted rotli, drowning in ghee," Rudy concluded.

Naina was going to love this. Jais went giddy with excitement as he picked up the wine and headed for the bathroom. Who would have thought that there would be real Gujarati food in the middle of a snowstorm in the middle of—wherever they were.

He raised a fist to knock on the bathroom door before walking in to leave the wine for Naina and tell her about the food. He froze just before his knuckles hit the door.

He no longer had the right to walk in while she was showering. Sure they were still married, but that was a technicality. Naina had made her feelings clear when she had asked him to leave six months ago.

His dropped his hand as his stomach tightened in sadness and slowly stepped back from the door. He raised his hand again to knock.

Maybe…maybe she'd had a change of heart.

The absence of regular conversation from the car ride came rushing back to him.

No. She hadn't had a change of heart. He lowered his hand and returned to the kitchen. It was time he stopped hoping that she would. She was with him, and it would still be a blue Christmas.

Chapter Three

Naina got in the shower to warm up. She was freezing, and the house did not feel like it was getting warmer. The excessive Christmas decor, though drab and old, was determined to put a smile on her face, but she knew what happened when she let her guard down.

She fell in love with a free spirit like Jais and convinced herself that they could both have a life together.

The reality was that that couldn't really happen. It wasn't long lasting. Opposites were most definitely attracted to one another, but they couldn't share their lives together. Forget that the attraction had never diminished—Naina knew that was more biology than anything else. But there you had it—Jais still made her heart beat fast every time he flashed that smile. Or grinned. Or frowned. Or breathed.

She needed to keep her feelings in check. He certainly was not interested anymore. He had been very clear about that when they'd learned they would have to attend the wedding together. *I'm going for Kaden. That's it. Then I'm going home.* Those had been his exact words.

Finally getting warm in the shower, her thoughts floated back to when they had met. Christmas Eve. A lifetime ago.

Naina stayed in the warm shower until she was wrinkled. She dried and changed into leggings and a T-shirt, throwing a sweatshirt over her head and fuzzy socks on her feet. It still didn't feel like the bedroom was getting any warmer.

She entered the living area to a wonderful aroma coming from two tiffins on the counter. Jais had set the table for two, and as she entered, he handed her a glass of wine and started doling out food from the tiffins.

"Wow. That smells amazing. Where did it come from?" she asked as she sat down at the table.

"Shant Uncle and Shanta Auntie sent it over," Jais explained.

"You mean Santa and Mrs. Claus." She grinned in spite of herself.

"*Rudy* brought it over." He met her eyes. "It's too coincidental."

"I know, right? He even has the belly. I mean, smaller, but still. Though I've never seen Brown Santa before," Naina said. Her stomach growled. She'd been up early to catch the flight to New York, and then the drive here had been slowed by weather. All they had eaten all day were the tepla she had thought to bring and not much else.

She glanced at the clock that was shaped like a green Christmas ball ornament. Five o'clock. She eyed the champagne and caught Jais doing the same. He questioned her with his eyes as they communicated without speaking. Like a married couple. Which they really were not anymore. She held his eyes for a moment too long enjoying the familiarity. Jais looked away first and she shrugged to hide the pain that had suddenly come over her.

"Might as well." She shivered.

"I checked the thermostat. It's not getting warmer in here," Jais said.

"I have an extra pair of fuzzy socks…if you want them." She tried to sound like she didn't care if he took them or not. But she did. His feet were always cold. He had been forever placing his ice cold feet next to hers to warm up. She could have bought him socks, but she never did. She warmed his feet herself.

He looked at her a moment before responding, "Yeah?"

She nodded.

"Well, sure, that would be…great."

She went and grabbed the pair from her bag. "Sorry about the color." Though she knew he would make light of it.

Jais grinned as he took the socks from her. "Hot pink is my favorite."

It almost hurt that she had been right about his response. That she knew him that well, and yet…

"Well, let's eat. Maybe by the time we're done we'll have heat. These are old cabins—maybe it just takes longer to heat them." She sat down while Jais poured champagne.

He took the seat across from her. Naina could hardly look at him. At her father's insistence, they had dinner together with him every other Saturday. But she couldn't remember the last time they'd shared a meal together like this. Just the two of them.

Not true. She did remember. But it had been a while ago. Jais handed her a glass, and she drank from it. She skipped the clinking of glasses. This was functional, not fun. If Jais noticed, he didn't say anything about it.

"How are you?" Jais asked as they sipped the sparkling wine.

"Let's not do that." Her voice sounded weary even to her.

"Do what?"

"Pretend to have normal conversation when there's nothing normal between us," Naina said as she took a large sip. At least the alcohol was warming her.

"So, we should sit in silence?" Jais ripped off a piece of rotli, scooped up some shaak and put it into his mouth.

"It was working in the car," Naina countered.

"Fine."

"Fine."

They ate quietly for a few minutes. The meal was incredible.

"So, your dad is getting serious about Romina Auntie?" Jais asked.

Naina frowned. "No."

"He's bringing her to the wedding, introducing her around to family," Jais said. "I think that's serious."

"He is not," Naina said as she took a bite of rotli with shaak into her mouth. "How do you even know that?" She spoke with her mouth full, annoyed.

"He told me."

Naina widened her eyes. "He told you?" Her annoyance increased and paired with a mild level of betrayal that manifested in her gulping down her champagne and pouring more.

Jais stared at her. "Yes. We FaceTime."

"Since when?"

"Since we got married. It's just now we talk without you."

"So, you talk to him behind my back?" she accused.

"Naina. *He* calls *me*."

"He didn't mention that Romina Auntie was coming to this wedding. It's too early for that," Naina said. How could her own dad be dating for real?

"They've been dating for nearly a year," Jais said.

She frowned. "Has it been a year already? He never mentions her to me."

Jais mumbled something she couldn't make out.

"What?"

"Probably because he knows you don't support him dating," Jais stated clearly.

"I'm just looking out for him. He's impressionable and too kind." Naina mixed the rice with the soupy dhal in her bowl.

"He's a grown man. He's perfectly capable of taking care of himself—"

"Why are you talking to him anyway? We're…separated." She choked the word out.

Jais narrowed his eyes at her. "Because he doesn't know we are separated. No one does. As far as he's concerned, I'm still his son-in-law."

Naina stared at him. It was true. She had not known how to tell her father, and then this wedding had come up.

Her dad was all she had left. Her mother had left when she'd been fifteen. She had no siblings. The only other person she had let into her heart was Jais.

But then Jais had walked out of their house six months ago.

Jais poured the rest of the champagne into Naina's glass and stood to clean up. The food had been delicious, even if the conversation had been difficult. He had been the one to walk out six months ago. But Naina had done nothing to stop him.

Or join him.

Now his best friend, Kaden, was marrying Naina's cousin, Savita. They'd all seen it coming. The two had met at Jais and Naina's wedding two and half years ago.

If you could call it a wedding. Jais and Naina had grabbed some of their friends for a weekend in Vegas when Jais had graduated law school. Naina had already been working for a small publishing company near her hometown of Baltimore.

They had gone to celebrate his graduation and a last hurrah before he started work in a firm also in Baltimore. It had started out as just the usual partying and gambling. They'd been truly in love and marriage had most definitely been in their future, they'd just wanted to take their time.

They'd been winning on the floor when Jais had caught sight of an Indian bride and groom getting a quickie wedding in their hotel. He had thought it was a sign. Naina was many things, but spontaneous was not really one of them. But when he'd suggested they get married, right then and there, she had jumped at the chance. Kaden and Savita had been their witnesses. Needless to say, his sister and her father had not been thrilled, having been robbed of a wedding, but they'd come around fairly quickly.

The cabin was not getting any warmer. Naina had grabbed a blanket and was currently making a bed on the sofa.

Jais finished the easy cleanup. "I'll sleep out here. You can have the bed. It's probably warmer."

"I can sleep out here. No need to give me the bed just because I'm a woman," she argued.

He stared at her. "It's not because— You know what? Fine. Have the sofa." He'd simply been trying to be kind.

Jais settled himself in the large bed. The Christmas comforter was musty, and a spring kept poking his back. Some animal was howling terribly outside.

Honestly, their separation was probably a good thing. He couldn't even be nice without her jumping down his throat. He tossed and turned as he recalled every irritating thing she had ever said or done.

Even so, her empty side of the bed continued to haunt him, just as it had for the past six months.

Chapter Four

The sofa was lumpy and hard. Not to mention it smelled funny. Like musty cinnamon. Naina pulled the thin blanket close, wrapping herself up in it. The cabin had gotten a bit warmer, but it was still chilly. She sat up and considered the logs in the corner. She had never started a fire, but how hard could it be? She shivered and glanced at the bedroom door.

This was the kind of thing she and Jais would have navigated together, each of them helping the other.

She turned away from the door. She was on her own. He was probably fine, all tucked into that giant bed.

He looked good. The thought floated into her head without invitation. She shrugged to herself. So what? Lots of men were handsome. It wasn't everything.

She picked up a log and placed it on the small stand inside the fireplace. Long matches were right on the mantel. She grinned to herself. Easy peasy. She'd be warm in no time.

She lit the match and held it next to the log. Some smoke, but nothing. Oh, right—she needed some paper or something. She looked around the room. A newsletter called the *Gingerbread Times* was on the coffee table. She lit the page and placed it under the log, then she closed the glass door and sat back to watch the log catch flame, anticipating warmth.

It did not.

Instead, smoke filled the small space and then started leaking out the glass doors.

She stood. Was this supposed to happen?

She opened the doors and instantly realized that she had done the wrong thing. Smoke started to fill the family room.

The bedroom door opened and Jais came out wearing only flannel pants and hot pink fuzzy socks, his hair ruffled.

He squinted into the light. "I smell smoke. What the hell is happening?" He coughed.

"I don't know. I was cold, so I tried to start a fire." She opened a window and yelped as snow was blown in on a cold draft and landed on her.

"Did you open the flue?"

"The what?" She shook herself, trying to get the snow off of her. She had no idea what "the flue" was.

He gaped at her a moment before grabbing an oven mitt. He then walked into the smoke, his hand over his mouth, and bent down in front of the fireplace, sticking his mitt-covered hand up into the chimney. Naina heard a click and felt a rush of cool air.

Jais backed up. "There. The smoke will now go up the chimney."

Oops. She'd had no idea. Though there didn't seem to be a fire anymore, just lingering smoke.

And now it was colder than before.

Jais grabbed a couple logs. She couldn't help but notice his muscles flex as he did so. He was shirtless after all. She mustered a grin. She'd loved that he had slept without a shirt.

"Come on—I'll start a fire in the bedroom."

"I'm not sleeping in that bed with you," she snapped—maybe a bit more harshly than she meant, given her level of irritation at herself at the moment.

"Duh," he said. "There's a sofa in there, too. I'll sleep on that."

"I'll take the sofa. Your legs will hang off the edge." No way was she going to be the reason that he didn't sleep well.

"Suit yourself." He shrugged and took the logs into the master. The bed was rumpled from him sleeping in it. Naina was suddenly hit with the memory of what it had felt like to sleep next to him. Warm and secure and he'd smelled like…home.

"…blankets. You should be fine. Naina? Did you hear me?" Jais was looking at her while she stared at the bed, lost in old memories.

"Huh? Yes. I got it."

Jais had started a lovely fire. It was already warmer in here. She grabbed her pillow and blankets from the sofa and returned to the bedroom. He was sitting on the edge of the bed.

"You sure? I can…" He motioned to the sofa.

"I'll be fine—I'm not a delicate flower. I won't break."

A smile twitched at the corners of his mouth. "No, I would definitely not describe you as a delicate flower." He rested his gaze on her for a moment before getting into bed. He mumbled something she couldn't hear as he turned off the light.

"What was that?" she said into the dark.

"You're as tough as they come," he answered her with a large sigh.

Chapter Five

December 23

Jais slept fitfully. The fireplace crackling, an animal continuously howling in the distance and Naina's soft breathing all conspired to interrupt his much-needed sleep. Though, after Naina had come in the room and the fire had warmed them, he found the bed was a bit less lumpy, the comforter no longer smelled of mold, and the pillow was just the right amount of firm. He found some peace in the wee hours just before sunrise. He woke to the sun fully formed in the sky. Naina was still asleep.

He smiled to himself. She very rarely slept past sunrise. She must've been exhausted, too. That sofa could not have been comfortable. He quietly used the bathroom and donned a plush robe he hadn't noticed before as he went to the kitchen. The smoke had dissipated, so he closed the flue and the windows, shivering in the cold. He got to work on coffee and breakfast.

A morning like this begged for masala chai. He glanced at the large tote bag that Naina had left out. Odds were pretty good that there was chai masala in there. He took a few steps toward the bag before he stopped himself. He couldn't go through Naina's things anymore, like he had when they'd really been together. Going through her stuff was a level of familiarity that he no longer had. Technically, of course, they were still together. But that technicality did not make it okay for him to go through her things. He stared at the bag, his craving for chai unsated and his heart heavy.

Jais backed away from her bag. He made some coffee and whipped up some spicy scrambled eggs with whatever he could find in the kitchen. The thermostat indicated that the heat was indeed starting to work. Naina still wasn't awake, so he sat down to eat and check the billion messages on his phone—mostly wedding related, some work related. He attacked those first, then dug into the ones from the groomsmen, the aunties and Naina's dad, all wondering when they would arrive and sending pics of what they had missed.

The mehndi party was tonight. He checked the weather in the hopes that they'd be able to get out, but it didn't look good. He was looking at train and bus schedules as he finished up his eggs when Naina emerged from the bedroom. Her dark curly hair was loose around her head, and, despite her late awakening, she looked tired. A familiar warm feeling came over him. He had always loved seeing her in the morning, before she'd had a chance to put her armor on for the day. She was a beautiful woman at any time of day, but he'd always found her most beautiful in the morning. Only he got to see her like this and he relished being the one person that was able to enjoy her beauty this fresh and uninhibited.

He pushed aside that feeling.

"Coffee?" he asked. Even though Naina usually woke at dawn, she was not a morning person. He had asked her about it after they got married.

"I just feel like there's so much to get done in a day, I have to get up early to get it all done. Dad needs things, I have work, bills, emails..." Her eyes had widened in anxiety just talking about it. *"But my body wants me sleep in."*

"You probably don't need to do things for Dad. He's pretty self-sufficient—"

"You'll see. Give it time. He needs someone to take care of him."

"Are you sure about that, Naina?" Jais had asked.

She had sighed, the deep deep sigh of a caregiver. "You'll see, Jais."

"Coffee? Um. Yeah," she mumbled as she sat down.

He scraped his plate clean and she let out a harrumph.

"What?" Jais looked up from his empty plate.

"Did you make eggs just for yourself?" She didn't even bother hiding the accusation in her voice.

Jais stalked to the stove and lifted the lid off the pan. He drew his other hand in front of her still warm portion in true Vanna White style.

She flushed. "Sorry. But you can't blame me."

"Excuse me?" Naina didn't look so cute right now.

"I mean, you are all about yourself. Isn't that why you left?"

"Why *I* left?" Jais's heart thudded in his chest, and his blood began to boil.

"Duh. Yes. You chose a job in New York." She said this as if it were common knowledge. Or even the truth.

"There were two jobs in New York. Two *great* jobs. One for you and one for me. You chose not to take yours," Jais retaliated.

"And you chose to take yours." She glared at him as if this were a sin.

"It was a once in a lifetime opportunity!" he growled. "Both jobs were."

She stood up. "I couldn't leave and you knew it."

"You could have left. You chose not to." He scraped the eggs onto a plate for her.

"There was no choice. I couldn't have left my dad alone in Baltimore and moved to New York. You knew it when we were dating, you knew it when we married. Nothing has changed." She paused. "You made your choice. You thought about what you wanted, what was best for you. And you made your choice and left."

He froze with the pan and spatula in his hands. He could not believe what he was hearing. "You made your choice and stayed," he said quietly as he set the plate of eggs in front of her, his hand lingering for the briefest of seconds before he stepped away.

"If I'd moved to New York, who would've taken care of him?" She paused. "I couldn't do what my mom did—she *left* when he was diagnosed with cancer. I took care him. I've taken care of him since I was fifteen."

"He's not sick anymore, Naina." Jais softened his voice and handed her the bottle of hot sauce he knew she would want. "He eats well, exercises, takes his meds. That diagnosis was thirteen years ago. He went back to work. He even learned to cook for himself—"

She glanced at him, her eyes softening for a moment. "You taught him how to cook."

Jais nodded. "And you didn't think it was a good idea and he turned out to be a great cook."

"Yeah, so?"

"So, Dad is doing well."

Her eyes hardened again. "So just because he can cook, he can be abandoned?"

"We weren't abandoning him," Jais grunted out.

"No you just abandoned me," she spat at him. "You made promises, and at the first chance for something more exciting, you broke them." Her nostrils flared with anger as she growled at him, "And I was alone again."

"Naina." He reached out to touch her, but stopped himself. "You are not alone."

"Of course I am," she stated as if it were fact. "I do not have the luxury of pursuing a career."

"Pursing a career is not a luxury, it's part of life."

"Then it's a part of life that I will not experience."

"Naina, Dad is fine," Jais insisted.

"You can't guarantee that he'll be fine." She threw the words at him.

"No, I can't, Naina. No one can." Jais shook his head in defeat. "But—"

"But nothing, Jais. I had no choice but to stay," Naina insisted. "It would have been easier if you and I had never..." She stopped.

"Never, what?"

"Never met. Never fell in love. Never married." She shrugged. "All of it."

He hadn't thought his heart could be anymore broken than it was already. He was wrong.

He should have let the eggs go cold.

Naina glared back at him as she scooped a forkful of eggs into her mouth. Jais had no idea what he was talking about. As if she could leave her poor father behind. She sipped coffee and took another delicious mouthful of eggs. It was hard being mad at him when he cooked like this. Had kept her eggs warm for her while she slept. She had not forgotten how incredible his cooking could be, she simply never let herself remember. It was easier to eat her own rubbery eggs.

She stared at her coffee. Hmm. Jais hadn't made chai? Weird. He loved chai in the morning. The food and caffeine had her feeling a bit more like a normal person, despite their argument. "You cooked. I'll clean up."

Jais waved her off. "It's literally just your plate now and this pan. I got it."

She checked her phone while Jais did the cleanup. She couldn't help but look at him. She had once told him that there was nothing sexier than a man doing dishes. He had taken that as a challenge and had spent the next couple hours showing her exactly how sexy he was. She heated just thinking about it. She tried to remind herself of their argument, how frustrating he was.

It didn't help.

He had on a plush red-and-green plaid robe that she hadn't

noticed yesterday. Maybe he'd brought it with him? The tie had come undone and the robe fell open, revealing Jais's bare, and very muscular, chest beneath it. She peeked at him over her coffee mug. Damn, but the man was fine.

The cleanup done, he turned off the water.

"It's still snowing," she said.

"Yep. No sign of stopping. I'm going to get dressed and go tell Auntie and Uncle that we'll need the cabin another day or two," Jais said, weariness in his voice.

"What about the wedding?"

"We can't leave until the snow stops. That doesn't seem as though it's happening anytime soon. The trains are cancelled, as are the buses. And even if we had a truck—" he grimaced at her "—we wouldn't be able to make it to the wedding today."

Wow. He'd been busy.

"Did you—" Just then both of their phones jingled. Naina peeked. Her dad was FaceTiming them both. Jais glanced at her before answering.

"Hi, Dad. What's up?" she said.

"Hey, Dad." Jais's face appeared on screen, though he was sitting a few feet from her.

"Ah! I got you both—perfect." Her father chuckled.

"We're pretty badly snowed in, Dad," Jais said. "I checked trains, buses."

"I thought so," her father replied. "Even here it is terrible. Luckily Romina Auntie and I had decided to come extra early. All the events are in this hotel, so everyone is here…except for you two."

"I'm sorry, Dad," Naina said. "Did you take your meds? And be careful of all the fried Indian food, huh? You remember what Dr. Robinson said…"

"I'm fine, beti." Her father sighed. "Where are you?"

"We're in a hotel—The Gingerbread Inn," she said.

"We're only about three hours from you, but the snow—" Jais started.

"And the car he rented is a Mini Cooper." She shook her head.

"Oh! You got the Mini!" Her father's eyes lit up.

"Yes. But it's not as good in the snow as we thought." Jais smiled.

What?

"You're together, nah?" her father asked.

"Yes, of course," Naina said as she shot a glare at Jais.

He shrugged. "Of course we're together. Naina flew in yesterday, and we rented the car and got on the road. We were doing fine until the storm."

Her father looked away as someone called his name. He nodded at them before turning back to his phone. "Well, as long as you are together." He smiled. "I must go! See you soon." He ended the call while Naina was still saying her goodbyes.

Well, okay.

Jais was already up and removing his robe. The heat seemed to be back, and the smoky smell was almost gone. He walked into the bedroom.

Naina sat there. Something wasn't quite right. She couldn't put a finger on it. "How did Dad know you were renting a Mini?" she called out. He had left the door open, and every so often, she caught a glimpse of him dressing. And undressing. Off with the flannel pajama bottoms. She really should not be looking. On with jeans. T-shirt. Sweater.

"We talked about it. I told you—he calls me from time to time," Jais said. It sounded like he was in the bathroom. Probably doing his hair. He had great hair.

He came out looking—and smelling— amazing. The sweater he had on was an ugly Christmas sweater she had gotten him last Christmas. It did not, however, look ugly on him.

"You brought the ugly sweater?"

Jais shrugged. "It's warm." He avoided looking at her. "Boston and the surrounding area is cold." His voice was clipped, distant. She remembered it from when he had first left. Anytime they had to see each other, he had used this voice. He was still upset from their argument. Clearly his normal, happy, easy-going self was not going to make an appearance. "I'll be back."

He left without another glance. Whatever. Though Naina's heart sank a bit. She had hurt him.

Naina changed into leggings and a large ugly sweater of her own. Her phone buzzed—Savita on FaceTime.

"Hey! What is going on?" her cousin asked. "I just saw your dad. Are you really snowed in with Jais?"

Naina sighed. "Yes. I'm sorry I'm not there for you. The snow just keeps falling and I'm not sure when we'll get out."

"You'll make it for the big day, I can feel it. And no worries, the other girls are stepping up. But I do miss you."

"I miss you too. Tell me everything that's going on."

Savita filled her in on all the drama and gossip as well as all the fun. Naina's heart ached that she was missing this important time in Savita's life.

"So, tell me how you're handling being stuck together." Savita asked. "Where did you sleep last night?" Savita raised an eyebrow and smirked.

"We're not getting back together just because we're snowed in." Naina rolled her eyes. "And I slept on the sofa. He slept in the bed."

"What?" Savita's smirk turned instantly to outrage. "You weren't kidding that he was selfish."

"Well, he offered the bed to me. I just chose the sofa," Naina clarified. And then he had made her eggs this morning.

Her eyes glinted again. "You should have just gotten into the bed with him."

"We are not getting back together."

"At least think about it while you're stuck there with him. Reevaluate," Savita insisted. "You two were really good together."

Were they?

"Aren't you getting married?" Naina changed the subject. Savita had both of her parents. She didn't understand.

She had thought Jais would understand her. After all, he had been raised by his grandparents and then his older sister.

"Jyoti got here yesterday with her family. She is the sweetest! And her twin boys." Savita sighed. "So cute!"

"How are you so calm?" Naina asked.

"What's to freak about? Kaden and I will be married no matter what happens now—I just need you to get here. And Kaden needs Jais."

"I know. I'll do what I can. Check out this inn." She turned the camera on her phone to show Savita the cabin. "It's like Christmas threw up—but in the weirdest way. Look."

"It's a Christmas winter wonderland! Looks like the bridal suite here," Savita said.

"What? It's all ripped and faded and—"

"Is it?" Savita furrowed her brow. "If you say so. Oh! Those cute twins are coming. Talk soon." She ended the call abruptly.

Naina stared at her phone. Weddings were busy. She sighed and decided to venture into the hotel as well. There wasn't much to do in the cabin. She grabbed her coat and found her way to the lobby. The covered walkway sported plastic holly and dried evergreen wreaths with dusty decoration. The nearly dead and dried Christmas tree in the lobby sported some old ornaments, some of which were cracked or broken. Every third light or so was out on the stringed lights which seemed like a fire hazard. A toy train was parked underneath the tree on broken tracks, alongside hasilty wrapped gifts. She was taking all of this in when she ran into Jais talking to the older couple.

"Well, hello." Shanta Auntie turned to her. "We were just talking to your husband about the anniversary party we're hosting tomorrow night. We hope the weather allows."

"Anniversary party?" Naina asked.

"Yes, a local couple is celebrating thier many years together.

Their family and friends have taken up most of the inn—we're just concerned about their caterer. They had chosen a specific person for their desserts. Apparently it was the dessert chef from their wedding, making all the Indian sweets they had at that time. But they're coming from New Jersey. They wanted to come in tonight so they could make everything fresh."

"Wife, it is only just noon. I am sure they will arrive shortly," Shant Uncle said calmly.

"Well..." Naina offered filling with pride. "If they don't make it, Jais is amazing at all sweets. He claims it's just a hobby, but he is passionate about it and the results are—" She made the motion for "chef's kiss."

Jais stared at her. "I...uh, haven't done that in a long time." He moved next to her. "I didn't think you remembered," he said very softly.

She leaned away to look at him, surprised. "Of course I remember that." She saw the older couple watching them. "I only eat the sweets he makes. It's just not worth it to eat anyone else's."

Auntie and Uncle smiled at them. Auntie sighed. "Ah... such beautiful young love. How long have you been married?"

"Two and a half years," Jais answered.

"Two years," Naina said at the same time.

They looked at each other.

Shant Uncle and Shanta Auntie glanced at each other, eyebrows raised.

"Well, two and a half, of course." Naina laughed. "Don't know what came over me."

"It seems the latest forecast is for more snow," Auntie said, glancing at her phone. "The roads are still not plowed around here. We tend to be low priority since we don't get much traffic."

Just then another couple approached Auntie. "Such a beautiful room, such lovely decor everywhere. Really feels like Christmas," the woman said as she held her husband's hand.

Jais elbowed Naina, and she turned to catch his eye. He raised an eyebrow slightly, just enough so that she could see but no one else. This had been one of their things, how they communicated with each other without anyone ever knowing. She fell right into its comfort and familiarlity without thought.

Naina widened her eyes just enough to let him know she agreed with him. The decor today was the same as when they'd gotten here last night. Overdone, drab, dusty, old. Clearly everyone else thought it was fine, or they were simply lying.

"It seems you may need to stay a bit longer," Uncle said.

Naina cleared her throat. "Well, this place is lovely, but we do have that wedding."

Jais nodded. "If the roads open up, we'll have to go."

"Yes. I understand. You're welcome to join us for dinner tonight, if you stay."

"Right. Of course," Naina said as the older couple turned away to other customers.

"Are we really staying another night?" Naina turned to Jais.

Jais shook his head. "I'd much rather be at the wedding, but look." He held up his phone with the weather forecast. Snow and more snow.

She tapped his phone. "No buses. No trains." She sighed meeting his gaze.

"We're stuck here," she said. *Together.* And the thought didn't really upset her.

"We'll just have to make the best of it." Jais sighed deeply and he did not look happy at all.

Her heart fell into her stomach at the discomfort she read on his face. Ironically, the fact that *he* was upset about being snowed in with her *did* upset her.

Chapter Six

Jais was still annoyed about the fact that Naina had insisted that he'd left her as opposed to her just not coming with him.

That didn't stop him from walking with her as they checked out the inn.

Huh. Even when she was irritating him, he wanted to be with her. He shook his head at himself. Kaden was right—he had it bad.

"You're unusually quiet," Naina said as they walked down what could only be the creepiest Christmas hallway ever. Christmas gnomes guarded every doorway, but each one was broken. More dead Christmas foliage lined the halls, and the pumped-in scent remained cloying.

He shrugged. "You told me to leave."

"You left. You looked out for yourself."

"Damn straight, I did. I've been looking out for myself ever since my parents died," he said.

Naina stopped in the hallway. "So, you admit it?"

"I admit that the New York job was the best decision for me, yes." He paused and looked into her skeptical eyes. "I asked you to come with me. You had a fabulous offer as well. The plan was for both of us to go—it was never to leave for New York without you. Looking out for myself came to include looking out for you, too." He softened. "You're a part of me. Leaving you behind was like leaving a piece of me behind."

Naina stayed firm. "But you did leave."

"You didn't want to come."

"You could have stayed."

He heard her voice crack, just a bit. He nodded. "I could have. But I believed from the bottom of my heart that you would see how great the opportunity was and join me. Why do you think I was looking at two-bedrooms places?"

Naina narrowed her eyes at him. "What do you mean? Why would we need a two-bedroom? It's New York—we'd hardly be able to afford a one-bedroom…" Her eyes widened as the truth hit her. She covered her mouth with her hands. "You mean—"

He nodded, a small smile coming to his face. "Of course. Dad needs some space when he comes to visit or whatever."

"You were including my dad?"

"Of course. We're married—he's my dad, too." He paused. "Especially since I lost my own dad."

"I didn't realize you felt that way."

"Naina. Even when we were living together, he and I went to movies and breweries and sometimes just hung out together. What did you think was happening?"

She shrugged. "I don't know. I guess I just thought you were doing those things, because we were married. I just thought you were being kind to an old man."

Jais opened his mouth but was interrupted by a sudden blaring of Christmas music. Bad Christmas music. He never would have thought there was such a thing as bad Christmas music, but there it was: "Let it Snow" coming through speakers riddled with static and squeaking.

He cringed and Naina looked at him before they both burst into laughter. They walked again for a bit and ended up in the lobby. The weather was on the TV.

"The roads are barely passable at the moment. With more snow coming in the next few hours, the best thing we suggest is to hunker down and enjoy another mug of eggnog." The meteorologist chuckled.

"Attention!" Uncle's voice crackled through the speakers, interrupting the weather forecast. But Jais had heard enough to know they weren't leaving tonight.

"Teatime. In the dining room," Uncle's voice said.

Jais looked at Naina. "What do you think?"

"Might as well."

They wandered until they found the dining room. It was almost completely full. At least sixty people were having tea and biscuits. No one seemed to be cringing from the off-key blaring of "Twelve Days of Christmas." The decorations were the same as they were around the hotel. Dead, dry, foliage, string lights with broken bulbs, dusty figurines and ornaments everywhere.

"Come on." Naina's face lit up and she took his hand and tugged. Jais was momentarily taken off balance, feeling Naina's hand in his like this again. "I want tea and biscuits." When she smiled, he melted.

"Yeah, I could have a biscuit. But the tea won't be good unless it's chai." Though from the thudding in his chest, they could serve cardboard and water and he knew he'd be happy just holding her hand. Jais followed her to the only empty table there was.

Shanta Auntie appeared almost immediately with a tray of biscuits and a teapot.

"Auntie," Jais asked, "any chance we can get chai?"

She grinned at them. "What do you think is in this pot?" She poured, and sure enough, the familiar aromas of cardamom and cinnamon reached him.

"Thank you, Auntie." He inhaled the scents of happiness. Of lazy Sunday mornings spent in bed talking or reading the paper while he and Naina drank their chai. Of staying in bed and making love all afternoon.

Auntie looked at them both, a smile on her face. "Enjoy."

Jais sipped his chai and took a biscuit. As did Naina. He bit into his biscuit and glanced around the crowded room, awkwardly sitting across from his wife.

"I'm sorry," she said.

He snapped his head to her.

"I'm sorry for saying that you were selfish and that you only think about yourself." She inhaled. "I know that's not true." She paused. "I was just…angry."

He nodded, surprised to hear her saying that after all this time. "Thanks. For saying that. For knowing that. About me." In his excitement, he was rambling. "What I mean is, okay. I get it." He wanted—needed—to touch her, but he didn't want to spook her, so he kept his hand on his chai mug.

"Yeah. Well. It's the truth. And I'm sorry I didn't say it sooner." She reached across the small table and opened her hand to him.

He did not hesitate to take it, relaxing into the warmth of her touch once again.

After a moment, he glanced around the room. It seemed cleaner, the lights emitted a soft glow. The foliage looked properly green. "Naina." He leaned toward her and whispered. "Are you seeing what I'm seeing?"

Naina followed his gaze and nodded. "If you mean the lights and foliage. Yes." She turned to him. "Did we just not notice when we came in?"

Jais frowned and shook his head. "It was not this nice when we came in. Unless we've simply lowered our standards in Christmas decor in the past day,"

"You mean as long as it's not broken and dusty, we're good." She giggled. "Even the carolers sound better."

Jais listened closely. They did sound better. Like actual music. He leaned toward Naina, spoke to her like he used to, softly, initimately. It felt natural like they had never stopped talking like this. "This place is amazing but weird, right?"

* * *

They returned to the cabin after dinner, warm from wine and good food. Naina was feeling quite relaxed, and they were still laughing. They stopped when they entered the cabin—it was freezing and the heat was off.

Naina called the front desk while Jais went to get wood.

"Shanti Auntie has no idea what's wrong. The heat seems to be out in the other cabins," she reported.

"There's no wood." He opened his arms and looked around as if the wood might be somewhere else.

"What do you mean?" Naina shivered.

"I mean the wood is gone. Just that one small log."

They looked over to where the stack of wood had been, only to find one log in the holder.

"Where did it go?" Naina asked.

"No idea. Call Auntie back," Jais suggested.

Naina called the front desk, but no one answered. She hung up and shook her head at Jais. "We should save that one log for morning in case the heat doesn't come back," she suggested. "But honestly, what kind of inn are they running here?"

"Naina. There's a record winter storm. There's no way anyone could have planned for that," Jais said.

She pursed her lips. "But still."

"Let's find blankets," he suggested.

They gathered all the blankets they could find, which was three thin blankets that might have seen better days. Naina took the sofa in the bedroom; Jais got in the bed. It was freezing.

"Naina." His voice came to her in the darkness. The sound of his voice calmed her, even if it did not warm her. A sliver of moonbeam was their only light.

"Hmm."

"Get in bed with me."

"Ha! Nice try." There was no way she was sharing a bed with him.

"No, I'm serious. It'll be warmer that way. Our body heat will keep us warm."

Silence for a moment. He wasn't wrong. Her body was tense from trying to keep warm under the thin blankets. There was no way she would sleep like this. She got up and ran over to the bed and hopped in. Warmer already.

"You have to move closer to me." He put out his arms for her to spoon like they used to.

She raised an eyebrow at him.

"Trust me, Naina. I'm not going to try anything. It's just cold. And we're fully dressed."

"I know." She trusted him, she just didn't trust herself to not to give in to what she wanted.

Chapter Seven

December 24

Honestly, it was embarrassing how good it felt to be in Jais's arms again. Her body immediately relaxed into him against everything her mind knew was right. He was warm and strong, and when he held her like this, his whole body surrounding her, she didn't want to be anywhere else in the world.

Naina closed her eyes and melted into the familiar strength of his arms. She had missed him, but it was now, in the comfort of his body that she realized how much she had missed him. She must have drifted off to sleep because the next thing she knew early dawn was peeking through the curtains.

She hardly remembered falling asleep. Well, she hadn't really slept the night before. Not to mention dinner had been so filling. There had also been wine. That was why she'd been knocked out. It had nothing to do with the fact that Jais's arms were still around her.

And they were still fully dressed.

It should've made her happy that he respected her boundaries. But had he wanted to try something and hadn't because... boundaries? Or had he not wanted to try anything at all? Had he moved on? She had kicked him out. They saw each other for dinner with her dad every other Saturday night, but he never asked to stay over and she never offered.

He moved. She closed her eyes, not wanting this time to end. He snuggled closer and pulled her to him. She inhaled the last traces of his cologne from yesterday, mixed with the warm scent of his body and snuggled closer.

Heaven.

She closed her eyes and let sleep take her again.

The next time she opened them, fabulous aromas were coming from the kitchen and Jais was not beside her. She used the bathroom and found him making eggs again. Coffee was percolating in the coffee maker.

Jais was working quickly and efficiently in the kitchen. He had on a fitted T-shirt and his flannel pants that he had slept in. She watched him move with grace and efficiency, chopping here, seasoning there, biceps flexing as he lifted the iron skillet with ease and flipped the omelet over. A smile fell across her face in spite of herself. Jais was comfort. Jais was home.

Not to mention, Jais in the kitchen was one of the hottest things she'd ever seen.

"Smells great," she said softly.

"Hey," he said, a huge smile filling his whole face as he noticed her. "Sleep well?"

"Yes. You?"

"Best sleep I've had in a long time." That was Jais, open and honest. "But I always slept better with you." He shrugged.

Naina tried to hide her complete pleasure at hearing this, but she couldn't stop the smile or the flush from revealing it.

"I knew you were just trying to get me in bed." She smirked as she poured them each a mug of coffee. She added half a sugar to hers and two sugars and cream to his, then handed him his mug.

"Why do you keep making coffee? You love morning chai," she said, sipping the coffee. She pulled the mug back and looked at it—it was so good. "Wow. Amazing coffee, though."

"The chai stuff is in your bag," he answered, suddenly engrossed with sautéing onions.

She stared at him, and her heart dropped. Of course. He wouldn't go through her things since they weren't really a couple anymore.

He plated eggs for them both. She sat at the breakfast bar, while he stood in the kitchen across from her with his plate in his hands.

"How's the new job?" she asked.

He snapped his gaze to her, his forkful of eggs frozen on the way to his mouth. "It's good. Great, actually." He took the bite.

She nodded. "Is it everything you hoped?"

"What's happening here, Naina? You never asked about the job before." He took a bite of omelet.

"I just want to know how you like job. If—"

"If it was worth leaving you for?" he asked quietly.

She wasn't sure she wanted the answer to that question. She shoved a scoop of omelet into her mouth. It melted in her mouth. Honestly, this man was wasted as a lawyer. Though he was excellent at what he did. "If you're happy," she said quietly.

"It's a fantastic job," Jais continued as he ate. "Challenging. Meaningful. Great potential for growth, for upward mobility. It's everything I've ever dreamed of in a job." He opened his mouth as if he had more to say, but then he stopped. His plate was empty. He set it down, continuing to lean against the stove behind him, his arms folded across his chest. If she hadn't known better, she would think he was showing off his very fine forearms. "But no. No, it is not worth being without you."

She froze. What? Had he just said what she thought he'd said? That he wished he hadn't left?

Naina dropped her fork. She had missed him like she was missing a limb. "Jais. I thought—" She didn't finish. She simply slid off the stool and walked over to him, her eyes never leaving his. "I thought all you wanted was that job." *Not me.*

She couldn't say the last words. But the way he was looking at her right now...

He shook his head, his eyes following as she moved toward him. "I need you."

All she had to do was lean toward him, touch him and she could have him back. She leaned toward him, her gaze never leaving his. She stood on tiptoe, her mouth millimeters from his. She dropped her gaze to his mouth. Full lips parted, waiting for her. She had missed him—his company, his laugh, his easygoing nature. She had missed his arms around her. She had missed his body, his kiss. She had thought he would love that job, never look back at her.

Much the same way her mother had never looked back. She was convinced that Jais would happier without her, just as her mother seemed to be happier without her too.

He was waiting for her to invite him in.

She closed the scant distance between her mouth and his and kissed him. She had meant for it to be soft, reconciliatory, tentative. But her heart took over, and her kiss was filled with longing, with demand.

One hand on her face, the other on her neck, Jais kissed her, holding nothing back. He never held back. His emotions, his longing for her were open to her. He stepped closer to her, closing the distance between their bodies.

They broke for air, both of them panting.

"Naina... I missed you." His voice was gruff.

"Me, too." She grabbed his hand and led him back to the warmth of the bed they had so chastely shared just an hour ago.

He pulled her close and kissed her madly, gently laying her down on the bed. She allowed it, surrendering herself to him as she had so many times before. She loved this man in every way possible.

And now she had him back.

Chapter Eight

Jais was acting on instinct. On need. On love. He didn't want to think about why Naina might have had a change of heart about him.

She smelled of flowers and citrus and coffee, and she was familiar and new all at the same time.

Her skin where his lips touched her was silken. Her sighs of contentment and gasps of delight as he undressed her slowly were a balm to his soul. He loved her. He had spent the last six months longing for her. Waiting for her to join him. Willing her to see that they were better together. That New York would be good for them. That she did not need to be a caregiver twenty-four seven. She could do this for herself. She could live her own life. With him.

Right now, he wanted to show her how cherished she was. She tugged his T-shirt off and pulled him to her. They were skin to skin.

"I love you, Naina. I never stopped." He kissed her neck, her shoulders, working his way down, not wanting to miss a spot.

"I love you, too. I never wanted you to leave," she whispered.

Jais stopped, his mouth hovering over her collar bone. "Then why did you tell me to leave?"

"I didn't tell you to leave." Naina's giggle felt forced. She kissed him. "I love you."

Irritation had Jais pulling back from her, rolling over to lay next to her. "You most certainly told me to leave." The pain of her telling him to "just go, then" was a moment he tried not to relive too often. Being rejected was one thing, but being turned away by the woman you had given your heart to—it was too much.

She sat up, pulling the sheet up with her. "You said you wanted to take that job in New York."

"Your dream job was in New York, waiting for you. I wanted us to go together." He'd said this many times—why was it so hard for her to understand?

"There was no way I was going to do that, and you know it. You wanted that job, so you left." Naina sounded as exasperated as he felt.

"I held out hope that you would see how great your father was doing, and start living your life. With me. In New York. At your dream job." Jais got out of the bed.

"You went without me," Naina shot at him.

"You said there was no more 'us,'" Jais said softly, a hitch in his voice. Those words had broken him.

Naina *had* said those words. She had meant them at the time.

"You were asking me to leave my father." She found her clothes and started putting them back on. "You've always been on your own. Your sister raised you—I thought you would understand what it meant to only have that one person as your family...but you're too carefree, too spontaneous. You don't know what it means to have to take care of someone—"

"You don't own the market on taking care of loved ones. I do take care of my sister. But our lives aren't just about me and her. She has a husband, children—all of whom I love."

"It's not the same. My father needs me close by."

"No, Naina. He does not. You think he does. You're afraid to let go."

"No. He does need me." Naina raised her voice. Jais had no

idea what he was talking about. He hadn't six months ago, and he clearly did not right now. "He can count on me, because I stay. You left me, just like my mom left my dad—and me."

Jais froze and locked his gaze with hers. Silence lay thick and heavy between them. He put on a sweatshirt over his T-shirt. "I'm not—" She had never seen such defeat and pain in his eyes. He simply shook his head as he left the bedroom. Naina just stood there. She heard Jais open the door and leave the cabin.

That was the second time she'd let him walk out on her.

Chapter Nine

Naina stayed put where she was, trying to process what had just happened. She had just compared Jais to her mother. Nothing could be further from the truth. Jais was everything to her, where her mother was just a memory. Just someone who was there until she wasn't, leaving a teenager to deal with the realities of a sick father all alone.

Jais might have left, but he had been going to something. He hadn't been running away. Isn't that what he had been trying to tell her all this time?

He was a good man. A man she loved, and a man she hurt with that awful comparison.

Was it possible that Jais was right? That she was afraid to let go?

She was about to hop into the shower when her phone rang.

Her dad. FaceTime. He was probably worried sick about her, waiting for her to show up.

His face on the screen, however, was all smiles. "Hi, beti," he said. He looked good. Relaxed. Laughing.

Huh.

"Hi, Dad. How's it going?"

"Oh, it's great. The mehndi night was such a wonderful party. We danced until past midnight. And the food…" He made a chef's kiss. "Out of this world."

"Take it easy, Dad. Be careful of what you eat and get some

sleep. Maybe dancing until midnight is too much for you. Did you take your medicine?"

He waved a hand at her. "I'm fine, beti. I haven't had this much fun in a very long time."

"Dilip," a woman's voice singsonged in the background. "I can't seem to open the safe."

"One second, Romina."

"Ah, I'm sorry." Romina Auntie came into the frame. "I didn't see you were talking to the children. Hi, Naina."

"Oh hi, Auntie." Naina tried to mask her surprise. Some part of her knew her father would be sharing a room with Romina Auntie. But it was weird seeing it…live. "Uh…how are the events? Are you and Dad…enjoying yourselves?"

Romina Auntie beamed and looked at her father with complete adoration. "You better believe it."

Oh. *Oh!*

Naina somehow managed to maintain her smile. "Oh great."

"I'll just go catch a shower, while you both chat. See you soon, Naina."

"You too, Auntie."

Oh god, they were sleeping together. Naina closed her eyes and shook her head. They were grown consenting adults…she just didn't want to think about it.

"Hey, Dad." Now she felt awkward.

"Hey, beti," he said watching her closely.

"I guess you and Romina Auntie are pretty serious?"

"Yes…" His voice held some caution.

"Just be careful, you know? Get enough sleep, eat properly. You're a cancer survivor—"

"Cancer survivors can have sex."

"Oh god!" She squeezed her eyes shut even as she heard him chuckle at her expense. "I know. I just need to you to be careful—"

"Naina. I am fine."

She opened her eyes. He did look good. Healthy, a sparkle in his eyes.

"I always remember to take my meds. I can take myself to the doctor. I'm not an invalid." He paused and looked at her. "Your mother left so long ago—I deserve to be happy, and Romina makes me happy." He smiled. "And I make her happy as well."

Tears burned behind Naina's eyes.

"You are my daughter, and I will always love you and need you. But I don't need you to take care of me. I know I allowed it in the past...maybe I shouldn't have—it wasn't fair to you as a child. But I'm setting you free now—I should have ages ago. Naina, your mother is never coming back. It took me a long time to come to terms with that fact. I know you took care of me because there was no one else at the time, but I'm an adult and I'm fine. And I want you to live your life for you. To do what makes you happy."

A tear fell before she could wipe it away. "You sound like Jais."

"He loves you, beti." Her father grinned at her. There was something...

"What do you mean?" She narrowed her eyes at him.

His eyes widened. "Oh, I hear Romina calling. Let me go open the safe. She forgets the code." He forced a laugh. "I hope you and Jais make it here in time—everything so far has been lovely."

Her father ended the call.

Naina stared at the phone for a few minutes. Her mom had walked out years ago when her dad had been sick. Naina had been a teenager. She had stepped up to take care of her father until her mother returned. But her mother had never returned, and Naina had never stopped being her father's caregiver. Her world revolved around him. It was as if she were somehow making up for the fact that her mother had left him. As long as Naina was there to take care of him, they were both able to survive.

Her mother was never coming back. And her father was just fine without her. Naina expected her heart to feel heavy. She waited a minute for the reality of him moving on with his life, instead of living in the moment her mother had left. Which was where she lived. Her father had a girlfriend. This was weird.

But not unheard of.

Her father absolutely deserved to be happy.

If Romina Auntie made him happy, who was she to stand in the way?

She gathered her things and once again tried hopping into the shower when the cabin phone rang.

"Hello?"

"Ah, Naina." It was Shanta Auntie. "Is it possible for you and your husband to make a few sweets for the anniversary party tonight? The chef cannot make it in today due to the storm."

"Oh, uh. Well, he's stepped out for a moment. He's really the one who makes—"

"Perfect. I'll find him and see if we can scrounge some ingredients."

"Oh—uh—" But Shanta Auntie had already hung up.

Whatever. Naina finally hit the shower.

Jais didn't even care that he was still in his flannel pajama bottoms. He needed to be away from Naina for a few minutes. He should have seen this coming when she'd told him that she would never leave her father's side.

She had told him from the moment they'd met.

And he still hadn't listened. That was on him.

He would not be making that mistake for a third time.

"Jais." Shanta Auntie found him staring at the oversized nearly dead Christmas tree that was in the lobby.

"Auntie."

"I'm sorry, beta. You seem distracted, but I need to ask a favor."

He turned to face her. "Sure. How can I help?"

"Well, that anniversary dinner is tonight, but the pastry chef is unable to make it from New Jersey. I was hoping you and your wife could whip up some desserts for the couple and their guests. You're welcome to join the party. And we'll comp one night of the cabin."

There was nothing Jais wanted to do less. But the older woman was clearly desperate, and Naina had bragged about how good his pastries were. It would be cold to turn her down.

He gave her a small smile. "I would love to help you out. But Naina is...under the weather, so—"

"I just spoke with her. She seemed fine."

"Oh, well—"

"She's happy to help you." Auntie smiled at him, a twinkle in her eye. "I just called her."

He sighed. "Perfect. When should I get started?"

Jais sighed and looked around. Now he and Naina were going to be cooking together. There was a time not so long ago that he had enjoyed being in the kitchen with her. Fact was, he had enjoyed being in any room with Naina. Still did.

Pathetic.

People thought he was the fun one because he was outgoing, always ready with a funny story or a joke. And it was true he was the extrovert of the two of them, but Naina was funny without being the center of attention. She was caring without needing to turn on any charm. It took some time to get into her heart, but once you did, you were there forever.

He should have known that Naina would never leave her father for something as superficial as a job opportunity, no matter how amazing or perfect it was. People mattered to Naina more than anything.

That was why he had fallen in love with her.

That was why he still loved her.

Jais started walking back to their room to change and get a shower when Kaden FaceTimed him. He found a small corner off to the side of the lobby and sat down.

"Hey. What's up?" he asked his best friend.

"You going to make it here tonight?"

"Doubtful. All the roads are still snow covered. And we ended up in some tiny town resort that isn't going to be high priority in terms of cleaning out."

"How's it going?" Kaden smirked at him.

Jais shook his head. "Don't even… She's not interested—or even if she is, all she sees is that I walked out."

"So, apologize. What's the big deal?" He leaned in. "You have to take her as she is. She's always going to take care of her dad. You love her, you love her dad."

"I do love her dad. He and I talk all the time. I don't have any issue taking care of him or doing whatever he needs."

Kaden shook his head. "Listen. You're stuck there with her. Make the most of it. Talk to her… Like really talk. No holding back."

"I don't know…" Jais glanced around. Were there even more people here now?

"Well, I do. She's crazy about you," his friend insisted.

"It might be too late for all that."

"Do you love her?" Kaden asked.

Jais stared at him.

"Do you love her?"

He nodded. "More than anything."

"Then fight for her. Tell her how you feel. Tell her why you went to New York to begin with." Kaden paused. "I assume you didn't tell her that you put in a letter of resignation?"

"Of course not." Jais shook his head.

"Talk. To. Her." Some commotion behind Kaden demanded

his attention. "Listen, bro, I have to go. Maybe you'll get here in time for the wedding? Day after tomorrow?"

Jais shook his head, smiling at his friend. "I'll do what I can."

He ended the call and stood. The weight of what Kaden was telling him to do…it was too much right now. He couldn't handle seeing Naina in the cabin. He gave up on his shower and went to find the kitchen and see what ingredients were available to work with.

Chapter Ten

The kitchen wasn't easy to find, as it was located almost separate from the main building. A small hallway connected the main house to the kitchen, and another small hallway connected to a private dining room, where tonight's anniversary dinner would be held.

Naina wandered in to find Jais already there, still in his pajamas, opening and closing cupboard doors. After this morning, it felt even more awkward to be in his presence. Especially since she could still feel his hands on her body and his mouth on hers.

The way he was opening and closing cabinet doors indicated that he was still agitated.

Still hurt by what she had said.

"Find anything useful?" she asked by way of greeting.

"Huh?" He turned to her. "Oh, hey. Um, well, yes." He started taking things out as he spoke. "Flour, sugar, corn flour. Some turmeric as well as cardamom and saffron."

"Jalebi for sure," Naina said.

He nodded, but his normal enthusiasm and passion was missing. He pulled out milk powder and condensed milk.

"Oh!" She recognized those—they were key for an "instant" version of her favorite sweet. "Peda. We could add red-and-green food coloring for a Christmas twist, since it's Christmas—" she paused, catching herself "—eve," she said softly, still watching

Jais. He was in the pantry, the door blocking his face from her. But she saw his body stiffen and pause movement.

They were clearly both thinking of that Christmas Eve four years ago, when they'd first met.

"I found food coloring," he said into the pantry.

Naina started hunting around the kitchen for the various pots they would need as well as something to fry the jalebi in. She heard him working behind her. She found a large bowl to mix the jalebi batter in and an empty ketchup squirt bottle. The batter would go in the bottle, and then they would squeeze it out into the hot oil, much like funnel cake. Then they would soak it in cardamom-infused sugar syrup.

Jais had already started the sugar syrup. Naina walked over to the stove and silently took over. This had always been one of her jobs as assistant. She stirred the syrup while the sugar melted. Jais scooped some flour, corn flour, turmeric and yogurt into the mixing bowl and began stirring with a large whisk. Not one measuring cup to be found near him.

Jais never measured anything, he just figured it out. Soon enough, they had a batter that seemed the right consistency as well as sugar syrup that Naina had added cardamom pods and saffron to. She poured oil into a deep pan and set the heat while the batter sat for a moment.

They hadn't spoken a word.

Jais was already at work on the peda mixture. This would have to cool before they rolled small pieces into balls and flattened them. The result would be a melt-in-your-mouth fudgelike confection that Naina loved. Her mouth watered in anticipation of her favorite sweet. Jais had made it for her all the time.

Naina froze as she was suddenly visited by a memory of her mother making this same sweet for her. Naina had forgotten—or maybe had subconsciously chosen not to remember—this particular thing.

That was it. That was the whole memory. Making something in the kitchen with her mother, who had been patient and kind and loving and—

"Naina? Naina!" Jais's voice came to her from faraway. "Naina. What is it?" Concern tainted his words, all the irritation and anger from their earlier argument completely vanished. He was standing right in front of her, his eyes intent on her.

He wiped a tear from her cheek.

"I...uh... My mom..." She cleared her throat as Jais used both thumbs to wipe away more tears. "My mom used to make peda for me, too. And at Christmas, we colored them red and green."

Jais watched her, his brow furrowed, his hands resting on her face. "You never mentioned that before."

She sniffled. "I forgot." More tears burned behind her eyes and she couldn't stop them. "I guess I forgot that my mom had loved me at one point."

Jais turned off the oil and nodded. The desserts could wait.

"Once she left, I focused on taking care of my dad, and it was like everything before didn't exist. I didn't want to remember that she loved me." Tears kept coming, and she was breathing hard as her sadness turned to anger. "Because if she loved me—" she was vaguely aware of Jais moving closer, holding her shoulders "—then why would she have left?"

"Naina." Jais's voice was firm but soft.

"No. Jais. Why would she have left? Maybe there's something I did that I don't remember... I mean, I didn't even remember making the peda—"

"Naina." This time it was more of a growl. "I don't know why, but it wasn't because of you. You are a rock. You're a solid fixture for the people you love. And I suspect you were born that way. The stories Dad tells about you prove that. You are dependable and loyal, all the things your mother was not."

Jais was staring at her, his expression soft, even though she had been shouting and crying. He wrapped his arms around her and held her tight as if doing so would make her believe his words.

It worked.

She stepped back. He didn't drop his arms from around her. "I pushed you away because I thought you'd leave me anyway," she said softly, looking down at her hands. "She left, so I guess I figured others that I love might, too." She looked up at him. "I'm sorry for what I said. You are not like my mom. Not even a little."

Jais grinned. "Neither are you, Naina."

"I'm not, am I?" Realization struck her, and she saw her actions from a new point of view.

Naina grinned at him as she wiped her eyes. "I'm me. I don't run when things get hard."

Jais watched her, his smile growing with hers. "No, you don't. But you don't have to go around proving it all the time. Your dad is fine."

"Well, he's gotten himself a girlfriend, so I suppose that's true." She nodded, clearing her eyes of tears, feeling much lighter than she had—ever. "He's living his life. I don't want to get in the way of that." She smirked at Jais. "Turn on that oil. We have sweets to make."

He grinned at her. "All right, then."

Chapter Eleven

Jais fried the batter, placing the hot jalebi into the sugar syrup while Naina got to work on rolling one-inch balls of peda dough. She also periodically stopped and pulled the jalebi from the syrup mixture. She found a bowl with a flat bottom and smooshed the balls of peda into round discs, sprinkling colored sugar on top in lieu of chopped-up pistachios or almonds.

He caught her sneaking a taste while she worked, and he swore he heard her mumble to herself, something about how he made the best peda ever. Pride filled him at those murmured words. All he'd ever wanted to do was make her happy.

Their argument of the morning past history, and Naina's latest revelation fresh between them, the energy in the kitchen was uplifting, promising.

They worked like a well-oiled machine. Like they had from almost the very beginning. Jais's heart warmed, and he filled with hope.

"You know what we need?" she asked, stopping suddenly. She washed her hands and ran out of the kitchen. Very unNaina like. Jais juggled the frying and sugar syrup dunking while she was gone.

She returned in ten minutes, holding a small bag of chai spice. "Add it to your hot chocolate. I saw it in a blog. We have everything we need to make a large batch."

Jais grinned at her. "Take over."

She moved closer to him and took over the jalebi. He pulled out a pot and made his hot chocolate, adding the chai spice when Naina instructed. The aroma of the hot chocolate mixed with the cinnamon, cardamom, clove, nutmeg and ginger in the most delicious way. Memories of the Christmases he'd shared with his parents and sisters flashed before him, all rolled into the memories of Diwali and Rakshabandan as well.

Some of it must have shown on his face because Naina walked away from the oil and came to him, wrapping her arms around him. "You always make the best hot chocolate."

"Not as good as my dad's." He gave her a small smile.

"Not according to Jyoti Ben." She grinned.

He widened his eyes. "My sister...said that? She said my hot chocolate was as good as my dad's?" He shook his head as tears burned at his eyes. "No way."

Naina was laughing and bobbing her head. "She did. And she swore me to secrecy, so don't blab."

"Oh, no. That's too good—I'm totally calling her on it." He laughed, the tears blurring his vision. This was how it was with Naina. He was free to laugh or cry or laugh and cry at the same time. Being around Naina felt right. Naina might've wanted to take care of people, but she was his rock. She was his home. He wanted to be the one who took care of her. To the point of having found that job for her in New York. He had found his *after* hers came available. It was always about her.

Her arms around him right now, that's where he wanted to live. She pulled away to continue their work and he felt it like a loss.

He arranged the jalebi and the peda on a few platters and poured himself and Naina each a mug of the chai-spiced hot chocolate.

He held his up, and they clinked mugs before tasting. The thick chocolate with a hint of cinnamon and cardamom and the sharpness of the clove was many holidays in his mouth. "Wow. This is fantastic."

She grinned as she sipped.

He looked at her and then into his drink as he leaned back against the counter. "Naina. There's something I have to tell—"

"Oh! It smells just lovely in here!" Shanta Auntie exclaimed.

"What's cooking?" Shant Uncle asked as he inhaled deeply. "No, let me guess." He closed his eyes and held his belly. He wore a red kurta that was testing the limits of his belly. "I smell jalebi. Maybe peda?" He opened his eyes and smiled widely at them. "Eh?"

"You got it, Uncle," Jais said.

"But there's something more..." He closed his eyes and inhaled. "I smell chai but hot cocoa as well." He popped his eyes open. "You didn't...?"

Naina poured them each a mug. "We did. Well, Jais did. He makes the best hot chocolate." She glanced at him, pride in her face.

"But it was Naina's idea to add the chai masala. And she makes masala herself." Jais rested his gaze on her. She'd pulled her dark hair into a high ponytail as they'd cooked, and right now her beautiful mouth was quirked in a smile as she joked with Uncle. She passed her gaze over to him, and his heart jumped at the intimacy he found in her dark eyes. He could never tire of looking at her.

"This is incredible!" Shanti Auntie looked at her husband.

"Would you mind if we served it here? At the inn?" Uncle asked.

Jais and Naina looked at each other. "Of course not," they answered in unison.

"I made enough for the party tonight," Jais offered. "I'll just heat it up when it's time."

Uncle took Jais by the shoulders and pulled him down for

a hug. "Ah, beta! That's wonderful. Thank you so much!" He looked around the kitchen. "I must sample."

Shanta Auntie shook her head and rolled her eyes, but her mouth quirked into a smile. "You enjoy, but be sure to leave room for the feast tonight." She nodded as her husband tasted the sweets and pronounced them fabulous.

"We'll let you finish up." She raised eyebrows at her husband and looked at the door. "My dear, we should let them work."

"Of course," Uncle said as headed for the door. "You two be sure to join us all tonight at the party."

"Oh, no, we couldn't impose—" Naina started.

"Yes. Sure we can," Jais said, looking at her, a small plea on his face. "The food will be amazing."

She sighed and capitulated. "I guess we'll be joining you." She glanced at Auntie's beautiful red sari. "We certainly have the clothes."

Chapter Twelve

Uncle and Auntie left. Naina and Jais finished up their hot chocolates and then started the long cleanup. "My dad called."

"Yeah?" Jais was scrubbing dishes as Naina put things away and straightened up.

"He and Romina Auntie are sharing a room." She'd thought this would be harder to say, but saying the words out loud, she found, did not hurt nearly as much as she might have thought. She shrugged. "Romina Auntie couldn't figure out the safe." She chuckled. "I didn't even think my dad knew how to operate the hotel safe."

"Why?"

"I don't know… I guess I'm so used to doing everything for him, I never even let him try." She looked at Jais, tears burning her eyes again. "That's pretty lousy, huh?"

He dried his hands and went to her, scooping her up into his arms again. "No. It's just you." She could get used to these arms around her, a strong secure place she could call home.

"I want a new me."

He chuckled. "I don't know. I really love the you that you are."

"You do?" She pulled back. "Even though I try to control everything and I kicked you out?"

He nodded. "I can't help it."

"Children," Shanta Auntie's voice called from the doorway. "Quickly, go on and get dressed. The party is starting."

"Okay, Auntie," Jais called. They quickly finished cleaning and hurried to their cabin to change.

As they approached the main lobby, they both slowed down.

"Are you seeing what I'm seeing?" Naina asked. She took in the surroundings. The train under the tree ran smoothly, tooting quietly every so often. The tree looked healthy, green in fact, with beautiful, intact ornaments hanging from now sturdy branches.

"I don't know." He took her hand. "Are you seeing Christmas decor that isn't gray and dingy?"

"Lights that work?" she asked, nodding. The lights were all on, no broken bulbs.

"Weird," Jais said.

They entered their cabin, still holding hands. Jais's hand in hers had always felt natural and right. They stopped in the doorway. The cabin was gorgeous. The holly was a plush green with soft white lights. The tree was strong and lush and tastefully decorated. Candles flickered a soft glow all around. Christmas might have thrown up, but the effect was a beautiful fantasy.

"Maybe they redecorated?" Jais suggested.

"Whatever. Let's get dressed. At least we get to wear some of our fun clothes." Naina tugged his hand.

"Wait." Jais tugged at her hand. Naina stopped. "It's actually warm."

They were dressed in record time. Naina threw on the sage-green lengha that she had chosen for the mehndi night. Jais wore the matching sherwani. They hadn't shopped together as they might have if they'd been together, but they had texted colors so they could match like a couple would.

The green in the sherwani brought out the hazel of Jais's eyes and the deep brown of his skin. He always had cleaned up nicely. But what struck Naina right now wasn't only how drop-dead gorgeous Jais was in that outfit but the way he was looking at her. Smile all the way out to his one dimple, he was adjusting the sleeve of his sherwani when he noticed her looking at him.

His smile widened and his eyes lit up, and she felt wrapped up in his bubble of love.

"You…" He shook his head. "You're beautiful in leggings and an ugly Christmas sweater. There simply aren't words to describe how you radiate beauty in this moment."

Naina opened her mouth to say something, but nothing came out. She flushed at his attention, speech failing her in that moment. But her heart thudded in her chest.

"Ready?"

She nodded again. He held out his arm and she took it, and they walked in comfortable silence, following the sounds of laughter, joyous chatter and music. They slipped into the party and looked for Shanta Auntie and Shant Uncle.

Auntie caught their eye and walked over. She was resplendent in the red sari they had seen her in earlier. "Don't you make quite the pair? Come say hello to our hosts."

She led them over to a couple older than Naina's father but not quite old enough to be her grandparents. There was still some black in the graying hair, and the wrinkles were laugh lines. The woman wore a beautiful pink sari, and her husband was in a matching sherwani.

"Welcome," the woman said with a wide smile. "I'm Lata and this is Vipul. Thank you so much for making our favorite sweets. I can't wait to try them."

"It was our pleasure," Jais said. "Thank you for having us."

"How long have you been married?" asked Naina.

"Forty-seven years," Vipul Uncle said, and he glanced at his wife fondly.

Naina's eyes widened. "Wow. That's a long time. How did you manage?"

"Love," said Uncle.

Auntie pressed her lips together and raised an eyebrow at her husband, trying to look stern, but a smile broke through her lips. "Sure, there is love. But we had to work. We had to talk to each other, say the difficult things. We spent some time angry with one another. But yes…" She looked fondly at her husband. "Love was the motivation, but friendship and vulnerability and talking—"

"Lots of talking." Uncle widened his eyes.

Auntie gave him a playful smack on the arm. "Lots of talking is needed. There's no secret, beti. It's hard work."

Uncle put his arm around Auntie and squeezed her tight. "Worth every minute of it."

Jais took Naina's hand, and she melted right into it. Her hand belonged in his. She hadn't believed it with her whole heart six monthe ago, but she believed it now. She knew it now.

Shant Uncle approached. "Come, have dinner."

Jais and Naina joined the party, enjoying the food and drink. They met Vipul Uncle and Lata Auntie's family. Most of them lived locally and were able to navigate the snow to get to the inn. Others had arrived before Naina and Jais and were staying at the inn. But everyone knew they weren't leaving for another day or so.

While Naina did not forget about Savita and Kaden's wedding, she did thoroughly enjoy this anniversary party. Jais slipped out into the kitchen after the meal to reheat the hot chocolate.

"I can help," she said.

"No. It's fine. I'll be right back," he said.

Shanta Auntie brought out the desserts to much fanfare as everyone helped themselves to jalebi, peda and either chai or masala hot chocolate. Everyone raved about the sweets and thanked them.

"How long have you been together?" Vipul Uncle asked

them over a delicious cup of masala hot chocolate. Jais had slipped back unnoticed by anyone but her.

"We've been together four years. In fact, we met four years ago today. Married two and half," Naina answered.

"One thousand two hundred and seventy-seven days," Jais said at the same time.

She snapped her head to him. Her heart thudded in her chest. Did he actually count the days—?

The whole crowd had turned their attention on him. Lata Auntie grinned, one eyebrow raised. "You don't have to be a math major to realize that those numbers don't add up."

Jais's smile was shy, as if he'd been caught revealing a bit too much of himself. "She's right." He dipped his chin in Naina's direction. "I simply didn't include the days that I didn't see her." His voice dropped. "Any day that I didn't see her, just didn't count."

Naina's heart thudded in her chest.

Shant Uncle furrowed his brow as he calculated. "You haven't seen her for close to six months?"

Jais glanced at her, sadness in his eyes. "Not really."

"Why?"

"Mistakes I made. Choices I made. Wrong choices." He looked at her. "Choices I wish I had made differently." The truth was in his eyes.

"What brought you together?" Lata Auntie turned to Naina.

She ripped her gaze away from Jais. His broken heart was in his eyes, and it spurred an ache deep in her heart. "Um…" She looked around. They had a rapt audience. She became aware that Christmas music played softly somewhere. Which was odd because they'd all been listening to Bollywood hits blaring just a minute ago. "It was Christmas Eve. We were both working in the soup kitchen on campus. I was working on a master's in creative writing, and Jais was in his second year of law school. I always work the soup kitchen during these holidays, but never before on Christmas Eve. Jais worked every Christmas Eve feeding people, but this was his first visit to that particular kitchen."

A collective gasp and low murmuring spread through the crowd.

"We hit it off right away and stayed all day, helping wherever we could." She smiled in Jais's direction.

He grinned, his eyes fixed on her. "By the end of the day, she and I had taught each other new recipes."

"He does the sweet stuff." Naina chuckled. "Which fits because…" She waved in his direction, her gaze not leaving. "He's sweet."

Jais raised an eyebrow at her. "She does the salty." He chuckled, and the crowd laughed with him. "But she's not salty. She's tough—don't doubt that. Her heart is pure and loving. She's fierce when she needs to be." His eyes softened on her. "And sometimes, even when she doesn't need to be."

Naina flushed, lost for a moment in his eyes. "Anyway…" She cleared her throat. "We went to have a bite, and then I went home," she told the crowd. "The next day, Christmas, we were back at the soup kitchen. I invited him to my house for dinner, where my dad always made a huge Christmas dinner—tandoori masala turkey is the highlight, and no one does it better than my dad. Jais came over. He and my dad worked the kitchen like they had always known each other." She stopped. It was one of her happiest memories—the two most important people in her life working together.

"Then we watched movies." Jais gave a sly smile.

"I let him pick." She smiled at the memory. She had braced herself for *Die Hard*, but Jais had wanted…

"Love Actually," he announced proudly to a chorus of laughter. "It's a must-watch at Christmas."

Naina giggled along with the crowd. "Now we watch it every Christmas."

"And on every Christmas Eve, we have the same thing we had that night, when we grabbed a bite to eat," Jais said.

"What's that?" one of the guests asked.

He looked at Naina and flushed as he shook his head.

She chuckled. "We had pizza, but we sprinkled the Indian pickling spice on it. Jais had it in his backpack."

The crowd applauded and laughed.

"You never know when you're going to need to spice something up." He laughed and looked at her.

In that moment, she knew. She had been a fool to let him walk out. The publishing job was the ideal position she had been looking for. He loved her Dad. It was about time she let go and lived her life. She had let fear and insecurity keep her from doing so.

From him.

Chapter Thirteen

Jais was thoroughly enjoying himself on the dance floor, holding Naina in his arms whenever he could. The music switched to an upbeat bhangra and the party really started. He simply could not take his eyes off Naina. Until he did for a moment, and then he couldn't find her.

"Shant Uncle, have you seen Naina?" he asked.

Uncle shook his head but didn't make eye contact. "I'm sure she's here somewhere." He tugged on Jais's sleeve so he had no choice but to go.

Jais followed Uncle to a section of the room that was set off to the side with a sofa, fireplace and small Christmas tree.

"So, you did redecorate," Jais said.

"What?"

"When we got here, all the decoration was old, broken, dusty, dead. But now..." He spread his arms wide. "Everything sparkles and is shiny and alive."

Uncle was silent.

"I'm sorry, Uncle." Jais turned to him, afraid he had offended. "I mean—this tree is beautiful. But the one in the lobby..." But the older man didn't look upset. He was looking at Jais with an eyebrow raised and a small smile on his face.

"When you came here, everything looked hopeless, drab and uncared for?" he asked, his voice low and soft.

"Well...yes."

"But now things look shiny, new, alive…loved, even?" Uncle quirked his smile, a knowing twinkle in his eye.

"Um…well, yes."

Uncle grinned and looked at the tree. "This is not a new tree. This has been here the whole time. Check out the lobby tree later. I'm sure you heard other guests comment on its beauty, eh?"

Jais narrowed his eyes. "Are you going to tell me that's the Christmas spirit?"

Uncle shook his head. "Call it what you want. But whatever it is, it's found in the power of love." He chuckled, a soulful thing that rose from his belly. "This tree has been here in this capacity since you arrived. Ask yourself why it is that you see it differently now, eh, beta?"

Before Jais could respond, his phone buzzed.

"You're going to want to take that." Uncle beamed.

Jais pulled out his phone and saw a text from Naina.

Can you come to the cabin? Please?

Jais walked into their cabin to find Naina waiting for him. A familiar aroma was in the air.

"Hey. Is that pizza?"

She nodded. "The frozen kind, because it's all I could find at the inn."

"We just ate—"

"I know." She watched him closely. "But it's Christmas Eve. And I went through your stuff, and I found—"

"The pickling spices?" He raised his eyebrows.

"Well…" She shrugged one shoulder, amusement in her eyes. "You never know when you might need to spice things up. Or so I've heard."

He nodded, his eyes never leaving her. "So very true. I assume you have *Love Actually* all ready to go?"

She nodded. "Jais, I…" Naina moved closer to him. "I've been an idiot."

He furrowed his brow.

"Hear me out." She paused and bit her bottom lip. "I love

you. I've loved you since that first Christmas Day when you and my dad cooked together. I felt…complete in that moment. I realized that my whole world was in that kitchen, and I've never felt so content and secure and loved."

Her eyes filled with tears. Jais took her face in his hands and wiped them as they fell. His heart pounded in chest as he listened to her.

"And then I got scared." She sniffled.

He nodded. "I know. That's why I married you in Vegas before you could overthink it." He sighed. "It's okay to be scared, to not always be in control. It's okay to let yourself just…be."

She nodded. "Jais." Her voice cracked. "I'm so sorry for everything. I love you, and these last six months have been completely horrible. If I'd never met you, I would probably have been fine. But I did meet you and I did fall in love with you." She paused. "And I have been loved by you." She shrugged one shoulder, a sheepish smile on her face. "So, now, there's no going back to 'being fine'. I don't want to give you up." Tears were flowing freely now. "You've always been my family."

"And I want nothing more than to be your family. There's nothing to be sorry for." He wiped her eyes. "We both have things we could have done differently. I have never been so miserable at the most perfect job. I've been wanting to tell you, I'm giving notice when we get back. I'm coming back to Baltimore to be with you." He tilted her chin up to him. "You are everything to me, Naina. You are my home."

"Well…" She sniffled, then chuckled. "That's going to be a small problem. Because I just emailed that publishing company to see if the New York position was still available."

Jais grinned at her and brought his lips to hers. She melted into him instantly, lifting to her toes to kiss him deeply. A beep went off in the kitchen.

"Pizza," he mumbled into her mouth.

She pulled him down onto the sofa and kissed him again as she worked the buttons on his sherwani. "It'll wait."

Epilogue

December 26

"Are you ready?" Naina called from the kitchen. She was gathering the spices they had brought with them. The plow had been by and the roads were clear thanks to a cozy Christmas Day without any precipitation.

"Yes," Jais said as he brought both bags out of the bedroom.

Naina froze. Jais was dressed in his navy sherwani for the wedding. "You look amazing."

Jais just stared at her. "Come here." He went to her, scooping her up into his arms. His mouth met hers, and she was lost. They had spent Christmas Day barely dressed, never leaving the warmth of their bed, which now had no poking springs, as well as a plush comforter and the softest sheets.

But it wasn't enough. They had six months to make up for.

Jais set her down, eyes dark wih desire as he spoke low and soft, his hands running along the silk of her sari. "How long will it take to get this sari back on?" he whispered as he tugged at the pleats, pulled at the tassel tie of her blouse and undid the hooks. The sari unwrapped and her blouse fell to the floor.

"Doesn't matter," she answered as worked his sherwani buttons.

Some time later, Naina and Jais piled into the car and left The Gingerbread Inn, this time, with Naina driving. She caught the inn in the rearview mirror and it was resplendent. A solid red brick structure adorned with softly glowing lights and Christmas trees tastefully decorated. Beautifully warm and inviting.

Naina caught Jais looking from the inn to her, an eyebrow raised. Uncle was right, the power of love. Only their best friends' wedding was keeping them from going back to that cabin.

Naina started down the driveway and the car skidded on black ice. Jais reached his arm out from the passenger's seat, pinning Naina to the seat, once again. Naina quickly regained control.

Jais took her hand. "Are you okay?" He brought her hand to his lips and kissed it.

Naina melted and brightened. "I'm just fine."

This was the world she wanted to live in. The world in which she and Jais had their lives to spend together.

* * * * *